PRIVATE PLEASURES

BERTRICE SMALL

PRIVATE PLEASURES

NEW AMERICAN LIBRARY

New American Library
Published by New American Library, a division of
Penguin Group (USA) Inc., 375 Hudson Street,
New York, New York 10014, U.S.A.
Penguin Books Ltd, 80 Strand,
London WC2R 0RL, England
Penguin Books Australia Ltd, 250 Camberwell Road,
Camberwell, Victoria 3124, Australia
Penguin Books Canada Ltd, 10 Alcorn Avenue,
Toronto, Ontario, Canada M4V 3B2
Penguin Books (N.Z.) Ltd, Cnr Rosedale and Airborne Roads,
Albany, Auckland 1310, New Zealand

Penguin Books Ltd, Registered Offices:
80 Strand, London WC2R 0RL, England

First published by New American Library,
a division of Penguin Group (USA) Inc.

ISBN 0-7394-4504-9

Set in Sabon
Designed by Leonard Telesca

Printed in the United States of America

FOR KATHE ROBIN,
WHO LIKES IT VERY, VERY HOT

CHAPTER ONE

"I think Jeff is having an affair," Nora Buckley said unhappily, looking about the kitchen table at her four friends.

The women of Ansley Court shifted uncomfortably, throwing quick looks at one another. It was a difficult situation.

"So." Rina Seligmann, the oldest of them, finally broke the silence. "What else is new, sweetie? I mean who hasn't Jeff hit on all the years we've lived here?"

The silence deepened appreciably with her words.

"Oh, my God!" Rina gasped as the truth hit her. She looked at Nora sympathetically. "You didn't know, hon? You really didn't know? Shit! I'm sorry, Nora. I didn't mean . . ." Her voice trailed off.

"What makes you think Jeff is having an affair?" Carla Johnson, Nora's best friend, asked quietly. "And don't pay any attention to Rina. She's got a big mouth, and a bigger imagination." She gave Rina a sharp look.

Nora Buckley swallowed hard, her questioning glance encompassing the other four women at the table. "Did any of you . . . ?" Her voice trailed off.

"NO!" they all chorused with one voice.

"Then why did Rina say it?" Nora looked as if she was going

to cry. She was a pretty woman with fading red hair and soft gray green eyes.

"Because," Carla explained, "there used to be rumors at the club about what a big flirt Jeff was. I suspect a few women even succumbed to his charms, but honey, it's all water under the bridge. No one took him seriously except one or two professional widows, or a divorcée hot to trot. We sure never did. Now, what's got you so damned upset, Nora? Why are you so suddenly certain that Jeff is having an affair, and with whom, for heaven's sake?"

"It's someone at his office, or at least connected with his business," Nora replied softly. "He's in town far more than he is here, isn't he? He's been home once in the last ten days. Just once. I don't know what to do, or think."

"And?" Carla probed as the others tried not to look too interested. Carla was the most sensible of them all. She had taken Nora under her wing from the moment they had met. Carla was no-nonsense. Nora was gentle, almost helpless except where her house and her two children were concerned.

"There have been more and more late nights when he does come home," Nora said. "And calls on the weekends to his business phone in the den. If I pick it up, the caller hangs up," Nora explained. She sighed. "I know the kids have more than consumed me, but raising children is hard work. Maybe I haven't been as attentive to Jeff as I might have been. And I've let myself go a little because I never seem to have enough time for me anymore. Suddenly I feel as if Jeff and I don't have anything in common. He's so distant when he is home. It's like he's paying his mother a reluctant visit instead of coming home to his wife and his family. He doesn't seem interested in us at all."

Rina nodded. "I think you've got it right, hon," she said stoically. "He's sure showing all the signs of a man on the prowl, and don't glare at me, Carla. What else can it be?" She reached for a jelly stick, and bit into it.

"How the hell did you get so smart? And how would you know such things?" Carla snapped. "Sam is so damned devoted to you that it's sickening. You're the luckiest woman on Ansley Court, Rina, and you know it."

"Hey, I read *Cosmo* and *Ms.* too," Rina snapped back. "I may be the oldest of us all, but I'm not dead yet by any means." She took another bite of the jelly stick.

Her companions laughed. Rina was the only one of them who would really stand up to Carla Johnson. They were six years apart in age, but very much alike in character.

"But what am I going to do?" Nora wailed plaintively. "I'm scared to death for the first time in my life. What if he leaves me?"

"Well, you have to consider if you're better with him or without him," Tiffany Pietro d'Angelo, silent until then, said. "Isn't that what 'Dear Abby' asks?" She was a pretty and petite blonde whose lawyer husband was in local practice with Carla's husband.

"I honestly don't know," Nora said slowly, "but if he's in love with another woman, I can't stand in the way of his happiness. But then, do I really want to throw away twenty-six years of marriage?"

"What have you got?" Rina asked bluntly.

"Got?" Nora looked confused.

"Yeah, got. In your name. The house? And if you're smart, you'll clear out all the joint bank accounts right away. Put 'em in your name," Rina advised. "And move your own bank account somewhere your husband doesn't know about. Jeff is at that dangerous age. When they get involved at this time in their lives they usually want to start all over again with the Jennifer."

"Jennifer? You know her name?" Nora looked confused, and the others struggled to keep from giggling. Nora was really such a sweet innocent even after two kids and all those years of marriage.

"The Jennifer is what they call the young girlfriend who usually ends up being the second wife. The trophy wife," Rina explained acerbically. "Who knows what her real name is? Heather. Courtney. Madison. Who cares?"

The others giggled.

"So," Rina repeated. "What have you got?"

"I don't think I have anything," Nora said softly with a sigh. "The house is in Jeff's name. The only bank account I have is a joint one with Jeff. I pay all the bills associated with the house and the children. He deposits my allowance into it once a month. That's what his father did for his mother."

"Jesus Jenny!" Rina exploded while the other three woman just looked disbelieving. "I thought women like you went out in the fifties, Nora. You don't own the house? Not even jointly? You don't have some money of your own put aside for emergencies? Shit! I think that you are in really big trouble, hon."

"Shut up!" Carla said. "We don't know anything for sure. You're scaring Nora to death with all your talk. How do we know Jeff is having an affair, or that he's going to dump his wife for another woman? You're letting that damned imagination of yours run away with you. You all are!" She put a comforting arm about her best friend. "Nora's just down in the dumps because Jeff is being a little worse than his crappy self. Mr. Workaholic. That's Jeff. Nora's lonely. Jill is finishing college, and working so she can support herself at law school. J. J. is graduating high school, and headed off to college in August. Nora's facing an empty nest. You know what I think, girls? I think Nora needs The Channel. I think it's time we shared our little secret with her." She looked about, grinning conspiratorially at the others. "Am I right? Huh?"

"Ohhh, yes!" Tiffany giggled. "I just love The Channel? What would we all do without The Channel? I remember how I always hated Joe's poker night until you introduced me to The Channel. But now Joe can play cards till the cows come home for all I care." She got a dreamy look on her pretty face, her slim fingers twirling a lock of her champagne blond hair. "Thank heavens for The Channel!" She sighed gustily.

"How come we've never told Nora about The Channel before, Carla?" Joanne Ulrich wondered aloud. Like Tiffany she was petite, but where the youngest of them was slender, Joanne was plump in a pretty and comfortable way. "We generally share everything as a rule."

"Do you really think Nora was ready for The Channel before today?" Rina replied with a mischievous grin as she reached for another jelly stick. She was one of those tall women who never gained weight. "Not really."

The other women laughed knowingly, nodding, sharing the secret.

"What channel?" Nora asked them. "What on earth are you talking about?"

"Yeah," Carla agreed. "I think it is time for us to share The Channel with Nora." She turned to her best friend. "It's this interactive thing we get through the television, sweetie," she began. "It's really difficult to explain. You have to experience it to understand it. The next time you're going to be alone for the whole evening, call Suburban Cable, and tell them you want The Channel. That's all you have to do. Try it. I'll bet you'll like it. We all use it, and we all love it. You'll feel a helluva lot better after an evening with The Channel, Nora."

"What channel?" Nora repeated, looking very confused. "Is it like House and Garden? And what's *interactive*?"

The women burst out laughing again, unable to contain themselves.

"House and Garden," Tiffany wheezed, laughing so hard that the tears ran down her pretty face.

Finally Carla managed to get ahold of herself, and said, "No, hon, it isn't at all like House and Garden. At least it isn't for me. It's different for everyone. But who knows with you, Nora? Look, have I ever steered you wrong? Trust me. Just ask Suburban for

The Channel. That's all you have to say. 'I want The Channel.' Now somebody pass me a jelly stick before Rina eats them all. Is this a coffee klatch, or not?"

"Like you need a jelly stick," Rina chuckled with a smile.

"What can I say?" Carla replied, biting into the pastry and quickly licking the jelly that squirted onto her chin. "Your home-made jelly sticks are the best! Besides, Rick likes me cuddly and huggable." She grinned at them.

The women of Ansley Court met every Monday morning for coffee and gossip. They had all moved into Ansley at Egret Pointe, an upscale subdivision, twenty to twenty-five years before. Rina and Sam Seligmann had built first on the cul-de-sac. They had been followed by Joanne and Carl Ulrich. The Buckleys and the Johnsons had by coincidence built at the same time. And finally Tiffany and Joe Pietro d'Angelo had constructed their house on the last lot on Ansley Court. Rina and Joanne were over fifty now. The other three were slightly younger.

They had raised their children together, while their husbands supported their families in the traditional old-fashioned way. Rina had once been a full-time social worker. Joanne an elementary school teacher. Carla was a nurse. Only Tiffany and Nora had never held down a job. Neighbors are not always the best of friends, but these five women were. They had done nursery school, PTA, Little League, and soccer together. They had gone trick-or-treating together in costume with their children and weathered chicken pox and flu seasons constantly, exchanging remedies. They even hung their Christmas lights out on the same day so Ansley Court wouldn't be lopsided, as Tiffany liked to say.

Long ago the five families had bought a ramshackle old Victorian house, called a camp, for their summers. The house was set on a mountain lake. They shared their camp together throughout the warmer vacation months, and often into autumn weekends. They taught their kids to swim there, and more important how to identify poison ivy. The children had named it Camp Cozy. It had been a very comfortable and predictable lifestyle neatly bordered by the changing seasons. But now with Nora Buckley's fears out in the open, something was changing, and not necessarily for the better. They could all feel it.

Nora's husband, Jeff Buckley, wasn't at all like their husbands, and he had never made any real effort to be friendly. Sam Seligmann was Egret Pointe's favorite doctor. He had an old-fashioned general practice, rare in this day and age, but he was the kind of doctor his father had been, and he was content to follow in his father's footsteps. Carl Ulrich owned the local hardware store, which continued to flourish despite the Home Depot in a nearby new mall. Carl gave his customers personal service. He was knowledgeable, as were his two longtime employees. They were unlike the kids working at the mall, who didn't know a wing nut from a Brazil nut. Joe Pietro d'Angelo and Rick Johnson had a small country law practice in the village. They handled wills, house closings, a few local divorces, and other small matters usual to a country village. Carla was Joe's cousin. Only Jeff Buckley, partner in a prestigious advertising agency, commuted to the nearby city.

Jeff had been very ambitious and career oriented. He had never been around a great deal. He missed his son's Little League games each year, and despite the fact that the boy, named after him but called J. J., was star of the high school varsity soccer team, Jeff had never seen him play. And his daughter had fared no better. He had never seen her perform in a dance recital or a school play. She had gone to college in California, and had recently been accepted at Duke Law. Jeff enjoyed bragging about Jill's accomplishments.

He showed up at Camp Cozy two weekends a summer: over the Fourth of July and Labor Day weekends. He was pleasant enough when he was around, but the other men had absolutely nothing in common with him. It was Nora they all knew and liked. They tolerated her husband for her sake. Jeff was definitely the odd man out, and he didn't seem to care at all.

Nora Edwards had meet Jeffrey Buckley in her freshman year at college. He had been a senior. He was the quarterback of the football team, captain of the baseball team, and a brilliant scholar. He was the quintessential big man on campus. He had come to the freshman mixer with some fraternity buddies to check out the girls, looking for the sluts who could be easily fucked, and the nice girls who might be eventually seduced. But Jeff Buckley was ambitious, and wherever he was going, he would go to the top.

He had met Nora, and known immediately that this was the girl he wanted for a wife. She was perfect for him. She had the correct ethnic, religious, and political backgrounds. She was pretty in a subdued and ladylike way with her soft trusting eyes and her pageboy hairstyle. She wore a powder blue cashmere sweater set, and a strand of dainty pearls about her neck. She was an only child, innocent, carefully sheltered. She wasn't stupid. In fact she was very intelligent, but she was unsophisticated. Her girlfriends told her how lucky she was to have attracted a guy like Jeff Buckley, and having fallen half in love with him that first night, she believed them. And she believed Jeff Buckley. A pat from him, a flash of his smile, and she was lost.

But most important of all to Jeff was that Nora was a virgin. And he made sure that she stayed that way until he married her. The word went out on the campus that pretty Nora Edwards was the property of Jeff Buckley, quarterback of State's championship football team. On her birthday, November 30, he gave her his fraternity pin. She was serenaded by his fraternity just before the Christmas break, while standing in the cold before her dorm wearing the long dark green velvet formal gown she had worn to the Christmas dance at his fraternity house. Candles burned in the windows of the dorm, and the shadowed figures of the other girls could just be made out. She had almost frozen to death, but she had never shivered because she wanted him to be proud of her.

Nora had gone home with a cold, desperate to get well, as she was to spend New Year's Eve at Jeff's parents' home. His mother had called her mother and invited her. And on New Year's Eve Jeff had put his hand in Nora's underpants for the first time, fingering her clitoris until she almost fainted. When she had whimpered with her pleasure, he had stifled her cries with his kisses. At the fraternity's spring formal he had asked her to marry him, and put a ring on her finger before she might answer, but of course he had known the answer would be yes.

Here, however, Nora's parents had stepped into the romance. Nora was just eighteen. They wanted her to finish her college education, and they did not want her married until she did. When she was twenty-one they'd consider it. Jeff agreed. He had things to do before he entered into matrimony. He just didn't want Nora to get away.

After graduating he had gone on to earn a masters' degree in business at Harvard, and done a brief military service. Then he had joined Coutts and Wickham, a very prestigious advertising firm in the city. Nora had remained at her studies, kept safe from other possible suitors, chaperoned by her fiancé's fraternity brothers to the various university social events when Jeff couldn't join her.

Any young man approaching Nora was warned away in the strongest terms possible. One boy who refused to heed the warning was beaten up by unknown assailants. After that, no males approached Nora Edwards, but she never knew the lengths that Jeff had gone to, to keep her for himself. She had her studies, and everyone was so very nice to her.

Two weeks after her graduation with a degree in English literature, Nora Edwards had married Jeffrey Buckley in a large, tasteful all-white wedding, with six bridesmaids in white linen sheaths with narrow green ribbons at their waists, and wreaths of baby's breath with white rosebuds topping their heads. After a honeymoon in Bermuda, they had moved in with his parents for a year while their own house was being built. The lot on Ansley Court had been a wedding gift from their grandparents.

When the house was finally finished they had moved into it. Nora had spent her days decorating and gardening, making their home a place that Jeff was proud to show off. And she had immediately made friends with her neighbors, and the subsequent neighbors to come. She had gotten pregnant, and had her two children, Jill and J. J., born four years apart. The others had gotten pregnant too, or already had children. Jill and J. J. had grown up with the Seligmann, Ulrich, Johnson, and Pietro d'Angelo kids. Becky Seligmann, and Natalie Ulrich had baby-sat J. J. Carla's daughter, Maureen, would be graduating with J. J. shortly, leaving only the Pietro d'Angelo twins, Max and Brittany, on the court. They would graduate next year. And Ansley Court would be one big empty nest very soon. But no one planned to leave. Their homes were where their children and their grandchildren would come to visit, and there would be plenty of room.

Rina was already back to work for the county. So was Carla at the nearby hospital. Joanne was subbing for the local school district. Even Tiffany had been taking some law associate courses at the community college. She was going to help out in Rick and Joe's law firm. Only Nora seemed firmly stuck in place until now.

"Pretty soon I'll be the only one left here at home." She voiced her thoughts aloud.

"So do something," Rina encouraged. "You've got a degree. Go take a computer course at the adult ed when J. J. goes off to college. I did it last year. I had to. You have to have computer knowledge today to do anything, it seems."

"All I have is a B.A. in English lit," Nora replied. "Where is that going to get me in this day and age? I never took any teaching credits because I was going to marry and stay home after college. I took home ec courses."

"The women's lib movement was going strong, and you didn't prepare yourself for the eventual possibility that you might be on your own one day?" Rina shook her head. "I mean what was going to happen if Jeff kicked the bucket all of a sudden? Or was in a fatal car crash?"

"Or got shot by an outraged husband," Joanne murmured beneath her breath.

Carla shot her a hard look.

"Back then we thought the women's lib movement was just a bunch of lesbians, radicals, and liberals," Nora said. "No nice girl was going to get involved with them. Besides, I'm sure Jeff has made provisions for us in the event of a tragedy, although he would never believe anything could happen to him. He's always been very good that way," Nora loyally defended her husband.

"How is he set up for retirement?" Rina continued to pursue the matter. "Does he have profit sharing, a Keogh, four-oh-one-k, a traditional pension?"

Nora shrugged. "I don't know. We never discussed it."

"Well, you ought to know, hon." Now it was Carla who spoke up. God damnit, she thought, Nora has always been so darned trusting. She isn't stupid. Far from it. She's just too nice. Too polite. And Jeff had taken full advantage of it. He was probably very well-fixed. And, Carla considered grimly, if he intended dumping his current wife for a younger model, he probably had already hidden his assets pretty well. Rick had mentioned such things. Nora was going to need help. "You gotta find out what he's got," she advised her best friend. The other women nodded in agreement.

"How?" Nora said. "I haven't the foggiest idea of how to go about such a thing. Besides, I don't want Jeff to think I don't trust him. He's always been very good to me."

Carla looked for a moment as if she were going to explode, and Rina snorted scornfully, saying quietly, "You've been good to him too, sweetie." She turned. "Carla, do you think Rick could make a few discreet inquiries? I mean, just to give Nora an idea of the situation she's facing in the event of the worst-case scenario."

"I'll ask him," Carla agreed. And Rick would do it, or she'd kill him, Carla thought. Rina was right, although she would never say it aloud in front of Nora. Jeff Buckley was up to something. No one had to tell her he wasn't coming home a whole lot anymore. If anything was going to happen, it would happen soon. With J. J. graduating, and going off to State in August, it was the perfect time for Jeff Buckley to bail on his wife and family. Carla stood up. "I gotta go, girls. I'm working the three-to-eleven shift today. Maureen's doing supper for her dad. which probably means she'll con him into bringing home some KFC." She laughed. "The kid won't eat red meat, but she does love her KFC. Teenagers! Go figure."

"Tell her to have Rick bring me some too," Nora said. "Jeff probably won't be home either, and J. J. is studying with his girlfriend. Or at least they say they're studying," she finished with a wry smile.

"Oh," Tiffany said, "then this would be a perfect night for you to get The Channel, Nora! You really are going to like it."

"Can I get it during the day?" Nora asked.

Tiffany shook her head. "It's only available at night," she replied with a giggle.

"None of you has told me yet exactly what The Channel is," Nora said. "Is it old movies? What?"

"It's whatever you want it to be, and it's different for each of us," Joanne said quietly. "We all see The Channel through our own eyes. It's your perfect fantasy. You'll see when you watch it tonight."

"Will I like it?"

"I think you will, but it depends," Joanne told her. She stood up. "I've got to go too. The school district wants me to help out during exam week next month. I've got some prep work to do. Rina, the jelly sticks were heaven, as always."

"Come on," Carla said, pulling Nora up and linking her arm in Nora's. "I'll walk you home. Thanks, Rina. See ya, Tiff, Joanne!"

"Why are you all so mysterious about this channel thing?"

Nora asked as they walked across the cul-de-sac. "And how come you haven't shared it with me before today? You don't usually keep stuff from me, Carla. Why this?"

Carla sighed. "Because The Channel is a secret," she answered honestly. "It's just for women, and it isn't for every woman. If you like it, you'll go back. If you don't, you won't, and you'll forget all about it. That's the way it is, and that's the way it's always been, I'm told. And most important, it's a secret no woman shares with a man. You'll understand once you've been there."

"That's weird," Nora responded. "I don't know if I want to get mixed up in something like that. Why can't any of you tell me what it is? Why is everyone so evasive? And all the hush-hush stuff. Is it something illegal?"

They had reached the Buckleys and stood outside continuing to talk.

"Joanne told you the truth. We all view The Channel through different eyes, Nora. I guess the best way to explain it is to say that The Channel lets you live out your fantasies. It's one thing for me, and another for the others. It will be entirely different for you too. Like I said earlier, it's an interactive thingy, sweetie. I don't understand how it works myself, but I sure love it."

"Oh," Nora said. She really didn't understand this computer and interactive stuff. It was all Greek to her. She supposed she was going to have to learn about it if she was going to survive in this strange new world that seemed to have evolved while she had been busy being a good wife and mother. With J. J. gone in just a few short months, it might just be the right time to take a few courses. Rina and Carla were right.

"Let me know how you like The Channel," Carla said, her brown eyes twinkling as she and Nora parted at the Buckleys' kitchen stoop. "See ya!" And she was off across the perfect green lawn to her own house next door.

Nora entered her house, walking through the kitchen into the den, where she sat wearily down in her recliner. Voicing her fears aloud to her friends this morning had finally made her wake up and think about what was happening around her. For twenty-six years she had devoted herself to Jeff, his wants, his needs, their children. Everything was for them. She had never asked anything for herself. Consequently she had grown into a pretty dull person, Nora admitted to herself. Jeff led an exciting life, but her life was so damned ordinary and colorless. Maybe The Channel could be her first step on the road to a new and exciting Nora.

When they had come to Ansley Court it had been exciting. She had loved being at home, decorating each room lovingly and thoughtfully, working out in her gardens with Mr. Handlemann from the nursery, choosing the plants and trees for their property. She had picked fabrics and paints. Bought furniture and carpets. Jeff wasn't interested in any of it. The house was hers, he told her. It was her realm to do with as she pleased as long as it was tasteful and elegant so they might eventually entertain his bosses and clients.

Jeff had gotten himself a job with Coutts and Wickham Advertising. In those days it had been a medium-sized agency. He was unusually clever at thinking up successful campaigns for the clients, and they liked him as well. Jeff had worked hard, but then, Nora thought, so had she. Their home was right out of *Country Living*. And in those early years she had entertained perfectly for the firm. Their Christmas parties had even been written up in the city paper's Sunday color supplement. And Jeff had been made a partner. The firm was now known as Buckley, Coutts and Wickham Advertising.

And the children had been carefully spaced four years apart. They were terrific kids. Jill had accelerated her college time. She would be through after the summer semester, having finished in just three years. Jill had already taken her LSAT exams and been accepted at Duke University's law school. She would start in late summer. J. J. was not as focused as his sister had been at eighteen. J. J. would take four or more years to get his degree, if Nora wasn't mistaken. But she had no doubt that when he found himself J. J. would excel in life.

Yes, Nora thought to herself, I really have to do something with myself. I've got to get a life of my own now. I've got a perfect house, a perfect lawn, and garden, great kids, but what the hell do I really want? If Jeff is really having an affair, if Rina is right, I could be losing everything. What would I do then? But Nora knew that there was no what-if about it. Her husband was obviously involved with someone else, and until she had said it aloud this morning, she hadn't been able to face it herself. Now she was facing it, and it scared the hell out of her.

What had happened to them? The revelation this morning that Jeff was a womanizer had been a bit of a shock, though. But hadn't she always looked at Jeff through rose-colored glasses from the moment she met him? Yes, she had, she acknowledged to herself. She was dewy-eyed, and he was an important senior on the State campus. She'd never really had a boyfriend until Jeff Buckley. The private school she had attended, Lane, had been an all-girls school.

Her late father had been very impressed with Jeff Buckley. "The boy comes from a solid family," Nora remembered him saying. Jeff Buckley. The perfect prospect. Quarterback. Senior-class president, head of the debating team, at a time when student bodies across America were protesting and rebelling. Jeff, however, did not rebel. Rebellion, he argued firmly, was both inefficient and time-consuming. You changed the system from within the system, not by encouraging anarchy. Jeff had been pure establishment. Nora had thought he was just wonderful, and he had won over her father immediately, calling him "sir." Her parents had met him that first Homecoming Weekend.

Nora's mother, however, worried that Jeff was a bit—what was the word she had used? *Bossy?* Yes! Bossy. But Nora hadn't minded. Her father had been controlling. It felt good to let someone else take charge. Now after all these years she wasn't so certain that her mother hadn't been right. Maybe her mother had been trying to warn her in some subtle way. But she wouldn't have listened to Margo at that time in her life anyway, Nora realized. She was in love, and it was wonderful! She had never dated anyone else. She was a virgin on their wedding night. She remembered he had been very pleased. It was obvious that Jeff wasn't a virgin, however, but his mastery had thrilled her innocent heart.

But he had never liked it when she showed what he considered undue enthusiasm in their lovemaking. He had once accused her of being whorish, which had hurt her feelings. She had thought he would be flattered by her newly awakened passions. That if you loved someone, you should show him that you did. Jeff was not of similar mind.

"I'd really be wondering about you, Nora," he had said to her, "if I hadn't popped your cherry myself. You really bled, baby."

The sex between them, at first red-hot, had quickly cooled. Not because Nora wanted it to, but because she wasn't allowed to really participate in a shared passion. The novelty wore off, and he seemed less interested. Looking back, it seemed to her as if his only interest in her sexually had been her virginity, and ability to give him children. Then five years ago sex between them had stopped entirely. She even remembered the date. It had been September 5, Labor Day weekend. Jeff had been drunk. He had called her Lanie. Oh, yes. The date was etched firmly in her mind.

Whenever her friends talked about their husbands' ardor, and the fact they weren't getting as much as they once had, Nora was silent. She knew they all assumed it was because she was reticent in discussing sex, but of course that wasn't it at all. If they had known about her situation, they would have pitied her. Nora didn't think she could stand being pitied because her husband no longer found her lustworthy. So she kept her mouth shut, and went on with her life as if everything were fine and dandy, but of course it wasn't. And now it appeared as if her husband was going to dump her like rubbish for another woman. A younger woman. There was no hiding from that.

"I'll bet they're having great sex," she grumbled to herself. She wondered what the other woman looked like. Probably blond. How old was she? Probably in her late twenties or early thirties, which was a good twenty or more years younger than Jeff. Women in their early thirties were really in their prime sexually. At least the kids were grown, or almost grown. There wouldn't be any nonsense about custody or visitation. Nora wondered how much they knew or suspected about Jeff's peccadilloes. Neither Jill nor J. J. had ever been close with their father. He had never been home enough to allow it, but she was very close with both of them.

Her thoughts led her right back to her problem. What was she going to do about it? Rina was right. Nora Buckley was helpless, and she didn't like the reality of that knowledge at all. What was the matter with her that she hadn't gotten a little bank account just for herself? Something for a rainy day. Jeff had never been really cheap with her, and she could have siphoned off some of her household moneys every month. He would have been none the wiser as long as it had been just a little at a time. But no. Nora Buckley had been too busy trying to please her husband to consider herself. What a fool she had been!

The phone rang, startling her. She picked it up.

"Hey, Ma!" J. J.'s voice came over the wire. "Lily's mom has invited me to stay overnight. She and Mr. Graham invited a friend to dinner. The guy's a bigwig at State. They wanted me to meet him. I told 'em it would be alright with you, right?"

"Why can't you come home afterwards?" Nora heard herself asking.

"Maaa!" J. J. sounded exasperated. "You'll make me look like a real dork if I have a curfew. What if this guy from State and I are in an important conversation? The clock strikes ten, and I have to get up, saying, 'I'm sorry, Mr. Blank, but my mommy wants me home.' Do you want me to look like a jerk?"

"No, of course not. What about clothing for tomorrow?" Nora asked her son.

"I'll jet over after school, grab some, and my toothbrush too. Okay?" He sounded anxious and so excited.

"Okay." Nora gave in gracefully. What other choice did she have?

"Great, Ma! See ya!" The phone went dead.

Nora set it down, but then as an afterthought picked up the phone again, dialing the Graham residence. Maris Graham answered. "Maris, Nora Buckley. J. J. just called. This isn't going to be a problem for you, is it? He can always come home."

"No, no," Maris Graham replied. "He can sleep in Peter's room. There are bunk beds there. Michael Collier is the director of admissions at State. I know J. J.'s gotten in without any difficulty, but I thought if Mike met J. J., he'd like him," she laughed. "What isn't to like? But I thought it might help J. J. get a better on-campus job, and maybe a bump in his scholarship money. I wish they could have met earlier, but Mike only gets down to see us once a year. He and John were at Princeton together."

"Well, fine, then," Nora replied. "And Maris, thanks so very much. You have been very kind to J. J., and we appreciate it."

"No problem. He's a good kid," came the response.

Nora had no sooner hung up the phone again when it rang once more. Her husband's voice came over the line.

"Don't you ever do anything but yak on the phone?" Jeff greeted her. "I've been trying to get you for hours."

Nora sighed. "Don't prevaricate, Jeff. I've been over at Rina's this morning. There were no messages." She pressed the caller ID. "You haven't called until just now, and I didn't get a beep. You must have dialed the wrong number. I was just on the phone with Maris Graham. J. J. is staying over there tonight. I wanted to make certain it was alright with Maris. What's up?"

"I can't get home tonight," he replied curtly, ignoring her explanation. "Big campaign, and the client is in from Detroit. By the time the meetings are over, and we've wined and dined him, it will be just too damned late. I'll stay at the company apartment."

"Of course," Nora said, an edge in her voice. "You stayed all weekend, Jeff, but of course I understand. Just remember that the Athletic Association awards at the school are Friday night. J. J. is picking up a scholarship for soccer from the local booster club. I damned well expect you to be there for your son!"

"What the hell has gotten into you?" he demanded. "The Change, I suppose. I work like a peon to keep you and the kids comfortable, and all you can do is bitch at me."

"I've been on hormone replacement therapy for two years now if you had ever bothered to notice. Are you having an affair, Jeff?" Nora shot back at him, astounded even as the words left her mouth that she had said them.

"I don't have to dignify that question with a reply, Nora," Jeff said loftily. "I'll call you later this week."

"Don't bother! Just be home for the awards. J. J. is your only son," Nora snapped. "At least the only one that I know of, dear."

The phone line went dead, but not before she had heard the sharp intake of his breath.

"Omigod!" she half whispered as she put the phone back down in its charger. He hadn't denied a thing. He had practically confirmed it by not answering her question. If he wasn't having an affair, he would have said so. But he hadn't said so. She was surprised that he hadn't asked her to define the word *affair*. When had Jeff become such a son of a bitch? Or had he always been that way, and she too blind to notice? You are in big trouble, girlfriend, she thought to herself. And you are all alone. Her father was dead, and she certainly wasn't going to go running to her mother. Margo had never really liked Jeff in the first place. She had no siblings. What the hell was she going to do? There was really no one to help her. It frightened her to realize that Jeff seemed to have all the cards in this terrible game they were playing.

Nora stood up and paced the room. She had no idea of the time, but it had to be afternoon because the sun was flooding the den with its bright light. She had never expected to come to this point in her life when she married Jeff. Nora believed when you got married, you stayed that way until one of you died. That was the way it had always been. That was the way it was supposed to be. It was like that here on Ansley Court, but then, they had all been lucky. No one worked at marriage anymore, it seemed. Divorce was so commonplace nowadays.

She walked into the front hallway and stared at herself in the large mirror over the hall table. Alright. She was heavier than the 120 pounds she had weighed when they were married. She wasn't a flaming redhead anymore. She pushed at the hair near her temples. It was faded even more than the rest of her head. She peered closely into the mirror. Okay. She had a few laugh lines around her eyes. But everyone she knew did too, damnit! But she wasn't a bad-looking woman. In fact she was in pretty good condition for a woman in her late forties if you overlooked the fact that her boobs were going south, and her waist wasn't quite as narrow as it had once been, and her thighs were a bit mottled. Weren't everyone's at this point?

Nora sighed. So she wasn't the girl he had married anymore. He wasn't the boy she had married either. But there was no doubt about it, unfair as it seemed. Men simply did age better than women in most cases. She knew that Jeff worked out at the gym in his office five days a week. He insisted on low-fat, low-carb meals when he was home. He didn't smoke, and drank rarely except very expensive wines. The truth was that he looked better now than he had when they were first married.

Nora wandered absently back into the den. He hadn't said anything to her yet, but he was going to, and she sensed it was coming soon. She flopped back on the couch. Damn! Damn!

Damn! Damn! There was that niggling question again. What was she going to do to survive this disaster? Suddenly Nora was exhausted with her newly discovered tension. She dozed restlessly for how long she didn't know. Her confusion and reverie were broken by a young voice calling.

"Mrs. B.? It's me, Maureen. I've got your KFC."

"Thanks, honey," Nora called back. "Leave it on the counter, will you?" She didn't want Maureen to see her, for she realized that she had been crying in her sleep. She must really look like hell. If Maureen saw her, she would call Carla at the hospital, and Carla would call her. There was nothing anyone could do for her right now.

"Okay, Mrs. B. I ran into J. J. coming in. He said he didn't want to disturb you. He'll see you tomorrow. Daddy got you mashed potatoes and coleslaw. I hope that's alright," Maureen said.

"Fine, sweetie, my favorites," Nora assured her. "Tell your dad I said thanks, and ask him to let me know what I owe him, okay?" She heard the kitchen door close behind the girl. Standing up, she went out into her kitchen to get her dinner. Taking a plate down from the cabinet, she opened the cardboard box. Rick had gotten her a breast and two wings. It was still hot, and it smelled good. She put it on her plate along with the biscuit, which she buttered. Then she emptied the container of mashed potatoes and gravy onto the plate, opened the coleslaw and took it into the den. Returning to the kitchen, she grabbed a fork, a napkin, and a glass of peach iced tea. Back in the den she turned on Peter Jennings, and sat down to eat. The news was the same as always. War and a fluctuating stock market.

Mick and Jerry, the family cats, appeared magically, licking their chops and meowing. They looked up hopefully at Nora. She laughed, pulled the meat from the two wings, put it on a napkin, and set it down on the floor for the two felines to devour. When the news ended, she turned the set off. The clock on the fireplace mantle struck seven o'clock, and as it did she considered her conversation with her friends this morning. She was alone tonight. No one but her and the cats in the house. She could order this channel thing. They all seemed to like it, and damnit, she could use a lift. She suspected it was some sort of X-rated channel, but why not? Carla was her best friend in all the world, and Carla wouldn't steer her wrong. Nora picked up the telephone and dialed Suburban Cable.

Two rings, and an automated voice was droning in her ear. "Thank you for calling Suburban Cable. If you are experiencing technical difficulties, please press one. If you would like to order one of our pay-per-view movies, please press two. All other callers, please remain on the line for the next available representative. Your call will be answered in the order in which it was received."

Was The Channel a movie? Nora wondered. No. Carla would have said so. She hung on the line as the elevator music kicked in, playing that golden oldie, and rather applicable to her situation, "These Boots Are Made for Walkin'." Nora felt a grin crease her face.

"Suburban Cable, this is Joyce. How may I help you?" a cheerful voice suddenly chirped in her ear.

"I . . . I'd like to order The Channel," Nora said, the words rushing out.

"Your telephone number, please," Joyce said, sounding totally disinterested in Nora's choice of entertainment.

"It's 567-2339," Nora replied.

"Buckley? At 720 Ansley Court?"

"Yes."

"And you are?" Joyce asked.

"Mrs. Buckley," Nora replied.

"Very good, Mrs. Buckley. You'll find your selection tonight on channel sixty-nine at eight p.m. Is there anything else I can do for you at this moment?"

"No. Thank you," Nora answered, and then she hung up. Omigod! She had done it. She giggled to herself, and began to finish her supper. She realized now that she couldn't wait until eight. It probably was a porn channel, she decided, but she didn't care. She and Jeff had once watched a couple of movies from the video store. Her husband had claimed to be turned off by them, or so he had said. Nora had thought the films silly, but they were certainly stimulating, she recalled. It was probably just what she needed. An evening of dirty movies, and a pint of caramel praline ice cream. She picked her chicken down to the bone and cleaned her plate of everything else.

Putting her dishes in the dishwasher, Nora went upstairs, showered quickly, and got into a clean nightshirt that had a teddy bear on the front of it claiming, "I don't do mornings." Giving her ice cream ten seconds in the microwave, she got a spoon and a glass of water, and set them on the table by her large recliner. Then settling into the chair with a contented sigh, she picked up the remote as the clock struck eight p.m., pressed it on, and coded in sixty-nine. The screen was black.

"Oh, for God's sakes," Nora muttered aloud. Did they forget to send her the signal? Damn! She had been looking forward to this.

But then suddenly the screen lightened, and a rather melliflu-ous voice said silkily, "Good evening, and welcome to The Channel, where your fantasies become your reality."

Well, that was certainly confusing, but absolutely intriguing. Then the screen changed again. Nora found herself looking into a rather large living room that came into perfect view. "Oh," she said softly. It was a beautiful room. Just like one she had always imagined, but certainly not one that Jeff would have liked. It was very modern and elegant. All glass and chrome and brass with large overstuffed white sofas and chairs, with emerald green and sapphire blue silk pillows. Even the carpet was creamy white. It looked as if when you stepped on it you would be ankle-deep in the pile. The lighting was indirect. There were candles on every table. In her imagination they would be scented and give off the faint fragrance of gardenia. She adored the smell of gardenia candles. Large windows offered a night cityscape. Dipping her spoon into her ice cream, she slid it into her mouth, enjoying the taste of the caramel praline on her tongue.

She heard the sound of a door opening and closing. A man came into her view. Nora gaped, the spoon halfway to her mouth again. The man, bronzed, and clad only in a white towel, was gorgeous. Absolutely, perfectly gorgeous! He appeared to be looking in her direction, and he smiled. The dazzling white teeth flashed against his tanned skin. All abs and pecs, and heaven only knew what else—she couldn't pull her eyes away from him.

His chest was broad and smooth. His waist and hips were narrow. He was tall with long, long legs. The full head of hair was raven black, cut short, but beautifully styled. Nora couldn't tell the color of his eyes beneath the bushy eyebrows, but hell! Did it really matter? Yeah, this was porn, but oh, baby! She couldn't wait to see the woman who would partner Mr. Gorgeous.

The man was looking directly at her, or at least it seemed he was looking directly at her. It was just the slightest bit eerie, Nora thought. Then he spoke, and of course the voice belonged with the buff body. It was deep with just the roughest edge to it. "Hello, Nora." He smiled again. It was a slightly crooked smile. "Hey, Red Rover, want to come over and play with me?" he crooned.

Nora smiled. When she was a kid they used to play a game called Red Rover. When she had first learned it she thought the boys were referring to her hair when they called to her, "Red Rover, come over." She stretched back in her recliner, waiting to see the hot babe who was undoubtedly about to appear. Why didn't Carla just say The Channel was a porn channel and let it go at that instead of making such a mystery of it? Probably thought I'd be shocked, Nora considered.

The man held out his hand. "Nora," he said quietly, "aren't

you coming? You did order The Channel, and it has created that little fantasy you've kept hidden all these years. Do you just want to stare at me, or do you want to have some fun with me?"

A sudden chill of surprise swept down her spine. He was talking to her! No! He couldn't be talking to her.

"Are you afraid, Nora? You don't have to be afraid, you know," he assured her with another crooked smile. "This is your fantasy, after all. We aren't going to do anything that you don't want to do, I promise you, but I assure you I know just what you want, darling. But you don't trust men right now, do you? Well, I can't blame you, considering what Jeff has done to you all these years." He held out his hand once again. "Come on, Nora. Come and be with me for a while. You'll enjoy it, I guarantee you."

For the longest moment Nora couldn't move. She was absolutely frozen in her chair. Her heart was hammering in her ears. He really was talking to her. He was! She swallowed visibly. Her throat felt tight, but she managed to speak. "Who are you?"

"My name is Kyle," he told her, and he smiled a third time. "You like the name Kyle, don't you?"

"Yes." It was in fact one of her favorite names. Nora wasn't certain that she shouldn't be very afraid, but she realized that she wasn't. Startled, yes. Surprised? You betcha! But she was not afraid. "How do you know me?" she questioned him.

"Well, I suppose you could say I was a part of you, Nora, because this is, after all, your fantasy. You've kept it hidden away deep in your subconscious for a very long time because fantasies are illusionary and not really meant to be lived out. And many fantasies wouldn't be considered respectable." He grinned. "By requesting The Channel, however, you allowed your fantasies to be released. It allows you to interact with your fantasies. This is the apartment that you always dreamed of, isn't it? You've furnished it in your mind a thousand times over, haven't you?"

"Yes," she said slowly. "But how can this be possible? How can I be seeing it on my television, and talking to you?"

He shook his dark head. "I have absolutely no idea," he answered honestly. "My reality seems to be your fantasy."

"Omigod!" she half whispered. "I'm asleep, then. Right?"

"Nope," he told her. "You're very much awake, Nora, my darling. Come and join me now." This time the smile he gave her was seductive and slow. It promised to fulfill her deepest desires.

"How?"

He placed his palm against the television's screen from the opposite side so that it faced her. "Match your hand to mine," he said, "and we'll be together."

"I'll be with you? In that apartment?" Nora sounded dubious. "And just how do I get back here to my own house, then?"

"Every woman visiting The Channel is returned at the end of the evening," he replied. "It just happens. Carla wouldn't steer you wrong, Nora, darling. You know she wouldn't. Come on over, Red Rover, and play with me. I play nice, and you know you really want to be with me."

"I don't think so," Nora answered him.

"Why not? Afraid?" he half taunted her. "You never used to be afraid of anything when you were a kid, darling."

"Maybe you haven't noticed," Nora remarked dryly, "but I'm not a kid any longer. I'm closer to fifty than forty. I've got about thirty pounds on me I didn't have way back when. My hair is showing signs of graying, and you, Mr. Gorgeous, should have someone equally gorgeous." She reached for the remote. It was past time to turn this thing off. She had to be dreaming, but if she shut The Channel down and woke herself up, maybe, just maybe, she could catch *Mystery* on PBS.

"Don't send me away, Nora, darling," he pleaded, divining her intent. "This is your fantasy, and you actually have the chance to live it. Here you can be whatever you want to be, and do whatever you want to do. If younger and sexy is what you desire, then you shall be young and sexy. The Channel allows you this unique opportunity."

Nora hesitated, fascinated by his words, surprised that she was actually beginning to consider them seriously. "You mean if I want to be thirty again, one hundred and twenty pounds, and have perky boobs again, I can?" This was crazy. Why was she even listening to him? Then she smiled to herself. She was listening because he was charming, and very tempting. It had been forever since a man had spoken to her as if she was a sensual and intelligent woman. Not someone's wife, or mother, or servant.

"You can be whoever you want to be when you're with me," he repeated. "Tell me what you would wear," he enticed her softly.

"Something sexy. I don't know," she said.

"I'd like to see you in a teddy. Black lace against your white skin, and red hair," Kyle murmured low.

"But no bikini bottom," she answered him, blushing at the vocal thought. "No, no teddy. I think one of those little short robes. Black silk. Just grazing the tops of my thighs."

"Yes, I'd like that. Just long enough to cover your pretty little pussy," he said.

Her cheeks were burning with his words. "Why do you prefer the robe?" she asked him.

"Because it would make it a whole lot easier to fuck you," he admitted frankly. Then he laughed. "You're blushing again. I can see it even with just the light from the television on your face. How long has it been since you were well and truly fucked, Nora, my darling?"

"Years," she sighed gustily. "Hell, you know the answer, Kyle. You don't have to ask me, do you?"

"The first time we do it," he told her, "we'll do it quickly because you need it badly. Then after that, we'll do it slowly. I'll make you scream with your orgasm. Jeff never made you scream, but I can."

"No," she said, "Jeff never made me scream. All he wanted to do was to satisfy himself. Still it was better than nothing, which is what I've been getting for the last few years," she finished tightly.

"Pity the other woman, Nora darling," he said. "Once the novelty wears off he'll start treating her the way he's treated you. She's going to be stuck. In ten years Jeff will be ready for Social Security, but you'll have me, and anyone else you want, for as long as you want," Kyle told her. "Would you like to have a threesome with another guy? Of course you would, Nora. And you can whenever you want to, Red Rover."

"Would you be jealous if another man screwed me?" she asked him.

"If all I could do was just sit and watch, yeah, damned straight, I would be!" Kyle said. "But it's your fantasy, Nora. You can do whatever you want to do with me. You might say I'm your slave." The quick smile flashed again.

Nora drew a long, slow, deep breath to clear her head. She was almost dizzy with the possibilities he offered. This was certainly the wildest dream she had ever had. While she was a little afraid of it, it was also very exciting. None of it was really happening of course. It just couldn't be. Yet, what if it was real? No, she thought. It wasn't real. Things like this just didn't exist. But the thought of Mr. Gorgeous as her personal slave, her boy toy, made her giggle. "Do you know Carla?" she asked him, suddenly curious.

He shook his head. "Only that she's your best friend. I'm your fantasy, Nora. Carla has her own fantasy. Every woman is different. Every woman has her own secret and private world. Some fantasies are sexual in nature, as yours. Some noble, or just plain fun. Some people, I am told, enjoy reliving a happier time in their lives."

She grew quiet now as he stood silent in his white towel looking longingly at her. How old was he? He was one of those ageless men with no hint as to his years. And who was he really? Some actor probably. But how would an actor know her name, and all her secrets? Especially from the other side of a television screen. What the hell was going on? How was any of this possible if she wasn't dreaming?

Nora pinched herself, starting as she felt the painful pressure of her fingers on her flesh. That was most definitely real. "Omigod!" she whispered again. It was very real, and very Faustian to boot. She looked directly at Kyle. "If," she said, "and it's a pretty big if, I came over to your side of things, what's the price I'd have to pay for it? Who controls The Channel, and what do they want in exchange for my buying into it?"

"Your soul," he said, and when she gasped he laughed aloud. "Just kidding. You'll get charged three ninety-five on your cable bill for a movie every time you visit The Channel, or you can add it to your program package for twelve dollars a month. That's all there is to it. Nothing sinister at all."

"Suburban Cable just thought it would be fun for its bored, discontented, overweight housewives to have a little interactive amusement, huh?" Nora said caustically.

He shrugged. "I don't know. Nora, my darling, why can't you just accept what's happening? The apartment. Me. We've been created out of your deepest imagination. Why are you unhappy with us?"

"I don't understand it," Nora admitted to him.

"Do you have to understand everything?" he asked. "Look, Nora, your friends turned you on to The Channel because they thought it was time, and they felt you needed it. Right now your reality sucks, and you need your fantasies if you're going to survive what's coming. Isn't that so? Damn, Nora, I want to reach out, take you in my arms, and comfort you. This isn't bad. It's good. Put your hand on mine, darling, and come over, Red Rover. I'll make the sadness go away, I promise you. I will." He stood directly before her, filling the television screen, pressing his big palm, fingers outspread, up for her to match with his. "Nora," he begged her, "please!"

This is not real, one side of her brain said. You are not having a conversation with a man in the TV. Well, if it isn't real, then why don't you put your hand on his and prove it? the other side of her brain taunted her. What if she actually put her hand up and was zapped into that dream apartment with this dream man, and he turned out to be a monster? She laughed bitterly. Would he be any worse than the man to whom she was married? Who was about to leave her for another woman? This was a dream. It was! So she was going to put her hand on his, and maybe she would be in that apartment, and then what?

Go ahead, the little voice in her head pressed her. Why are you always so afraid to try something new? Whatever you do with Kyle, at least it's only in your imagination. Not like your cheating husband, who is probably banging his girlfriend right now without a thought for you, or the children you share.

She put her spoon aside, and arose from her recliner. Kneeling before the television, she matched her hand to his. One hundred and twenty pounds and a pair of perky boobs, here I come! And Nora smiled to herself as she thought it. Still it wasn't going to happen, and she knew it. But what the hell! It was only a wild dream. A wonderful wild dream. And then her head began to spin.

CHAPTER TWO

S he actually felt a popping sensation within her body. Her head began to clear, and there was the distinct feeling of arms about her. Strong arms, and a very hard body. Nervously Nora opened her eyes and looked up into a pair of leaf green eyes laughing down at her. "Kyle?" she whispered. God! He was even better looking close-up. She closed her eyes again. This was not happening.

"Yes, Nora, darling, it's me," the rough-edged deep voice assured her, and she felt the kiss he pressed to the top of her head.

Nora's eyes flew open again. It was happening. It really was happening!

"I'm glad you finally got up enough courage to come over, Red Rover," he teased gently. Then taking her hand, he drew her over to a mirror, understanding exactly what her next thoughts were going to be.

Nora gasped softly. She stared hard at her image in the polished glass. She looked about thirty! Her hair was bright again, a long and luxurious mop of red gold curls that tumbled with reckless abandon over her shoulders. There wasn't a dimple of cellulite to be seen on her milky thighs or rounded knees. And she was wearing the most deliciously scanty garment, what little there was of it.

"Oh, my," Nora breathed, admiring herself in the very short black silk robe that was covering what appeared to be a voluptuously ripe and lush body.

Fascinated, she watched as standing behind her, he reached out to pull the sash of the garment open. Sliding his big hands around her torso, he displayed two perfectly firm breasts to her view. "These are very nice," he admired, fondling her gently. "Very, very nice, Nora." His hands were warm. His touch was wonderfully sensual.

"Ummm," Nora murmured. She closed her eyes, reveling in the pleasure his hands were giving her. She could feel the moisture already forming between her nether lips. She pressed herself back against the hard body, grinding her buttocks slowly into his groin. All her fears were gone. This man, or whatever he was, had no intention of harming her. She sensed it. He wanted only to please her. This was a fantasy, and she was in charge. Suddenly all her inhibitions drained away. Nora Buckley was entitled to something of her own even if it was only in her imagination.

According to Kyle she could demand all those tantalizing things she had always wanted to try. Things Jeff wouldn't even consider doing with her because he thought that wives should just lie still and get fucked by their husbands. He was probably doing those things with his girlfriend, the bastard! He always said if she obtained no pleasure in their lovemaking, it was her fault, not his. But how did you gain pleasure from being slammed on your back, screwed quickly, and then told to shower before you slept? There had never been any foreplay, and it was always done in the dark.

Well, damnit, it hadn't been her fault. It had been his, and she had always known it. He used her to relieve his lust, and nothing more. In the beginning she hadn't understood that, being a virgin, and not particularly well-informed. But she had heard her friends talking, and it had encouraged her to read more about sex. Once in an effort to spice up his performance she had suggested he spank her, and she put her fingers in her mouth and told him that she had been a very bad girl. Jeff had recoiled, and angrily demanded to know where she had gotten such a perverted idea. After that, she didn't dare suggest he use his tongue on her. She had read the tongue was a terrific and sensual organ. Her husband had never even French-kissed her.

Nora opened her eyes and looked at herself in the mirror again. She turned slowly to admire herself. Wow! What a body she had imagined. It was perfect. She hadn't looked that good since she was twenty. Hell, she had never looked this good. She turned around herself in his arms so they were facing one another, her hands fastened onto the towel wrapped about his lean loins. She pulled it away. "Turnabout is fair play," she told him softly.

"You just want to see my dick, you naughty creature," he answered with a wicked grin. Then he stepped back so she might get the full view.

Nora's pulse raced as she stared at his male member. She was certain that Jeff's penis was a normal size. Kyle's, however, was very definitely supersized. Even in its current quiet state it was very long, and thick. Reaching out, she took him in her hand. Her fingers wandered slowly, teasingly, down the length of him. Almost immediately she felt him begin to harden. Her hand slipped beneath him, cupping the sac containing his balls in her palm. He was, to use an old expression, heavy hung. "Very nice." She smiled up at him. "Very, very nice."

He chuckled, and the sound was rich. It warmed her all over. "We're going to have fun, Red Rover, aren't we?" he said.

She nodded slowly. "Yep," she agreed. "We're going to have lots of fun, Kyle. I still don't know how all this is possible, but I think for now I'll stop trying to figure it all out. I don't really care anymore." She gave his balls a gentle squeeze.

"Good girl!" he approved. Then he took the hand playing with him and said, "Come on, Nora. We're both anxious for that first fuck, aren't we? And just look what that wicked little hand of yours has done."

She gazed down, and her mouth made a small O of surprise. His penis was swollen, the tip of it almost ruby red in color now. *Supersized* didn't even begin to describe it now. She had never imagined a male organ that big. But she must have if he was standing there with it practically waving at her.

She followed him across the living room, as he opened a pair of double doors into a spacious, luxuriously furnished bedroom. The same city skyline view she had seen through the living room windows was available through the bedroom windows. And similar French doors opened out onto a large planted terrace. A Kwanzan cherry tree in full pink bloom pressed its branches against a corner of the doors. But she had no time to really inspect her new surroundings because he was pushing her back onto a bed covered with black satin sheets.

"Open wide for Papa," he said, kissing her. The mouth exploring hers was hungry and wet. Next it pressed slowly on her eyelids, her cheeks, the tip of her nose, as his big hands held her head between them. "You are so sweet," he murmured low. "So very, very sweet!"

I am in paradise, Nora thought as his gentle passion began to claim her. She felt him nudge her thighs apart with a knee. She spread herself without argument. He filled her with one smooth thrust. "Oh, God!" Nora moaned, but after just a few hard strokes of that thick, long penis she came, her juices mixing with his as he exploded inside her. "Oh, Kyle! That was so good," she exclaimed, sighing gustily. His weight on her felt wonderful. Suddenly she realized that he hadn't withdrawn his penis from her vagina. She could actually feel it throbbing and very hot within her. She looked at him questioningly.

"I told you the first time it would be fast because we both

needed it," he reminded her, "but the second time is gonna be real slow. I'm going to make you scream, Nora. I'm a man of my word." Still buried within her he drew her up slightly and, leaning forward, began to lick at the nipples of her breasts. His mouth closed over one nipple, and he sucked hard on it.

"Do it to me again!" she hissed at him.

"Not yet," he said, releasing the nipple, and looking into her eyes. "I'm going to teach you that it doesn't have to be fast. That you don't have to grab at your satisfaction, Nora. It will be there for you whenever you want it." His lips moved to the other nipple.

The tug of his mouth on her flesh was maddening. The sensation of his thick cock filling her but not yet fully pleasuring her was beginning to anger her. "Do it to me!" she insisted. She wiggled slightly against him, pressing down. "Do it to me now!" She was being wanton. She had always wanted to be wanton. Just as she had always liked sex, but hadn't been allowed to have enough of it in the years she had been married to Jeff. But no more! This was her fantasy, and Nora Buckley was going to get everything she had always wanted. Wouldn't her friends be surprised if they knew that their nice friend was a sex-starved wanton. She laughed aloud. "Do it, Kyle!" she commanded him. "Now! I want to be fucked hard, and mindless. You can do it! You can!"

He bit her nipple sharply, and then a slow smile lit his features. "At my lady's service," he told her.

"Yes!" Nora cried. "Isn't that what you're here for, Kyle? To service me in any way I want it, and any time I want it?" She felt the thrill of control race through her.

"That's exactly what I'm here for, Nora," he acquiesced, laying her back down again, kissing her fiercely.

Sex! Pure raw sex without any entanglements. Without guilt. Sex with a man whose sole aim was to please her. To make her feel good. Love had absolutely nothing to do with it. Nor did duty, or whatever else anyone expected of her. For the first time in her life Nora felt the taste of freedom. Spread shamelessly on black satin sheets. A handsome man with a very large and very talented cock plunging in and out of her. And it was wonderful!

His mouth demanded her full attention as it worked its way across her face, her throat, and her lips again. His penis was driving her into a frenzy of pleasure such as she had never, ever known in all of her life. Why couldn't it have been this way with Jeff? she thought briefly. Jeff, whom she had once loved, but was startled to realize she no longer loved. Other husbands and wives remained lovers. Why hadn't they? But it didn't matter anymore.

She wrapped her long legs around Kyle's muscled torso, groaning as each new position gave him greater access to her body. He plunged deeper into the hot, wet maw of her boiling sex. "Do it! Do it!" she screamed as she kissed his ear, and then nipped the lobe. Her fingers dug at his muscled shoulders, the nails clawing down his long back. She strained against him, almost resisting.

"Little bitch!" he growled at her. "Can't get enough, can you?" His groin slammed violently into hers as he worked his penis back and forth. "This is just the beginning," he told her. "The things I'm going to do to you and make you do to me, baby, you're going to love it. You are so hot, Nora!" He thrust and pumped harder, and even harder as he saw the subtle changes beginning to take place on her face, felt the faint quiver beginning deep inside her body. "Come on, Nora," he taunted her, licking at her ear, pushing the tip of his tongue to and fro in it, simulating there what he was doing with his penis in her hot, slick vagina. "You want to scream, baby! I can feel what's going on inside of you, Nora! Let it happen! Let it happen!"

She was burning up. She was ready to combust. He seemed to be getting harder and longer with each jab of his talented cock, and she loved it! She had only climaxed once in her entire life. The second time she and Jeff had had sex after they were married. He had scolded her for crying out. Unladylike, he told her.

Decent women didn't howl like banshees. But now the spasms rocking her very being were turning into violent tremors. Nora opened her mouth, shrieking with the pleasure her lover was engendering in her. "Oh, God, yes! Don't stop, darling! Don't stop! Ahhh! Ahhhhhh! Oh! Ohhh, Godddd!" She shuddered violently, and then for the first time in her life fainted.

But she revived herself quickly, shutting her eyes tight, praying, Oh, don't let me be back in that damned recliner yet! Let me still be on the bed with the black satin sheets, and the marvelous Mr. Gorgeous by my side. Then she felt a kiss on her forehead. Her eyes flew open in spite of herself.

"Told you I could make you scream," he said, pleased with himself, and smiling his warm, crooked smile at her. "You're going to come every time I fuck you, Red Rover. Every. Single. Time," he told her with emphasis on each word.

"Threat or promise?" she asked, recovered, and smiling up at him. "Either way is okay with me, darling Kyle."

He laughed. "Want to take a shower now?" he asked, getting off the bed.

"The bathroom's through there, right?" She pointed to another set of double doors on a far wall.

He nodded.

"It better have one of those great big tubs as well as a shower," Nora said, rising.

"It's your fantasy," he responded. "Want to go look?"

It was exactly as she had always dreamed it would be. Not some small utilitarian room with a tub/shower, sink, and toilet. This was a great big light and airy chamber with long arched windows offering another view of the cityscape. The Italian-tile floor was heated. It felt wonderful beneath her bare feet. The commode—because in a room like this you wouldn't call it a toilet— and the bidet were set behind lacquered white doors that could be closed for privacy.

Kyle sat her on the bidet. Then, kneeling, he adjusted the

water for temperature and direction, turning the bidet on. After a moment he reached between her thighs and washed her with a soft flannel cloth, then let the water caress her sexual anatomy for a moment or two more. It was the most sensual and intimate thing any man had ever done to her or for her. Turning the water off, he drew her up, and gave her a lingering kiss. "Come and see the rest of the room, Nora," he invited her.

In one corner of the room was a large curved glass and tile shower. And the tub was an enormous rectangle of marble sunk into the floor. There were two steps leading down into the perfumed water. A mirrored wall was fitted with two marble sinks, each set on its own single column, and no tacky cabinets beneath. The large closet in the bathroom was opened to reveal shelves filled with black and white towels of thick Egyptian cotton terry, along with matching robes and wraps.

"Gold fixtures," Nora murmured almost to herself. "Jeff thinks gold fixtures are vulgar," she told Kyle, "but I like them. Where's the masseur?"

"He's available whenever you want him," Kyle said, not even blinking at her request. He pointed to the small cell phone affixed on the wall by the sinks. "We can call when you're ready for him."

"He's blond, right?" Nora asked. "Austrian with one of those cute accents, and his name is Rolf?"

Kyle nodded, his leaf green eyes twinkling. "Yes, ma'am. He's exactly as you want him to be."

"I don't think I ever want to go back to reality," Nora said, sighing.

"Everyone has to face reality eventually, Red Rover," he answered her. "That's what makes our fantasies so very special." Then, walking across the room, he opened the shower doors and turned on the faucets. "Come on. We're both pretty rank, and the night is young. You still aren't satisfied. I can tell."

"I've probably never been, considering all the years Jeff has ignored me while he played around," Nora said bitterly. "And what happens if whoever invented The Channel takes it away?"

"You're asking me questions I can't answer, Nora," Kyle told her. "Don't worry about what hasn't happened yet, if it ever happens. Let's just enjoy the moment." He held out his hand to her. "Come on, baby."

Taking the hand, Nora let him draw her into the shower. There were water jets spouting at her from every angle. She could have sworn that the shower water was perfumed too. But was such a thing possible? Hey, why not? It was her fantasy, after all.

"This is a liquid-soap dispenser," Kyle said as he showed her a small spigot and matching button in the tiled wall. He pressed it, and began rubbing the slick substance across her shoulders. His big hands worked down her back, and over her rounded buttocks. Then he let the water jets rinse her back clean before turning her about and washing her breasts, her torso, and the luxuriant curls covering her pubic mound. The water rinsed her again.

"My turn!" Nora told him gaily. She pushed the button, and her hand was filled with the sweet smelling soap. She began to wash him in the same manner as he had washed her, hands smoothing over hard flesh. His shoulders were broad. His torso was narrow. His butt simply adorable. She couldn't resist giving it a little squeeze. "You've got the cutest tush," she told him. Then she let the water rinse him.

He turned about so she might wash his front. Her hands worked leisurely across his chest while his hands began to caress her breasts, moving down along her rib cage, and finally to her belly. Her hands followed his every move. She soaped his pubic hair, fondling his hairy balls with a teasing motion, washing his penis, which was growing harder with each stroke of her hands. His response was to be expected. Reaching down, he pushed between her nether lips into her vagina with two fingers to tease her back. Then they were kissing again while the hot water pouring over them began to feel cool in relation to the heat their bodies were generating with their rising sexual arousal.

His hands cupped her buttocks as he backed her into the tile wall of the shower. The fingers were withdrawn, replaced by his hard penis as he lifted her up, then lowered her onto his eager organ. She sheathed him entirely, her arms tightening about his neck. Fuck! That was all it seemed she wanted to do. Fuck! She was soaking wet from her head to her toes, and all she wanted to do was pleasure herself on this man's talented cock. She groaned almost angrily as she felt her climax coming much too quickly. "No, damnit!"

"Let it happen," he hissed in her ear. "There's going to be more where that came from, Nora. I never get tired. Let it happen, and just enjoy."

"Ahhhh!" She could help herself, and she immediately wanted more.

Kyle laughed softly, and kissed her tenderly as his arms went about her. He set her down on her feet again. "Poor Red Rover," he said. "I can only imagine what it has been like for you with Jeff. He didn't give a damn about you. Just grabbed his own pleasure and left you hanging. A wham-bam man, right?" His big hand stroked Nora's wet hair. "Once you get used to me, Nora, you'll see that you don't have to rush. I told you. I'm tireless. I can go on just as long as you need me to go on. I'm going to teach you to take your time and get all the pleasure you want. Trust me."

She could feel his heart thumping beneath her cheek. The hot water was hitting them from all sides as she stood there getting her breath back. "I never," she began, "in all the years I've been married got the kind of pleasure from Jeff that I'm getting from you. I wasn't even certain this kind of pleasure really existed except in the minds of romance novelists. But you're right. I'm so afraid you'll come before me that I climax too quickly. We've got to work on that, Kyle. It's my fantasy, after all."

"We're going to, darling, and won't it be fun," he answered with a grin.

"Let's get out of here," Nora said. "I'm starting to prune. And I do believe that I'm ready for Rolf, my masseur, now."

"Shameless and insatiable," Kyle chuckled as they stepped from the shower. "The two qualities I like best in a woman. Here." He handed her one of the large towels. "Dry off while I call down for Rolf." He wrapped a towel about his lean loins, and walking across the floor, he picked up the cell from its wall cradle, speaking softly into it.

Nora wrapped her hair in the towel he had given her, taking another to dry herself off. She felt so alive. She had been fucked three times in what? An hour? Two hours? She had absolutely no conception of time here. Did it matter? How long could this last, and could she order The Channel again whenever she wanted it? Surely they didn't put a limit on something as wonderful as this. That would be too cruel. She wondered if Kyle knew.

"Rolf will be right up," Kyle said, coming across the heated floor from the phone, and toweling himself as he walked. "Turn around, and I'll get your back, baby."

"Can I order The Channel whenever I want it?" Nora asked him. "I mean, do they put a limit on it?"

"Not that I've ever heard," he responded. "Does that mean you want to come back?" He slid his hands around to cup her breasts, teasing the nipples, which responded immediately to his touch.

"Hell," Nora said, "I don't ever want to leave. Stop, or I'm going to go down on you, Kyle. You're getting me all hot again."

"Hi there!" A voice with an Austrian accent.

They turned to to see a blond man standing in the wide doorway of the bathroom.

"I'm Rolf. Shall we do it here, or in the bedroom?" He was carrying a folded table with him, and had a pouch slung across his barrel chest.

Nora's eyes wandered boldly over the young man. Medium height. Muscled, but not ugly muscles. A stocky hard body. Blue eyes. Rosy cheeks. Naked. She licked her lips. Well, hell, they were naked too. It made it all so much easier. His genitals were very nicely formed, and she admired them. Rolf would do a lot more than just give her a massage, and she found she could hardly wait. "Set your table up in here," she told him. "Kyle, darling, why don't you take a break."

"Don't I get to watch?" he demanded.

"Do you want to watch?" she teased him. God! This was so exciting.

"Only if you want me to," he countered, but she could tell he did.

"I'll call you when I want you, then," Nora told him. She was in charge here, and she wanted to punish him just a little because she could. The jealousy she saw flare in his eyes gave her a great sense of satisfaction.

Rolf set up his table near the bathing pool. Taking a pale peach-colored percale sheet from his pouch, he flipped it over the table. "Let's start you on your back," he told her, helping her up onto the table. "Ever had a massage before?"

"I'm a virgin," she told him provocatively.

The blue eyes danced. "I'm very good with virgins," he replied. "Close your eyes now, and let me do my thing, sweetie."

"Are you?" she answered him boldly.

"So I've been told. You be the judge, Nora. If I'm a bad boy, you can spank me," he teased. "Gardenia or almond oil? I've got both."

"Gardenia." She closed her eyes as ordered, and imagined Rolf bent over the couch in the living room while she spanked him with a hairbrush, turning those plump white cheeks pink. It was something to think about, and where in the name of heaven were these lascivious thoughts coming from? Nora wondered. "Oh, that feels good," she told him as his hand began to knead and smooth her shoulders.

"I've only just begun," he responded. "It's going to get better and better before I'm all through with you." He was behind her, slicking the scented oil over her skin.

How was it possible that she could feel all of this? She was deep into a fantasy, yet she not only felt but smelled the oil. And she certainly had all her other senses intact as well. Why was she questioning how it was possible? It actually made her brain hurt. Just relax and enjoy it, she told herself. She pushed the confused thought away, and concentrated on the hands with their supple fingers that were now digging into the aching muscles of her shoulders and neck. She hadn't realized before now just how sore those muscles were. While she had never enjoyed the delights of a massage, she instinctively knew that Rolf had a great talent for it. Did she want him to have other talents? She smiled to herself. Oh, yes, she did!

She was relaxing beneath the skilled touch. His hands were now working on her left arm and hand. My God, Nora thought, if this is my fantasy, how long and how deep has it been buried in my imagination? This is one helluva daydream, but I love it! I've been married so very long. I married too young. I put aside everything I wanted to be the perfect wife and mother. And what did I want? It's been so long I don't know, if I ever did. Jeff has the morals of a mink and the ethics of a weasel. My kids are to all intents and purposes grown and gone. I'm all alone.

"Stop thinking!" Rolf's voice barked, piercing her consciousness. "You're starting to tense up again, sweetie." He was finishing her right arm, and now his hands moved to smooth oil over her chest. His fingers closed about her breasts. "Nice pair," he observed, squeezing lightly. "Round, firm, and big nipples, kinda like blown roses."

"I'm not going to relax if you keep doing that," Nora laughed up at him. "Oh, that is sooo nice, Rolfie!" Her nipples puckered, and a shiver ran down her backbone as his thumbs rubbed insistently at the soft flesh.

"This isn't about sex," he scolded her. "I'm here to give you a nice massage, sweetie. Now stop thinking with your cunt, and I'll get on with my job."

"But don't you want to—" She didn't get to finish the sentence.

"Sure I do," he answered her, "but not yet. Firrst a nice massage and then . . ." Leaning over, he grinned engagingly into her face. "Now, shut up, and let me do one of the two things I do best."

"Do I get to guess the other?" she murmured mischievously. Lord! She hadn't had so much fun in years. She hadn't ever had so much fun. And it wasn't just the sex. She was being admired as a beautiful woman. She was being spoken with as an intelligent being. If nothing more happened this night, she would be content. No! She most certainly would not be! This was fun. Sex was fun. And she had never really believed it until Kyle had shown her earlier. She had enjoyed every moment with him. She was going to enjoy little Rolfie too before the evening was over. Whenever that was.

And Kyle was going to watch. He had shown a delicious dash of jealousy earlier, and she wanted him jealous. Jealousy by a man, for her, wasn't something she had ever experienced. She had liked it. It made her feel powerful, and power, Nora realized, was almost as good as sex. She contemplated Kyle watching as Rolfie fucked her. Imagining him wanting her even as another man had her was exciting. Her own desires began to stir again, and she murmured.

Rolf's hands had finally departed her bosom, which felt firmer as his fingers moved away to slide over her belly. Tonight she possessed a belly only slightly rounded, and not pulled out of shape by childbirth and too many years of comfort eating. The pressure of his facile hands was stimulating, particularly when he pressed the heel of one palm down on her pubic bone. A jolt of sensation shot through her, and her eyes flew open. "Oh!"

"Eyes closed!" he ordered her sharply. "You don't want to look. Just sense, sweetie." He cupped her cunt with the same hand. His fingers played gently with her labia, rubbing oil into the twin lower lips with a light touch. A finger slipped between her moist nether lips, finding her clitoris. He used the ball of that finger to rub the tiny sentient bit of flesh until she began to squirm with her rising pleasure. Bringing her to a quick clitoral orgasm, he moved on and began to massage her thighs.

Damnit, Nora thought. I want more. Aren't I supposed to be the boss here? Then she smiled to herself again. Don't be impatient and greedy, girl. Rolfie is doing just great without any instructions from you, so just enjoy. The night is young. She purred with pleasure as his fingers kneaded her calf, and then began to massage her foot. Why had she denied herself the delights of massage until now? she wondered. Because Jeff wouldn't have approved of a man massaging her, and he would have made suggestive remarks if she had a female masseuse. He would have told her that a respectable woman didn't do things like that. Well, she wasn't so sure of that, but now she had her fantasy, and oh, yes! Yes! Yes! Yes! Massages were wonderful.

Rolf had finished with one leg and began to work on the other. He was skillful, and he was efficient. When he had finished with her legs he said, "Over we go, sweetie," and he helped her turn onto her stomach and get her face down into the headrest.

Nora felt the warm oil flowing onto her shoulders again, and she sighed appreciatively. The gardenia fragrance was subtle yet haunting. She absolutely loved it. It was definitely her scent, but next time she'd use the almond oil. And was there such a thing as freesia oil? She adored the smell of freesia. Rolf's fingers dug into her flesh as he worked to massage the knots away.

The hands moved slowly down her back, smoothing away the tensions of twenty-six years of marriage to Jeffrey Buckley. Nora suddenly realized that she didn't care if he left her for another woman. They had nothing in common anymore, if they ever did.

They had done what was expected of them in the time in which they grew up. It was what their families wanted. What generations before them had done.

Jeff had chosen a respectable virgin several years his junior. He wooed her, won her, and had then gone off to grad school and the military while she remained safe and loyal in her college dorm, studying diligently, and just waiting for the day when they would marry. He could trust her to be faithful. Nora Edwards was what was known in their youth as a good girl. And after their marriage came the house, the two children, and the membership to the right country club.

And while she remained at home raising the children, and making it all perfect for him, and Jeff made a great success of his career. The golden boy became a partner within five years of joining Coutts and Wickham Advertising. With each success he had made it his goal to top himself in the next campaign for the next client. He had quickly grown away from the wife he had so carefully chosen, the two children he had sired. Work and other women became the most important things for Jeff Buckley.

And she had never noticed because she had been so busy with Brownies or Boy Scouts; Little League or soccer; Sunday school or the church choir. Nora had taken pride in her children because Jeff never discussed his work with her. Work and Nora were two different things in his mind. So she had focused on their children, who needed her, especially as their father came home less and less. Now Nora Edwards Buckley, who had graduated summa cum laude with a degree in English literature, was suddenly forced to face the fact that she had no husband and no life.

What the hell was she supposed to do with the rest of her life? She wasn't fit for anything. Not in this new century with all its technology. A degree in English lit with a minor in home ec. What the hell had she been thinking? But how could she have known it would end up this way? She had no teaching skills. But she didn't want to teach. No computer skills, but she would need them now. Whatever happened with Jeff, she had to make a new life for herself.

Hell, she wasn't fifty yet. Close, but not there yet. No one retired at sixty-five anymore. Not if he or she could help it. She wasn't brain-dead. She could work twenty or more years, have a nice little 401(k) and collect her own Social Security. She could build a separate investment portfolio as well. She could do a lot of things if she could just get her act together and decide just what it was she really wanted to do.

"You're thinking again," Rolf chided, giving her butt a smack. "This is supposed to be relaxing for you, sweetie."

"I'm trying to figure out my future," Nora told him. "Carla and the girls are right. I have to make a life for myself. Rina's probably right too. Jeff is going to dump me. Besides, I have to be someone other than his wife and my kids mother. I have to find me again. I know I'm there somewhere, Rolfie. What do you think?"

"I think you're a very smart lady, Nora," he replied as he kneaded her buttocks. "You just need a little time to figure it all out. You need to restore that confidence you once had before you met Jeff. You don't need a man to take care of you, sweetie. You can do it yourself."

"Yep, Rolfie, but I still need time. I wonder if I'm going to get it. I guess the first thing for me to do is take a computer course, but the high school adult ed doesn't kick in until autumn. Still, that's the logical place for me to start, isn't it?"

"You're thinking again," Rolf said. "This is supposed to be relaxing for you." He was massaging her buttocks now, and the heel of his hand slipped deeply between the twin halves of her ass.

Nora caught her breath as he rubbed her. "I'm thinking about my future," she told him. A single finger was now gently rubbing at her anus. She tensed, but when he did nothing more than continue to rub her there, she began to relax a little bit.

"That's better," he said softly. The oily finger pushed itself one joint into her ass.

Nora gasped, and tensed again.

He bent and kissed the back of her neck, whispering, "Not yet, Nora, but one day that sexy little ass of yours is going to take my cock. You'll like it, I promise."

"Will I?" Her voice was tight.

"Yep, you will," he promised. Then he removed the invading digit, and smoothed his hand over her butt. "All done now, sweetie."

She drew a long breath, feeling a strange loss as the finger had been withdrawn. She had never considered anal sex, or had she? How much of what was happening came from her subconscious, and how much was just spontaneous? "All done?" she repeated.

"I don't think so, Rolfie," she told him boldly.

Rolf was at one of the sinks washing his hands. He laughed. "I can see you are a very bad girl, Nora. I really do believe you need a good spanking. That cute little ass is just begging for it, I'm thinking."

"Kyle," Nora called. "Rolfie wants to spank me. Then I think he's going to fuck me. Come and watch like a good boy, darling." Good Lord! A couple of delicious bangs and an erotic massage, and she was talking to these two men as she had certainly never talked to any man. But Carla always said men loved it when a woman talked dirty to them. She really couldn't believe herself. She suddenly felt strong. Maybe she always had been.

Kyle stood in the bathroom door. He was handsome in a rough-hewn, almost barbaric way. Her eyes couldn't help but go to his male member. It was so wonderfully big, and so deliciously talented. His eyes were still jealous as he spoke. "You probably do deserve a spanking, Nora. I've never known a hotter little bitch than you. If you're through, Rolf, we can all adjourn to the bedroom."

They helped her from the massage table, and led her back into the bedroom. There was a roll-armed love seat in a seating area before the fireplace. They brought her over to it, bending Nora over one of the arms.

"Are you going to tie me down?" she teased them.

"A couple of good smacks shouldn't bother you, baby," Rolf said, "but Kyle will be kneeling on the love seat and holding your shoulders down for me," he told her as Kyle knelt on the silk cushion before her, his groin at eye level. Rolf delivered the first smack on her round bottom, causing Nora to squeak with surprise, for she hadn't been expecting it quite so soon. "Just a few little love taps to warm you up, Nora," he told her. His hard hand descended again, and again, and yet again.

"Ohhh!" she squealed, but strangely it didn't really hurt. Rolf's big wide palm just stung. She began to feel a rather sensuous and delicious warmth spreading across her buttocks, not to mention a faint tingling in her sexual organs. And then came the startling knowledge that she liked it. God! Her conscience kicked in. What kind of a pervert was she that she liked this tender abuse? She wiggled her bottom at him, and his hands grasped her hips to steady her. He leaned over, murmuring hotly in her ear, "I am so hot for you, Nora. I'm going to fuck you now, sweetie."

"Where?" The words were out of her mouth before she knew it.

He chuckled, and dropped a kiss on the nape of her neck. "You're not ready for that yet, but I suspect we'll get to it eventually. Right now I'm going to stuff your cunt, and you're going to love it."

Her heart was beating with excitement. She had never in all her life been taken in this position. Jeff had never let her off her back, and when once she had tried to mount him, he had thrown her off him roughly, slapping her angrily, and demanding to know where she had ever gotten such a damned disgusting idea. She hadn't dared to tell him that the girls had been talking about sexual positions, and other things unmentionable.

"Wooo!" she exclaimed, feeling Rolf's penis penetrating into her hot, wet softness. His member was shorter than Kyle's, but thicker. But he was extremely skillful with it. He moved very slowly into her, withdrawing himself as slowly. Over and over and over again. It was an incredible tease. She was close to screaming with the pure unadulterated pleasure he was giving her. "Oh, God! That is so good, Rolfie!" she sighed. "Don't stop, and that's an order! Don't you dare stop. Ahh! Yes! Yes! Yes! Ohhh, that is sooo good." She wiggled her buttocks into his groin, unable to stop herself.

"What a divine wanton you are," Rolf said, laughing. "I think she can take both of us, Kyle. What do you say?" His fingers pressed into the tender flesh of her hips.

"Yeah," Kyle agreed. "Naughty Nora needs two cocks because she is very, very hot tonight, aren't you, darling?" He stroked her hair gently. Then his fingers closed about her hair, and he pulled her head up. "Open your mouth, Nora." He rubbed his penis against her lips. "Ah, there you go, baby." He pushed his penis between her two lips, and into her mouth. "Nice and easy does it, Nora. Keep your teeth away from it. Just use your tongue, and then your throat. I'll bet Jeff never let you suck his cock, although plenty of other women have." His eyes closed a moment. "Ahhhh, that's it, darling. God, Nora, you're a natural at this," he told her.

At first Nora thought she was going to choke, but then as she became intrigued with the realization that she had a penis in her mouth, she felt him burgeoning, and her throat relaxed. Fascinated, she began to lick and suck him. The taste was fleshy and salty with just a hint of musk. She could hear both of the men moaning with their own rising pleasure. They were going to all come together—she knew it! This was incredible. She felt her climax exploding even as she found herself being spermed from both ends. Rolf kept coming, and coming and coming; and Kyle's cum was so copious she could barely swallow it fast enough.

Then without warning Nora's head began to spin. There was a feeling of aloneness. She was being reluctantly dragged through time and space. Or at least that was how it felt to her. Suddenly her eyes flew open, and her body jerked with an orgasm that suffused every inch of her body. But she was in her chair. In the den. Her eyes went immediately to the television. The screen was blank. The set was off.

"Omigod!" Nora gasped. What had happened to her? What the hell had happened? Who had turned off the television? The remote lay on the table next to a melted pint of caramel praline ice cream. "Omigod!" she said again. She distinctly remembered turning on the television. She remembered kneeling before it. Matching her hand to Kyle's and being with him. There. In that gorgeous apartment with the incredible skyline view.

But it was obviously a dream. It must have been. None of it had really happened. It couldn't have. Stuff like that didn't really happen. She had let her imagination run away with her. But she suddenly smelled the fragrance of gardenias on her skin. No! It was a dream. But then why was her hair damp, and why did it smell freshly washed?

Nora tried to stand up, but fell back into her chair. Her legs were weak. She was taken aback by the slick and salty taste in her mouth. By the fact her vagina was very sore. Like she had had sex. Lots of sex. The house was quiet. Outside it was still dark. The clock on the fireplace mantle struck the half hour, but what half hour? Reaching for the remote, she turned the television back on and saw that it was four thirty in the morning. Where had she been for the past eight and a half hours?

Nora turned the set off again, and sat in the dark of the den. It hadn't been a dream as much as she needed to believe it had been. It had all been very real. Kyle and Rolf had taken her a total of four times. Nora could never remember being fucked more than once in a night in her whole life. And she had been so wanton. She shivered with the chill of the predawn hour. Her brain felt as if it were going to explode with the knowledge of what had happened to her during these past few hours. She had to stop attempting to analyze and understand it or she was going to go nuts.

Nora breathed slowly, deeply, in an effort to calm the frantic beating of her heart. Then she attempted to stand up again. This time she was successful. No lights, she thought. If anyone is up peeing and sees lights at this time of morning, theyll come running over. I can't face anyone right now. Carefully she made her way from the den to the center hall of the house, and up the stairs to her bedroom. She literally fell into the bed and was instantly asleep.

She didn't awaken until the sun was shining brightly in the room. She didn't need to look at the bedside clock. It was after noon. The sun only came into the bedroom in the afternoon. She rolled over onto her back. She was exhausted. And she was still sore. She hadn't ever in her life had such a workout as she had last night. And she smelled of sex. She hadn't smelled that odor in years, but it wasn't a scent you forgot. I want to go back, she thought. But Jeff would probably come home tonight because she had made him feel guilty yesterday. And she couldn't go to The Channel if J. J. was in the house. What was today? Oh, shit! It was Tuesday, and she hadn't put the garbage out for the weekly collection. If Jeff came home, he'd bitch at her over it. She'd have to make a dump run so he didn't know.

The school Athletic Association awards were Friday. Jeff would definitely be home then, because how he appeared to the public was very important to Jeff. And he'd probably stay for the weekend. Could she annoy him enough so he'd go back to the city, and his girlfriend? Maybe. Maybe not. Damn! She really wanted to go back to The Channel. The place was an aphrodisiac and she had been quickly hooked.

Nora got up and showered, soon smiling at the dried semen she found in her matted pubic hair before she stepped beneath the water. It had been real! Oh, yes! It had been very real, and she could hardly wait for it to be real again. She winced as she accidentally banged her elbow on the tile wall. It was like bathing in a coffin, she thought. No lights. No view. She needed to talk to Carla. Getting out of the shower, Nora wrapped herself in a towel, grimacing as she realized that her body was back to normal! The sides of the fabric didn't overlap on her frame.

I don't have to be fat like this, she thought. I've really let myself pork up in the last few years. I need some exercise. Maybe I'll start walking with Carla. I hate the way I look in my clothes. My height is all in my torso, and so is the fat. She pulled on a pair of cotton briefs, fastened her bra, squeezed into her stretch jeans, and yanked a bright yellow T-shirt on over her head. Then perching herself on the edge of the bed, she called Carla.

"Hi, it's me. We've got to talk before the kids get home from school. Yeah, I'm here. Just barely. Come on over. I'll get out the wine. It's afternoon, and I need wine."

Several minutes later Carla Johnson came into the kitchen with a plate of turkey sandwiches, and sat down at the table across from her best friend. "It's only one, and I'll bet you haven't eaten. You're going to be sick as a pig if you drink wine on an empty stomach. You went to The Channel, right?" she said matter-of-factly.

"I went to The Channel," Nora said. "Perfect night for it. Jeff stayed in town. First time I didn't mind he did. J. J. stayed at his girlfriend's house to meet some bigwig from State." She sipped the wine nervously, and then began to eat one of the sandwiches, surprised to learn she was very hungry.

"Well?" Carla demanded, cocking her head to one side, her brown eyes curious. "What did you find there? And did you like it?"

"It's my dream apartment," Nora began. "The one I've always talked about. It is so beautiful there, and I'm not a plump matron pushing fifty either. I am this sexy redhead about thirty. And I had sex with two men. Wild animal sex!" Nora laughed.

Carla grinned. "I wouldn't tell this to anyone else but you and the others," she said. "I'm Captain Raven, the pirate queen.

I sail the Caribbean, and have sex with whoever takes my fancy. Two nights ago I captured an English vessel bound for the Indies. There was a very handsome and wealthy young duke aboard. He was willing to do anything I wanted him to do to effect his release. At first he was quite difficult, but I made him walk the plank. When we fished him out he became much more reasonable."

She giggled. "Isn't The Channel great? We can have all the sex we want without venereal disease, AIDS, unplanned pregnancies, or guilt. I don't know who invented it, but it's terrific, and we owe them a vote of thanks."

"Nothing is for free," Nora said slowly.

"We pay for it," Carla replied glibly. "You'll see it on your cable bill. Movie. Three ninety-five."

"Doesn't Rick wonder about all those movies?" Nora asked.

"Nah, I pay the bills," Carla said. "And I took the twelve-dollars-a-month deal."

"I thought you loved Rick," Nora said.

"I do love Rick, but sometimes I want a change. I want to be young and sexy again. Doesn't everyone? I mean, hell, men do it with different women. Why are women expected to confine themselves to only one man? At least our generation thought that way. Tiffany loves her harem romance novels, so she's the sultan's favorite. Rina won't say."

Nora laughed. She couldn't help it. "Yeah, I'd expect Tiff would be the sultan's favorite. Carla! It was so real! I mean I'm actually sore."

"It is real, girlfriend. Now tell me how many times you did it with them, and who are they?" She leaned forward eagerly, her brown eyes sparkling.

"Four," Nora said, blushing with her memories. "Three times with my lover. His name is Kyle, and he's absolutely hunky. The last time was with my masseur. He's blond, has an Austrian accent, and is named Rolf. Kyle watched us while we did it, but he got jealous, and put his dick in my mouth. We all came together! It was so wild, but then suddenly I was back. God, Carla, I want to go back there!"

Carla grinned. "I am so glad you had such a good time," she said. "You're a whole different person today. How long has it been since you and Jeff were intimate?"

Nora sighed. She had never wanted anyone to know, but what difference did it really make now that she had The Channel? "Five years," she said softly.

"Jesus!" Carla swore. "Your husband really is a prick."

"I can't go back unless I'm alone in the house," Nora said. "I wouldn't want J. J. to find me, or see what's on the TV when I'm there."

"That's right. The only television you've got is in the den," Carla said. "Hell, Nora, get a TV for your bedroom."

"Jeff wouldn't pay for the extra hookup, and since each time I go it costs three ninety-five, I can't go too often. Even though I pay the bills, I have to account for every penny he gives me," Nora explained. "Too many movies, and he'll wonder why. But it's like your favorite cookies, or potato chips. Once you've tasted the pleasures The Channel offers, you're addicted."

Carla nodded. "I know," she said. "So what about Friday night?"

"We've got the AA awards. Jeff will probably come home. He'll stay the weekend. Doesn't like to look bad," Nora said.

"So you've got a couple of days to get all hot and bothered again," Carla teased her best friend. "I pity Kyle, Rolf, and whoever else you dream up come your next visit to The Channel." She grinned mischievously. "Monday nights at The Channel. Are you ready for some fucking?" she paraphrased a commercial for the autumn football programming.

Nora laughed. "You're impossible, Carla Johnson, but you sure are fun. Tell me how you manage to use The Channel? I mean Rick is always home at night."

"Ah, but my darling spouse is usually asleep by nine or nine thirty. If Maureen doesn't have a date, she locks herself in her room and plays her music with her earphones on while she does homework. Then she's on the phone. I don't see her from the time she finishes supper until the next morning when she grabs a granola bar on her way out to school," Carla explained. "So I just slip down to my basement craft and sewing room, where a television is located for my soaps. I lock the door and party on. No one ever bothers me. We all have our little methods, because The Channel is addictive."

"I wish they had it in the daytime," Nora said.

Carla chortled. "Then we'd all be caught for sure. Imagine having to come home and fix dinner for a family of four after a day of you know what? Pirates, masseurs, sultans, and meat loaf. All those delicious men who spring out of our very active fantasies, and whose sole reason for being is to please us."

"And meat loaf," Nora added, grinning. Then she said, "I wonder why Rina and Joanne won't say why they go to The Channel."

"Joanne's embarrassed," Carla said. "I don't understand it, but she is. But Rina, I think she maybe thinks it's disloyal to Sam. After all he is a most attentive husband, and there is no doubt they love each other But he is almost twenty years her senior. She's his second wife, you know."

"I didn't," Nora answered.

"Yeah, his first wife died. Cancer, I think," Carla explained. "I think Rina feels as if she is betraying Sam, but she still goes to The Channel like the rest of us."

The telephone rang, and Nora picked it up. "Jeff," she said, and she made a face at Carla. Then she listened. "You'll be home tonight? How nice. What would you like for dinner? Lamb chops. Alright. No problem, I haven't shopped yet. You just caught me on the way out. Because I've had other things to do, that's why."

Carla gave Jeff the finger, and Nora almost laughed aloud.

"Yes, I'll have dinner ready at seven the way you like it. Bye." She set the phone down. "I am not in the mood for him. I really am not. I hope he's not forgotten he's coming Friday."

"I've talked to Rick about your situation," Carla said.

"I won't do anything until Jeff does," Nora told her friend.

"You ought to file first," Carla said. "I mean the guy is hardly ever here, and hasn't been for years. That ain't a marriage, sweetie."

"No, I'll wait for him to make the first move," Nora replied. "If I'm in the terrible position that you all think I am, it's better if I'm the victim, isn't it?"

"You're not dumb," Carla said. "But Nora, you've got to be protected. With everything in Jeff's name, you really are in a lousy position." Carla sounded genuinely worried.

"I know," Nora agreed. "It's beginning to dawn on me that I've been living in a world where nothing changes, and Jeff has been living in the real world, where dog eats dog." She stood up, swaying slightly. "I better get down to Waldbaum's, or there won't be any food in this house tonight."

"I'll drive us," Carla said. "I didn't have the night you did, nor as much wine as you've been consuming with the sandwiches. You've almost killed a bottle," she chuckled. "Never saw you do that before." She pulled her own car keys from her jeans. "Come on, babe. I need stuff too, but it wouldn't do for the mother of Egret Pointe High's Athlete of the Year to get busted for DUI. My God, what a scandal that would be, especially with your pristine reputation."

"The old me is gone," Nora said. "The new me is just likely to cause a scandal," she responded with a grin.

And then the two women left the house, walking out into the late May sunshine.

CHAPTER THREE

"We have to talk," Jeff Buckley said to his wife as they came into the house.

"Very well," Nora replied. "Now is as good a time as any. J. J. is off partying with his friends, although I have told him he has to be home by midnight." She walked through the front hall, and into the kitchen. "Do you want something to eat? I can fix you a sandwich. You didn't arrive until just before the awards."

"Yeah, I could use something," Jeff said, and sat down. He was one of those men who just got better with age. He was tall and lean. There was hardly any gray in his dark hair, but his blue eyes were cold. They always had been.

Nora pulled out a loaf of fresh rye bread and smeared honey mustard on the two slices she cut, piling it high with Black Forest ham and tissue-thin Havarti cheese. Placing the sandwich on a plate, she cut it neatly in three slices, and plunked it down in front of her husband. Then she poured him a glass of iced tea, which she set on the table before him as she sat down. "Eat first, and then we'll talk," she said.

He nodded, biting off large chunks of the sandwich and chewing. "You always made a good sandwich," he said, and then he swilled his tea.

This was it, Nora considered calmly. He was going to do it tonight. Would he remain then for the weekend? Or would he hot-foot it out of the house, back to the city and his girlfriend? She didn't care, she thought, surprised. The sooner he was gone, the sooner she could get back to Kyle and Rolf, and whomever else her fertile imagination could think up. She almost grinned. And then the old Nora asserted herself, and she wondered what kind of a woman threw away a longtime marriage. What would her mother think? How were the kids going to react? Wasn't it up to her to try and save her marriage?

What's left to save? the voice in her head asked caustically. The man's been cheating on you for years. He isn't the same person you married. Or maybe he is, and you just didn't realize what a jerk Jeff Buckley was when you were that starry-eyed virgin who fell in love with the college quarterback. You did what was expected of you by your family. By his family. You were the good girl who saved herself for marriage, but the son of a bitch never really cared. He expected it just like he expected you to behave as you always have. Dutiful. Chaste. Patiently waiting. Waiting for what? To be scraped into the garbage like yesterday's mashed potatoes?

"I'm finished," Jeff said, breaking into her thoughts. He pushed his plate and glass at her.

Rising, Nora rinsed them and tucked them into the dishwasher, smiling to herself. She was so deferential, the good wife. She turned to him. "Would you like to go into the den to talk?" she asked.

"No, here is as good a place as any," he told her.

Nora nodded, and sat down again.

"I guess," he began, "you realize that we haven't been getting on, or rather that we've been growing apart, for the last couple of years."

"You want a divorce, Jeff. Is that it?" Nora said, surprising him.

"Yeah, I do," he replied, a little taken aback by her calm.

"You don't think we should try to mend this breach between us?" she pressed him. Well, for her own conscience' sake she had to at least make an effort, she thought.

"I think we're past that," he answered her, but a wary look was creeping into his eyes.

Nora sighed. "If you don't love me, I can't hold you, Jeff," she said quietly. "If you want a divorce, you may have one. I assume there's another woman."

"No tears? No recriminations?" He was at once suspicious.

"Jeff, I'd have to be a complete fool, and God knows I've been near to it over the course of our marriage, not to realize you weren't happy these past few years. You grew in one direction. I grew in another. It's no one's fault. These things happen. And there is another woman, isn't there?"

"You can't prove adultery," he said quickly. "Besides, those aren't grounds in this state. I want a divorce. Plain and simple."

"And I said you could have one. Plain and simple," Nora responded. So he had already checked out grounds, had he? What a bastard!

"Then I'll have my lawyer set it up, and you can sign the papers when he has them," Jeff Buckley said to his wife.

"No, I think you should have your lawyer call my lawyer," Nora told him, almost laughing at the surprised look on his handsome face.

"When did you get a lawyer?" he demanded.

"Every woman has a lawyer, Jeff. That's something you had best keep in mind, for future reference, of course." She was enjoying his discomfort immensely.

"Who's going to represent you?" he asked suspiciously.

"Rick and his firm," she said softly.

He looked relieved. "Oh." Obviously he didn't consider Rick was going to give his lawyer any difficulty. "Okay, I'll have Raoul call him on Monday."

"Do you want me to tell the children?" she asked.

"Yeah. They'll understand, and it's better coming from you, Nora. When they see how on board you are with this, they won't be so angry." Then he grew wary again. "You're not going to blame me for this, are you? I don't want you turning the kids against me over this. Hell, they must have seen how it was between us these last years."

"You're their father, Jeff. Sadly I can't change that," Nora told him.

"You were hot to be my wife," he answered crudely. "If I hadn't been certain of your virginity when we married, I would have really wondered about you, Nora. But then you were always my good girl, weren't you?"

"The girls in my generation were raised to wait, Jeff. How clever of you to understand that. But that doesn't mean we don't like sex," Nora replied. The arrogant son of a bitch, she thought. He had always been like this, and she just hadn't seen it.

"Like sex?" He laughed. "You haven't had sex since I last banged you. Do you even remember when that was?"

"I don't remember nonevents," Nora answered him softly.

"You know, you're turning into a real bitch," he said, and then he stood up.

Nora laughed. "Good!" she told him.

"I'm going to go back into town tonight," he said. "Drive me to the station."

"Call a cab," Nora responded. "As of this moment, I am no longer at your service, my lord. Tell me, does your girlfriend cater to you the way I always have? Or is it her independence and fuck-you attitude that turns you on, Jeff?" There was just the hint of a smile playing about her lips as she saw his jaw tighten.

He pulled his cell phone from his pocket and dialed the local cab company, ordering his transportation. Then he said to her, "I'll wait out front."

"Aren't you afraid of what the neighbors will say?" Nora taunted him.

"Oh, I think they already know," he snapped back at her. "Even your friend Carla isn't as dumb as you've been, Nora."

"I trusted you, you bastard!" Her anger rose up.

"Like I said, Nora, dumb," he told her, and then he walked out the door.

She stood in her foyer for the briefest moment, shaking. Then she shut the door firmly behind him. She hated him. She never wanted to see him again. How could she have fallen in love with him all those years ago? Dumb! Yes, damnit, she had been dumb! But she wasn't going to be dumb anymore. And if he thought he was going to get away with leaving her in poverty, he was sadly mistaken. What was it Ivana Trump had once said? "Don't get mad. Get everything." Well, she didn't want everything, but she wanted her house. And alimony until she could get on her feet. The house should be hers. But she wouldn't take a penny more from Jeff than it took to get her started moving in a new direction. And the kids' schooling had to be paid for because she didn't want them starting out burdened by debt. Especially Jill. Law school wasn't cheap, but at least her daughter would be able to support herself if she turned out to be as dumb as her mother where men were concerned. Jeff couldn't leave their children out in the cold. His children. What if the girlfriend had a child? Well, God help her if she did, Nora thought.

She needed The Channel tonight. She wanted to get away from all of this, and be the woman she really was. But J. J. would be home by midnight. Unless, she considered, she told him he could stay over at one of his buddies'. She heard a car honk outside, and peering through one of the sidelights edging the front door, she saw her husband hurrying to get into a Cassandra's cab. Schmuck, she thought, using one of Rina's favorite terms. Nora turned to go into the den so she could call The Channel and escape from all this nasty reality.

"Nora!" The back door slammed shut.

Damn! She said the word silently. It was Carla.

"What happened?" Carla came into the hall. "I saw Jeff leaving."

"He's asked for the divorce," Nora said sanguinely. "And he thought he'd just have his lawyer draw up the papers so I could sign them." Then she laughed. "You should have seen the look on his face when I said his lawyer should contact my lawyer."

"The bastard!" Carla exploded.

"No, it's alright. I almost feel relieved now that it's happened. I've been such a naive little fool all these years, Carla. With Jill going to law school and J. J. off to college, what would I do with myself? Join the Garden Club? The Egret Pointe Ladies' Reading Circle? I'm only just realizing how out of touch with reality I truly am."

"You are not out of touch with reality!" Carla responded loyally.

"Yes, I am," Nora answered quietly. "I've got a college degree, and yet I've spent the last quarter of a century looking after the needs of a selfish man, and two children. I have no idea how to operate a computer, or program the VCR. But I'm going to learn, Carla. And I'm going to survive on my own, and pay my own way. Not at first, but eventually. I'm glad to be rid of Jeff. I don't really know him anymore, but what I do know, I don't like."

"Oh, honey!" Carla put her arms about her friend and hugged her.

"Now if you're convinced that I'm not going to kill myself, get out of here," Nora said, drawing away from the other woman. "I'm going to let my son stay over with his buddies tonight, and I'm going to get The Channel."

Carla giggled. "Yeah," she replied with a grin, "a good screwing always makes a girl feel a whole lot better. Have fun! Oh, Rick says come into the office on Monday at eleven a.m. so he can get started on protecting you in this mess. Night!" And she was gone with a wave of her hand.

Nora heard the door slam behind Carla as she left. She went

into the kitchen and turned the lock. Then she went into the den and called the house where the party J. J. was attending was being held. It took a while, but finally someone picked up the telephone.

"If you're bringing more beer, come on over!" the voice said.

She could hear the *thumpa-thumpa* of the music in the background. "It's Mrs. Buckley. Find J. J. for me, Peter," she told him.

"Oh, gee, Mrs. B. just kidding," he replied.

Nora laughed. "Just don't go driving, okay?" she said.

"I'll get J. J.," Peter responded.

She waited, not surprised that Peter Mulligan's parents weren't there. They were a very liberal, let's-be-friends-with-the-kids type. And being friends with your son meant few, if any, rules and regs. She began to have second thoughts about letting J. J. stay out.

"Ma? Is everything alright?" J. J. sounded anxious. He was really such a sweet kid.

"If I let you stay over with someone," Nora said, "who would it be?"

"I don't have to come home tonight?" J. J.'s voice was excited.

"Answer the question, J. J.," Nora said.

"The twins, Mike and Joe Carter, asked me," J. J. said.

"I'll call the Carters and tell them if it's okay with them, it's okay with me," Nora told her son. The Carters were stricter than she was.

"Ma? Why?" His voice sounded so young, and he really wasn't that young anymore. He was heading to college in a few weeks. "You sure everything is okay?"

"Everything is fine, J. J. But you're eighteen now. It's almost graduation, and I remember how I wanted to be with my friends then. I mean by summer's end you'll all be scattering, honey. So I decided it was time I was a little less uptight. If you don't hear back from me, just go along with the twins. I'll see you sometime tomorrow."

"Ma, you are the greatest!" he said, and hung up.

Nora chuckled. Ma was horny. She reached for her school list to get the Carters' telephone number and, finding it, punched the number in, humming under her breath as she waited for someone to answer.

"Hello?" It was Marian Carter.

"Marian, Nora Buckley. J. J. said the twins invited him to spend the night. Is that alright with you?"

"Of course it is, and they have a twelve thirty a.m. curfew," Marian Carter said. "I hope you don't think that's too late, but it's such a special time for them."

"No, no, twelve thirty is perfect. Thank you so much for having J. J.," Nora responded.

"He's such a nice boy," came the reply. "Did you know that Mike will be at State with J. J.? He doesn't have a soccer scholarship, but he's going to try for the team. Joe decided to join the marines. He says he can make a good career with the marines."

"And if he decides not to," Nora said cheerfully, "he'll probably get college money out of it. Marian, thanks for having J. J. Send him home when he gets to be a pest tomorrow."

"Any time, Nora." And Marian Carter hung up.

Nora set her phone back in its cradle. She went to her front door, locked it, and threw the extra bolt. Returning to the den, she poured herself a glass of wine and sat down. Had she really had a sexual adventure with two men on Monday night? Or had it just been a dream? Well, she considered with a little grin, the only way to find out was to call the cable company and ask for The Channel again. She picked up the phone again.

"Thank you for calling Suburban Cable," the automated message came on.

Nora waited patiently.

"Suburban Cable. This is Francie. How may I help you?"

"I'd like to order The Channel," Nora answered calmly, and gave the requested information.

"Just go to channel sixty-nine, Mrs. Buckley. The Channel's already operational this evening," Francie told her. "Anything else we can do for you tonight?"

"No, thanks," Nora replied, and hung up. She put the phone back, and sat back in her recliner for a long few minutes. Then she took a gulp of wine. She got up and turned off the lights in the room. She took another gulp of wine as she sat down again. Then, drawing a deep breath, Nora pressed the ON button on the channel changer, punched in sixty-nine, and waited anxiously as the darkened screen began to grow light, and her dream apartment came into view. "Kyle?" Her voice sounded jittery in her ears. Oh, let it all be as good as it was last time. Especially the sex. She wondered if she would take up where she had left off the last evening, with one cock in her cunt and another in her mouth. Where was Kyle? She was beginning to get nervous, and then she heard his voice.

"You don't need my hand, darling. You just need to put your own hand on the screen. You left in a hurry Monday night. I lost track of the time. Sorry."

Nora put her hand on the screen, felt the pop, and was back in the apartment. Before she could turn, his arms were about her waist, one hand sliding between the folds on her satin shorty robe to cup a full and firm breast. Nora sighed with utter pleasure. "I didn't mean to go," she said. She could feel the sticky wetness already beginning.

"I forgot to tell you that The Channel closes down between four and four thirty a.m.," he said, his tone apologetic.

"Does anyone have a watch around here?" Nora said. "The last thing I remember was Rolfie coming like a raging river, and you blowing off down my throat. The next thing I knew, I was back in my recliner." She turned about so she could see his handsome face. "We can't have that happen again, Kyle, can we?"

"Just pick up the phone," he told her, pointing to the elegant little portable on the living room table, "and press one. Tell them you want a wake-up call at four a.m. They'll just ring through, and that will let us know we have a few minutes to finish up our business," he said with a grin. "I didn't get my turn," Kyle murmured, kissing her ear.

"You had more than your turn last time," she chuckled.

"But Rolf got last licks," he pouted.

"No, I got last licks," she teased him, reaching down to fondle his penis. Then she turned away, pulling out of his embrace, and, picking up the phone, pushed number one.

"Concierge," a crisp voice answered.

"I want a wake-up call for four a.m.," Nora said.

"Very good, Mrs. Buckley," the crisp voice replied, ringing off.

"How did she know my name?" Nora wondered aloud.

"You're in the penthouse," Kyle responded logically.

"Oh." Was she going mad? Well, who cared!

"You didn't eat at the awards dinner," Kyle said. "I fixed you something."

"How do you know that?" She set the phone back in its cradle.

"It's my job to know everything about you and to fulfill your fantasy, Red Rover," he told her.

"I think I like that, even if it is a little creepy," Nora said. "What have you prepared for me, my handsome slave?" She caressed his face, and catching her hand in his, he kissed her palm, then licked at it, before releasing it again.

"We're going to start with raw oysters," he began. "Then asparagus with a nice tart hollandaise, some steak tartare, and finally, for dessert, strawberries, whipped cream, and maybe a little chocolate."

"Ummm," Nora replied. "It sounds delicious. Could we start with dessert first?"

"No," he told her firmly.

She pouted. "Why not? Besides, it's my fantasy. Don't I get to have my way?"

"Not a hundred percent of the time. We're going to need those oysters, Red."

"Why?" she demanded.

"Because I'm going to fuck the ears off of you tonight, that's why," he said in his deep rough voice. "After what happened earlier this evening you're going to need a whole lot of loving tonight, and I'm going to see you get it," he told her.

Nora was silent for a very long moment. If only there were men like Kyle out there in the real world, she thought sadly. Then shaking herself, she undid her blue satin robe, and shed it. "I always wanted to eat naked," she said.

"Me too," he agreed, and dropped his white silk shorts. Then he took her hand. "I set up supper for us out on the terrace."

"What if someone sees us?" Nora gasped.

"Up here?" He laughed. "I don't think so. But so what if they did?" He led her outside.

The flooring of the large terrace was made of red tile. It was warmish beneath her feet. The air temperature was comfortable too. Above them the night sky was like black velvet, dotted with sparkling stars. She had heard you couldn't see the stars in the city, but there they were, floating above her. Well, it was her fantasy, and if she wanted stars, she was damned well going to have them. There was a black terry cloth double chaise lounge. Next to it was a table covered with the food he had described. It looked wonderful.

"Get on the chaise," he said. "I'm going to feed you, Red Rover."

"But how will you eat if you're feeding me?" she asked, positioning herself in a half-upright position on the chaise.

"I'll manage," he told her. Then he took an oyster. "Open up, Nora."

She complied with the request, and he dropped the oyster into her mouth, and then took one for himself. He kept feeding her, and himself, taking just enough time for her to swallow the oyster before he fed her another. When the silver bowl of oysters was emptied he bent over and gave her a slow kiss, his tongue playing with hers. And while they kissed, he began to play with her clitoris, laughing as she grew quickly wet, and pushed two thick fingers into her vagina as far as he could, then stopped.

"Nora, darling, I want you to feed me some of that steak tartare. It's already on the crackers. I have an urge for meat."

She could feel his fingers inside her, and her lust began to boil up. She wanted him to use those big fingers, and frig her till she came, but instead she reached out to a round silver platter and, taking a cracker spread with the raw steak off of it, fed it to him. Then she took one for herself, chewing slowly, trying to ignore the heat rising from her body. She had never imagined sex could be this good, and while she was impatient, she knew he was teaching her. It was going to get even better.

"Do you like the menu, Nora?" he asked her softly, and gently moved the fingers inside of her vagina just enough to send a jolt of sensation through her.

She nodded.

"Did you even imagine eating like this?" he pressed.

"I must have, or we wouldn't be doing it," she murmured back.

"Not everything that happens here will be your will, or your desire," he told her. "But I know you, Red Rover, my girl. You are a firebox of passion, and that stupid bastard you married never knew, never took advantage of it, never cared."

"Nice girls of my generation don't do things like this," she replied.

"Nonsense, Nora! Every woman has secret fantasies of private pleasures. And every woman is entitled to live her fantasies."

She didn't answer him; instead she fed him more of the steak tartare. But he was right. Women did have fantasies, but they rarely if ever really talked about them to anyone. She fed herself another cracker and meat.

"Lie back," he said, and when she did he frigged her until she came, moaning with the pleasure he gave her. Removing his two fingers from her vagina, he put them in his mouth and sucked them free of her come. "You taste very good," he told her softly.

"Do you want more?" she asked wickedly. She could feel the pounding of her heart in her chest. She had never felt so bold or confident as she did here in this mysterious fantasy world.

"Later, Nora. Later, I promise." he said, and their eyes met.

They finished the crackers and raw meat, feeding each other now as they sat cross-legged on the double chaise. Finally Kyle lifted the silver cover from an oval-shaped silver dish. Inside lay at least a dozen perfect asparagus, long and firm and a lovely shade of spring green. Reaching out for a small pitcher, he poured a stream of perfect hollandaise onto the vegetable. How the hell did anyone keep hollandaise so absolutely flawless? Nora wondered, remembering the Easter dinners and how if the damned sauce wasn't carefully watched, it would curdle. Hell, hollandaise curdled at the whisper of a butterfly's wings, but this hollandaise was indeed perfect.

"Open your mouth," he said softly, holding a stalk of asparagus dripping sauce over her mouth.

"Ummmm," Nora answered him, sucking the offering suggestively. "More, darling Kyle. More!"

"Are you sure it's asparagus you want, Red?" he teased her.

"You know what I want," she told him, "but I'll wait. This is the best meal I've ever eaten, darling. Did you cook it all with your little hands?" She sucked vigorously upon another stalk.

"I called room service," he responded, then licked a bit of sauce from the corner of her luscious mouth. "The management is very particular about their service."

The management. Who was the management? Nora wondered, and then she decided for the interim not to ask questions.

She didn't want to spoil her evening, or possibly be banned from The Channel. "Do we have any wine?" she asked him.

He poured her a fruity red called Sweet Scarlet that came from a Long Island vineyard. "Try this," he said.

Nora sipped the wine slowly. She was certainly no connoisseur of wines, but she liked it. It had a clean taste on her tongue. "Good," she told him. "Where's Rolfie?"

"Aren't I enough for you?" he demanded. There was almost a petulant tone to his rough deep voice. "Do you need two men every time?"

"I don't think I ever imagined a threesome until last time. I thought it was fun," Nora said, ignoring his tone.

"It isn't enough for me to come in your mouth, Red," he told her. "And last time when there were the three of us, that was the only option open to me."

"You can have me any way you want, Kyle," she told him seductively, and reaching down, she stroked his big penis. "Any way you want, darling."

"You think you're a big girl now, Nora, but you aren't. You're just beginning to explore your sexuality. I'm here to help you. You've never had a cock up your ass, and that's going to be a next step. But not until you are ready, baby."

"I want both of you tonight," Nora said stubbornly. "Last night was fun until I woke up again. Please, Kyle. Pretty please with sugar on it?" she teased him.

"I want you!" he said in a hard voice.

"You can have me, but you have to share me with Rolfie too," she told him. "At least tonight."

He laughed. "You are a little bitch, but it's going to be his dick you suck tonight, Red, because I really need to fill you full of cock. Okay?"

"Okay," Nora agreed. "Call down, and order up my masseur, lover."

"Not until I've fed you some strawberries," he said mischievously. And he popped one into her mouth.

Nora retaliated, and shortly they were both covered with juice from the ripe berries. They licked each other's faces and hands clean. Before Nora might request Rolf again, Kyle was drizzling a thin stream of chocolate all over her torso, and then spraying cream on top of it. Nora squealed with surprise. He began to lick the chocolate and cream off of her body. His warm tongue lapped at her, and she felt her lust beginning to reassert itself strongly. He dripped chocolate onto her clit, and began to lick at it. Then suddenly he reversed his position so that his penis was near her mouth.

Nora took up the bottle of Hershey's syrup and filled her mouth. Then, reaching out, she took his dick into the newly made bowl, and began to suck and lick at him. He filled her cunt with cool cream, and began to eat her. She sucked him harder and harder as her own senses blazed up.

"I don't want to come in your mouth," he groaned. "When I tell you stop, stop!" He frantically licked the cream he had spread into her sexual cavity, clearing the way for his penetration. "Stop! Damnit, Nora, stop!"

Reluctantly she did, because she wanted him to stuff her with his swollen penis. She opened her mouth and released him. He reversed himself so quickly that she was almost breathless as he plunged into her wet vagina. "Ohh, God, yes, Kyle!" she sobbed in his ear. "Fuck me, darling, and don't stop!" She wrapped her slender legs about his hard body, panting as he labored over her with enthusiasm.

He pulled himself out of her so far that she could feel the very tip of his dick at the mouth of her vagina. Then he pushed himself back in, slowly, slowly. He did this several times until she was sobbing.

"No! No! Faster!" she demanded of him. "Faster, Kyle!"

He complied, and before he wanted to he was coming in hard,

thick spurts, and Nora was clawing at his back and mewling with her own pleasure.

"Omigod! Omigod!" she gasped.

"Amen to that," he said, rolling off of her. Then, turning, he looked down into her face. "Feel better, Red?"

She nodded slowly. "Much better," she told him, curling up against him. "But I still want Rolf to join us."

He laughed. "I give up," he said.

"Then call him," she ordered. "And then let's go take a shower. Good thing we didn't do this in the bed."

"We'd just call housekeeping to send up the maid to change the sheets," he told her.

"Is the maid pretty?" Nora asked him.

"She can be. Why?"

"We might try a foursome sometime, or perhaps a different kind of threesome," Nora said suggestively. "Would you like that kind of threesome, Kyle, my lover?"

He nodded.

"Then we'll have to do it sometime," Nora replied daringly. "I've never thought about it before, but it might be fun to watch you get turned on by me and another woman playing together." She slid off of the double chaise, standing. Her pointed red tongue touched her upper lip. "Could two women turn you on even more?"

He nodded again.

"Call for Rolfie, then, lover, and if you're a good boy, maybe next time our threesome will be you, me, and the maid. I'll be in the shower. Come and join me when you've done your duty." With a smile she disappeared back into the apartment.

He followed behind her, picking up the cordless phone on the table in the living room on the way, and pressing a button on it. "Send up Rolf," he said. "Madame would like a massage." Then he entered the luxurious bath, where Nora was already in the shower.

"Wash me," she ordered him, handing him a soap-filled sponge, standing straight and facing him. "I like it when you take care of me."

He took the sponge from her. "Lift your hair up," he said. "And you have to learn how to take care of yourself, Nora."

"I know," she agreed, holding her wet hair off of her shoulders as he began to wash her. "But in a sense I've been taking care of myself, and everyone else, ever since I got married. It's nice having you around. Even if you are just a fantasy."

"Maybe the world which you think you inhabit is the fantasy," he told her, swirling the sponge down and around her chest. He lifted each breast separately and washed it. "Maybe this is the reality."

"No such luck," Nora sighed. "What is it my friend Carla says? Life is a bitch, and then you die. No, Kyle, this is definitely the fantasy, I'm sorry to admit. And when I wake up again, I'll be the plump, middle-aged woman in her chair whose husband is about to dump her for a younger woman. And since, it seems, he's got control of everything, I will have to fight him for my very survival. Hell, I might not be able to afford Suburban Cable, which means I won't have you."

"You wouldn't let that happen, Nora, would you?" The sponge moved over her belly, and down to her pubic area.

"No," she said. "I wouldn't. The Channel is the only thing keeping me from being scared to death right now. And you, darling Kyle, are keeping me sane."

"How about me?" The shower door opened, and Rolf stepped in. "Don't I figure anywhere in this equation?" His blue eyes were twinkling at her.

"Indeed you do, Rolfie," she said, pushing Kyle away and pressing up against the young blond man suggestively.

He gave one of her breasts a squeeze, and with his other hand pulled her head toward his for a kiss. His mouth was fleshy and seductive. His tongue pushed between her lips to play with her tongue as he kissed her with ill-disguised hunger. He rubbed himself teasingly against her pubic mound. "Where do I figure?" he asked her softly.

The hot water poured down on the trio, steaming the glass of the commodious shower.

"Wherever you want," Nora answered him teasingly. His penis was already hard against her. It was so exciting to elicit such a reaction from such attractive men, she thought. Kyle was silently washing her back with a vengeance, but his long hard cock was rubbing between her ass crease. She smiled, turning her head to him. "Almost done, lover?" she asked sweetly.

He nodded with a grim smile. Ohh, he really was going to fuck the ears off of her, and she was going to enjoy every minute of it. "All done, Red."

"Want to play?" she teased wickedly.

Both men grinned broadly.

"First I want my massage, Rolfie," she told them.

"Table is all set up for madam," he answered her.

The two men toweled Nora off, and then when Kyle had pinned up her damp hair, he helped her onto the table. Nora almost dozed off as Rolf massaged her front side. His hands were both gentle and strong. Her firm breasts seemed to grow even firmer with his attentions. The heel of his palm, pressed firmly on her mons, however, brought her fully awake again. His handsome face was devoid of any expression, but she knew he had done it deliberately. A finger massaged oil into her clitoris and the hood over it, but just as she was beginning to feel a little tingle he spoke.

"Turn over, Nora." And he helped her to flip.

He massaged her shoulders and she could feel the tension draining away. His strong hands smoothed down her long back, finally reaching her buttocks. Rolf's fingers kneaded her now-firm ass, the edge of one hand sliding down the crease between her buttocks. Fascinated, she forced herself to relax as the hand moved between the cheeks of her ass as deep as it could go. The room was silent. She did not see Rolf nod meaningfully to Kyle, but she felt the two halves of her ass being pulled apart, and as quickly the sensation of something rubbing against her anus very softly.

"Wha . . . ?" she tried to speak.

"It's alright, Nora. We're just showing you something new," Rolf told her. "We aren't going to do anything you aren't ready for, sweetie."

The slick finger stroked a spot she had never thought to be touched. It was rather exciting, and sent a small frisson of pleasure through her. Nora didn't know whether to be shocked by her reaction or not. When she felt him begin to blow softly there, she shivered. She actually wiggled a bit. The hands holding her ass cheeks apart released her, but the finger remained, and Nora could not help herself. She squeezed that finger even as she felt her face grow warm with a guilty blush.

"I think someone is going to be ready soon for a nice ass fuck," Rolf said.

"Not yet." Kyle's voice was almost angry.

Rolf actually laughed as he withdrew his finger and, going over to the double sink, washed his hands before resuming the massage. When he had finished with her legs, thighs, calves, and feet, he smacked Nora's bottom a light whack. "All done, sweetie." Then he helped her off the table.

"Let's have some of that wonderful wine I had earlier," Nora said in an attempt to break the tension. What an incredible fantasy world this was. Kyle was jealous of Rolf. And Rolf was enjoying torturing Kyle over her. Could her sense of self-worth get any better? She wanted that sense to carry over into her other world. She needed it to fight Jeff and win.

They went into the bedroom, with its huge bed, and Kyle poured them three goblets of Sweet Scarlet. He raised his glass. "To Nora," he said.

Rolf nodded. "To Nora, and to new sexual explorations."

"To the both of you, who make me feel so damned good," Nora toasted them back. Then she downed half of the wine. "I want to make love again before my wake-up call, boys," she said to them. "Drink up!"

But the two men put aside their wine, sandwiching her instead between them.

"Too much wine always leads to too little cock," Rolf said. He was standing behind her, his penis between the cheeks of her ass, his hands wrapped firmly about her breasts, thumbs rubbing against her sensitive nipples.

He needed to be brought down a bit, Nora considered. Rolf was getting a bit above his station. She drew away from him, her eyes meeting Kyle's in a silent understanding that she knew pleased him. "I believe I'm the one directing this ménage à trois, Rolfie. You are my slave, aren't you? And your mistress is in the mood for a little cunnilingus. Is your tongue as skillful at that task as it is talking, Rolfie?"

He took her by the hand and led her to the bed. "If my mistress will lie back, I will endeavor to pleasure her," he said with a counterfeit show of deference.

Nora lay back on the bed, spreading her legs open for him. She gestured at Kyle. "And you, slave, give me your cock to play with else I be bored." She could see he was already half aroused. He too needed a lesson. He had been behaving in too dominant a manner tonight. She felt Rolf kiss her vulva even as Kyle positioned himself atop her chest, careful not to let his weight hurt her. Unable to help herself, she ran her hands lightly over his muscled thighs. Then she took his penis in her hand, holding it gently as she breathed softly on it. Her other hand lightly tickled his balls as the tip of Rolf's tongue lightly touched her clit.

Nora put Kyle's cock in her mouth, but she did not suck on him. Instead she slid her lips up and down the long shaft. When her tongue encircled the tip of it several times, he shuddered. He was getting harder, and it was more difficult for Nora to concentrate on what she was doing because Rolf's skillful tongue was caressing her clit. She began to suck hard on Kyle's penis, which grew firmer and firmer in her mouth.

"She's ready," Rolf said suddenly.

"So am I," Kyle groaned. "Let go, Red, if you want to be fucked."

She released him immediately, and the two men reversed positions, with Kyle thrusting hard into Nora's vagina, and Rolf kneeling behind her head and leaning forward to push his cock into her mouth. This time they all came together, and when their bodies had untangled themselves Nora cuddled against Kyle contentedly.

"That was nice," Nora said softly.

"Better than nice, mistress," Rolf told her. "I'm going to shower and go if you don't need me anymore tonight."

"No, go on," she told him. She wanted to be with Kyle now. Just Kyle. She dozed, only to be awakened by the sharp ring of the telephone. Confused for a moment, she rolled over and looked about. A portable was on her bedside table. Reaching for it, she pressed the ON button.

"It's four a.m., Mrs. Buckley," the crisp voice said. "The Channel will be closing in a half hour."

"Thank you," she responded groggily, pressing the phone's OFF button. "Kyle?"

"I'm here," he said, coming into the bedroom. "Go shower. I've got a nice cup of cappuccino for you."

"You are perfect!" she told him, stumbling from the bed into the bathroom. She showered quickly, washing away the strong scent of unbridled sex from her skin. Toweling herself off, she walked naked back through the bedroom and into the living room. To her amusement he helped her into her short navy silk robe, and she cocked an eyebrow at him. "You don't like me naked anymore?" she teased him.

"We don't have much time, and I just want to enjoy your company for a few minutes," he told her, handing her the footed cappuccino cup. "When are you coming back to me, Nora?"

She sat down, and to her surprise, he sat on the floor by her side, his dark head in her lap. "I can't come tonight. It's Saturday, and if I let J. J. stay out with friends two nights in a row, it will look odd. And Sunday night is a school night, and he'll be home. Probably not until Monday night, Kyle." She sipped at the cappuccino. "Umm, this is really good."

"I'm going to miss you," he said softly.

"I'm probably going to miss you more," she told him. He was a fantasy, and you didn't have feelings for a fantasy, Nora reminded herself. But she did have feelings for him. He was her creation. The perfect man. The perfect lover.

"Let's just be together, the two of us, then, on Monday night," he said.

"Okay," she agreed. "No Rolf and pretty maid."

He looked up at her. "I'm falling in love with you," he told her.

She was startled. "You can't," she said. "You don't really exist, Kyle."

"I exist for you, Nora," he reminded. "I am as real for you as anything else is."

"But not in my world of reality," she said. "You're my fantasy, Kyle. Nothing more than a fantasy."

"I'm going to teach you to love again," he told her.

"If you can do that," she said wistfully, "it would be a miracle."

"I can do anything you want me to, Red Rover," he told her, looking up into her gray green eyes.

She smiled softly at him and, reaching down, caressed his jaw, but as she did she felt herself sliding away from him. Damn! Nora thought sadly. And then she woke up in her recliner once again. Sighing, she stood up, turning off the television with the channel changer. Another wonderful fantasy evening. Yet the taste of cappuccino lingered strongly on her tongue, and her body felt more alive than it had in years.

CHAPTER FOUR

"So, how bad is it?" Rina Seligmann asked, coming through the Buckleys' kitchen door. She was carrying a covered plate of chicken salad sandwiches on whole wheat bread she had made up at Trader Joe's this morning. She set the plate on the table, and pulled off the plastic wrap. "Tiff, where's that iced tea?"

"Right behind you," Tiffany Pietro d'Angelo said, plunking the pitcher and paper cups on the kitchen table next to the sandwiches.

"Worse than we even anticipated!" Carla said dramatically. She had driven Nora to her husband's office that morning, waiting while Nora had her first conference with Rick. "Absolutely everything is in the son of a bitch's name. Everything! He even tried to close down Nora's little household account this morning, but Rick put a stop to that."

"How did Rick know?" Joanne Ulrich was wide-eyed. This was even better than *General Hospital*.

"Well," Carla said with just the slightest air of self-importance, "when Rick got to his office this morning, he found a whole bunch of papers that had been faxed to him by Jeff's lawyer in the city. Only one bank account was listed, and it was the one here at Egret Pointe National Bank, and it was marked as closed. Well, Rick got on the telephone to Paul Williams at the bank. Paul said the request had come in this morning. Rick explained the situation, and told Paul to hold off until he could get back to the other lawyer. That the account was the only one Nora had, and if he would check back in the statements, he would see only she signed the checks, and they were mostly for household bills and personal expenses even if the account was in both names. So Paul said he'd hold off until he heard from Rick again."

"Well, that news will be all over town by closing time at the bank," Rina said dryly.

"How do you figure that?" Nora asked.

"Paul's secretary, Mae Taylor. She always listens in on his calls," Rina said. "She's the biggest gossip in town, and everyone knows it."

"Then why does he keep her on?" Joanne asked.

"He inherited her from his father-in-law, Lew Burnside," Rina replied. "Lew founded Egret Pointe Bank, and Paul is married to his daughter. When he retired, and Paul took over, Lew insisted he keep Mae on because, he said, she wasn't retirement age yet. But he really wanted to be sure he still knew everything that was going on at the bank. And before you ask, Sam plays golf with him twice a week. Will you all sit down? I'm starving." She reached for a half a sandwich and began to eat.

Joanne poured everyone a paper cup of iced tea, and then they looked to Carla.

"Rick called Jeff's lawyer back again, and told him the account couldn't be the only one Jeff had, because the one he had instructed the lawyer to close was Nora's household account, the only one she had, and she would need it to pay the household bills. That Jeff never used the account. He just made monthly deposits. Rick said the other lawyer seemed surprised at that, and said he'd call him right back."

"And did he?" Tiffany asked.

"Yeah. About ten minutes later," Carla said, grinning. "He told Rick that it was all a mistake, and he'd fax Paul Williams immediately that the account was to remain open. Rick told him he wanted Jeff's name off the account."

"Did he agree?" Tiffany asked.

"Oh, yeah, he agreed. Then he said that Rick should know that Jeff was under no obligation to put any more money into the account until a hearing."

"The bastard!" Rina said. "So he's going to play hardball, is he?"

"Yep," Carla said.

"It's worse," Nora told them quietly. "The kids' college funds have disappeared. They weren't on the list of stuff faxed to Rick. Jeff started an investment account for each of the kids when they were born. For college, he said, and he was always so proud of himself for looking ahead like that. You know how the market was after 'eighty-seven, and into the nineties. Jeff's a smart investor. Every Christmas he would show the kids and me their year-end statements. He said he didn't want them to come out of school with debt, like so many kids today. He said his father had done it for him, and he wanted to do it for his kids. That's why Jill was able to think of law school. There was more than enough money in each account, and now those accounts are gone."

"You're sure?" Rina asked.

"We called Jill up at school. I hadn't planned to tell her over the telephone about the divorce, but I didn't have any choice under the circumstances. She said her father had come to her about six months ago with some papers to sign. When she asked what they were, he said they had to do with the changes in the tax laws with regard to her account, and since she was of age, she had to sign the papers herself because he couldn't. She had no cause to distrust him."

"Nora hasn't had a chance to talk to J. J. yet, but Rick thinks he pulled the same or a similar stunt with him too," Carla said.

"My God," Rina said softly. "He's been planning this for months." She turned to Nora. "So what's Rick going to do now?"

"He's thinking about it. It has to be what's best for Nora and the kids," Carla said. "He doesn't want to make a mistake. This lawyer Jeff has hired is a pretty big-name, recognizable divorce attorney."

"Tell him not to take too long," Rina said acerbically. "So, what are you going to do while Rick is thinking?" she asked Nora.

Nora sighed. "I'll have to call my mother and tell her. Dad left her very well fixed. I think she'll help out until we get this straightened out. Of course I'll pay her back. She's not going to be happy to have her life disrupted, I'm afraid."

"Where does she live?" Rina said.

"In one of those elegant, perfectly manicured little retirement communities on the Carolina coast," Nora replied. "Dad moved them down before he died. It's a life-care community. He wanted her taken care of when he wasn't around to do it. I've been taking the kids down twice a year to visit. She never really liked Jeff. She'll be surprised, but not particularly devastated."

And Margo Edwards, Nora's mother, was indeed surprised by her daughter's news, but not because of the divorce. It was the timing that she found curious. "I thought he would have done this ten years ago," she said.

"What on earth would have made you think that?" Nora demanded of her parent.

"Well, other than the illusion that his marriage created for all to see, it was obvious he didn't love you anymore," Margo responded. "Didn't you realize what was going on, Nora? Of course I never told your father of Jeff's infidelities. It wasn't really necessary that he know unless, of course, he had divorced you while Dad was alive. Then I would have said something."

"I'm surprised you kept something from Daddy," Nora said. "He did rule the roost in our house."

Margo laughed. "There were a lot of things I didn't discuss with your father, Nora, and he only thought he was in charge, darling. A wise woman lets a man believe that, and she picks her battles carefully." Then she sighed. "At least the house is in your name. Is it paid off?"

There was a long pause. Nora swallowed hard, and then she said to her mother, "The house isn't in my name, Mom. Nothing is in my name."

"Jesus Jenny!" Margo Edwards swore volubly. "The lying SOB! When you bought your house Jeff had the ten percent for the down payment. Your father gave him an additional ten percent so the mortgage would be smaller. It was done on the proviso that Jeff put the house in your name. I put that idea in dad's head so you would always be safe. And I was there when your father brought it up to Jeff, and he agreed he would do it in exchange for the additional ten percent. You're sure the house is in his name?"

"Yes, Mom, I'm certain. But it is paid off," Nora said.

"How much money do you have in the bank?" Margo asked.

"It's the end of the month. Probably not more than fifty dollars," Nora replied.

"No, honey, not your household account. Your other accounts. CDs. You know."

"Mom, I've got a bank account for the house. Jeff puts money in it once a month, and I pay the bills. I don't have any other bank accounts, or CDs."

"Why not?" Margo's voice had suddenly hardened.

"Where would I get the money from?" Nora said helplessly.

"I used to take money out of my household account and squirrel it away," Margo said. "Why didn't you, Nora? I didn't think you were that stupid. A woman has to think of herself."

"Mom, Jeff gives me just enough money each month to pay the household bills. If I run over the previous month's amount by more than five percent, I have to show him the bills, and justify every expenditure. I am allowed one credit card, and before I use it I have to tell him what I'm buying and why. He's always been a bear where money is concerned. But he has always kept us comfortable. I have had no cause for complaint until now. I thought people got married till death did they part. My grandparents did. You and Dad did. Jeff's folks did."

"Why didn't you tell me this, Nora? Why didn't you tell me that your husband is a control freak? This borders on abuse, darling, and you have been standing there, and taking it. I don't understand it!" Margo was now sounding exasperated.

"I was only doing what you did, Mom," Nora said. "Jeff always said you had set me a wonderful example of how to be a good wife."

"Good grief!" Margo said. "Listen to me, Nora, although frankly it's a little late for me to tell you this, but I will anyway. Your father was raised by his grandparents, who had been raised in the Victorian era. He thought a wife should be meek and mild, and defer to her husband. That was the kind of wife he wanted, and I loved your father dearly. So I gave him that kind of a wife. But I was never that kind of a woman. Ever! Your father never controlled me the way Jeff has obviously been controlling you, darling. If I thought Dad was going in the wrong direction, I would cajole him into turning about. You know how he always wanted to invest in so many crazy schemes he was sure would make him rich, yet he never did. It was because I convinced him otherwise, and I did it in such a way that he always believed he had come to the conclusion all by himself. And when those schemes blew up, he would brag about how astute he had been to avoid it all. Don't you remember?"

"I do," Nora said slowly. "But Jeff is different than Daddy. Daddy had a sweet nature, Mom. Jeff has always been bound and determined to have his own way. Once I loved him dearly too."

"I never liked him," Margo said, "but then, you knew that, didn't you?"

"Yes."

"There was something about him, but I could see that nothing I would say was going to change your mind, and Daddy thought he was just the right man for you. I tried to show him otherwise over the term of your engagement," Margo said, "but that was the one thing in which I failed. I am sorry, darling."

"Oh, Mom, didn't you always say I had to learn the hard way?" Nora half laughed.

"Well," Margo responded, and her voice was brisk, "now the question is, what are we going to do? Do you have an attorney?"

"Carla's husband, Rick. Jeff has some big-city divorce guy," Nora told her mother.

"Who?" Margo was instantly alert to danger.

"Raoul Kramer, I think his name is," Nora answered.

"Certainly isn't stinting himself," Margo said dryly. This was not good. Raoul Kramer was a vicious divorce lawyer who always got his clients exactly what they wanted. He was ruthless, and was apt to make mincemeat of that nice Rick Johnson. Still, there was no need at this point to frighten Nora. "Tell Rick to call me tomorrow, darling, and I'll send him a retainer for you. I know he'd do it for free until it's settled, but no need for that. And give me your bank account number. I'll wire you ten thousand dollars to keep you going, Nora. And Nora, if you need more before a preliminary hearing, I want you to call me immediately."

"Mom . . ." Nora's voice cracked.

"Oh, shut up!" Margo said. "Now, darling, I have to run. There is a very delightful gentleman waiting to play tennis with me."

"You have a boyfriend?" Nora had never heard her mother speak of another man.

"I haven't decided yet, darling. One thing I do know. While I do enjoy sex, I am simply not of a mind to marry again, and break another man in," and she laughed at her daughter's small gasp. "Nora, I may be past seventy, but I do enjoy a good bang now and again. Gotta run, darling. Taylor is beginning to stamp his feet." And the phone went dead.

Nora put the portable down. She had learned more about her mother in this one phone conversation than she had in all her life. She was rethinking her parents' marriage, but then, no matter what Margo had said this afternoon, she had never said that she and her husband had been unhappy. Nor had Nora seen any evidence to the contrary. What a jerk I've been, she thought. Jeff was right. Dumb! She had been dumb, and now she had to live with the results of her stupidity. She stood up and, walking from the kitchen, went out the door and across her back lawn to the Johnsons' house. It was after five, and she knew that Rick would be home. "Hello!" she called as she walked into Carla's kitchen.

"We're in the family room," Carla called back.

Nora joined them, accepting the glass of wine Carla handed her. "I just talked with my mother," she began. "I'll give you her number, Rick. She wanted to send you a retainer. Says she knows you're a good guy, but you should get paid something. You can tell her anything you want. I've just discovered something I never knew."

"What's that?" Carla asked, curious.

"My mother is cool," Nora said with a smile. "When we got finished talking she told me she was off to play tennis with a gentleman. And that she enjoys a good bang now and again."

Carla shrieked with laughter, and even Rick grinned.

"Omigod! If my mother ever said anything like that to me, I think I would die," Carla said, but she was still giggling.

"I know. I would have never expected it from Mom," Nora admitted. Then she continued. "She's wiring me some money so I can keep going, I feel terrible having to have asked her, but I had nowhere else to turn."

"Jeff's name is off the account," Rick said quietly. "At least your moneys will be safe. Nora, I have to tell you that I don't think much of a guy who would try and cut his wife off without a penny."

"My mother says my dad gave him ten percent of the house's down payment so we could put twenty percent down, but on the proviso the house was in my name," Nora told Rick.

"Any paperwork on that?" Rick asked anxiously.

"You would have to ask my mother, but I suspect no. Dad was trusting. I guess that's where I get it from." She drained her wine and stood up. "I've got to go home. J. J. and I are having supper together before he goes to the movies."

When she had gone, Rick Johnson looked at his wife. "This isn't just going to be messy. It's going to be nasty. Jeff wants to put the house on the market so it can be sold before school starts next autumn. Seems there's a co-op in town he and his next wife want to buy outright, without a mortgage. I suspect that's where the kids' college money has gone to as well. And don't you tell Nora that. I'm trying to keep her calm and strong for what's going to come. When Raoul Kramer gets a wife like Nora on the stand, she suddenly becomes a gold digger who has been leeching off her husband's hard work for years. Judges don't like women like that."

"But Nora isn't like that at all!" Carla said.

"Raoul Kramer will make her seem that way. I've got to make her the victim of a husband who's discarding the wife who has been loyal and faithful, for a trophy wife," Rick said. "Funny thing is, Nora is really reasonable about this. She wants her house, Jill and J. J.'s education taken care of, and enough support to get her through until she can get some training and enter the job market. I'll bet she runs that house on a dime."

"Rick, honey, you have to get her what she wants," Carla said.

"Baby, I don't know if I can. Jeff has planned this very carefully, and Raoul Kramer is the best. I'm just a small-town lawyer. This is really out of my league," Rick told his wife.

"You'll do it," Carla said. "You may be small-town, but you're a fighter, honey. Nora is in good hands with you behind her."

"I'm going to try," he said. God! Carla's blind faith in him made it even harder. He dreaded going into the office tomorrow and calling Raoul Kramer. The guy's client list read like a who's who of the rich and famous. They loved him, but he had the reputation of being a snake who devoured his opponents whole. Poor Nora! Other than her fidelity and good reputation as a wife, Nora didn't have a leg to stand on. How could Jeff Buckley be so rotten? He couldn't be certain until he spoke to Kramer what he'd do, but he was going to fight like hell to get Nora Buckley an even break.

The following day he called her. "Hey, kiddo, it's Rick. Make me a sandwich. I'm coming by 'cause we gotta talk."

"Turkey or ham?" she asked.

"Turkey," he replied.

"What time?"

"About twelve thirty."

Nora was irritable. She hadn't been able to get back to The Channel since Friday night because J. J. was home in the evenings studying for his finals. She missed Kyle. She missed the raw animal sex she had enjoyed those two nights she had been with him. For the first time in her adult life she felt there was someone who cared about her. Really cared. And she wanted to be with him again. If only there were a television in her bedroom, but Jeff would never hear of it. She wondered how much it would cost to have the cable company put in another connection. But then, Jeff had exited her life but for the formalities.

Rick arrived exactly at twelve thirty. "Carla's out," he said to Nora as he came into the kitchen, and sat down. "I knew she would be. I didn't want her over here sticking in her two cents, and she would be."

"Tell me," Nora said quietly as she set the sandwich before him, and sat down with her fat-free yogurt.

"He wants to sell the house right away. He's got a bid in on a co-op in the city," Rick began.

"Let him get a mortgage," Nora said. Her heart was racing. If he took the house, where was she going to go? Where were the kids going to go when they came home?

"The lease on your car is up, and he's not renewing it. You can buy the car from the dealer for eighty-seven hundred dollars," Rick said. He bit into his sandwich, unable to meet her eye.

"With what?" Nora said.

"He's canceled the car insurance on your car, J. J.'s, and Jill's," Rick continued. The sandwich tasted like sawdust in his mouth. He gulped some iced tea.

"What else?" Her voice seemed to her to be coming from a very long way away.

"He's paid Jill's first year at Duke Law, but says that's it. She'll have to manage to get student loans for her other two years. He won't pay for J. J.'s college. He says his son is eighteen now, and he's not legally responsible."

"And?" Nora's face was emotionless.

"No alimony," Rick finished.

"What am I supposed to do, Rick?" Nora asked quietly.

"He says you've got a college degree, so get a job," Rick told her.

"What about the eight thousand dollars my dad gave him to buy the house? He told my father he'd put the house in my name."

"Jeff's lawyer says there is no proof of that, and that the money was a gift to Jeff. Unless your mother can help us prove otherwise, we're stuck. But listen, Nora, this is just the opening gambit in this game. Now we negotiate to try and get you and the kids better terms. Will your mother buy the car for you?"

"It's too much money right now," Nora said. "She's already given me ten thousand to tide me over. And she's sending you a check. Did you speak to her?"

Rick nodded. "Yeah. And you're right. She's a cool lady."

"We can turn J. J.'s car into the family car. He won't be happy, but I told him he couldn't take it to State in his freshman year anyway. But how much is the insurance going to cost me?"

"We can handle that for you," Rick said. "We'll put J. J.'s car in your name 'cause it will give us a better rate. Jill is working for her pocket money, so she'll be okay. J. J. got a summer job yet?"

"At Handlemann's Nursery," Nora said. "He's already working weekends, but it's too late to get him any student aid for this year. How could Jeff do this to his own son? And because he wants to buy a co-op for his girlfriend! Rick, what am I going to do about J. J.'s college? The scholarship covers tuition, but he's got room and board."

"We'll work that one out," Rick told her. "State is cheap for in-state kids. The big problem is the house. We can't let him sell it out from under you, Nora. I'm going to go into court tomorrow and get a restraining order. His lawyer can get it lifted, but we can tie them up long enough to get through the summer. And at that point we will have come up with something, or maybe he will be more reasonable."

"Don't bank on it," Nora said grimly. "When Jeff wants something badly enough, he will move heaven and hell to get it. You don't know what he's like."

"Well," Rick said, "we'll just have to move heaven and hell to keep him at bay."

Nora gave a small laugh. "I never realized you were a knight in shining armor, Rick," she said.

"I'm second-string, honey, and I'm up against the first string, but I'm not going to let Jeff leave you homeless and penniless, Nora." He stood up. "Thanks for lunch," he said.

"You only ate half your sandwich," she admonished him.

"I'm not hungry, except for a victory over Jeff Buckley," Rick told her, and then he was gone out her kitchen door.

The telephone rang. It was her daughter. "Ma, you okay

with all of this?" Jill asked. "It must have been one heck of a shock."

"It's bad, baby, but Rick is going to do his best," Nora said.

"I wish we had the best to handle this," Jill said. "This kind of thing is really over poor Uncle Rick's head."

"He's all I can afford," Nora answered, "or rather, Grandma can afford. She sent him a retainer. Your tuition has been paid at Duke for the coming year, but you'll have to get student aid for the other two years. Daddy says he won't pay. And I don't know where we're going to get the money for J. J."

"He's not paying for J. J.? Ma, that is so unfair! Why not?"

"I think he's taken your college funds for the co-op he wants to buy. He's trying to sell the house out from under us too," Nora told her daughter.

Jill shrieked, "Ma! This is terrible. It's like he's trying to punish you, but you didn't do anything. Are you sure I shouldn't come home this summer?"

"You've got another course to complete if you're going to Duke this fall, Jill. You were accepted on the proviso you finished. I don't want you deferring law school. There is nothing you can do to help, and we don't want to give your father an excuse to not pay that first year. Rick says this hardball is just a negotiating tactic."

"Ma, this is really gross of Daddy," Jill said.

"There is more, sweetie. Your car insurance is going to be changed, but don't worry," Nora said. "But I did want you to know when you get the paperwork. Okay?"

"Why is the car insurance changing?" Jill demanded.

"Because I'm going to be paying for it," Nora told her. "Now, Jill, I don't want to discuss it any further."

"You aren't telling me everything, Ma," Jill Buckley said.

"Jill, the divorce between Daddy and me isn't your problem. It's my problem, and I'm going to solve it. Your brother understands that, and is studying his brains out for his finals. I want you to understand it, and finish up so you're ready for law school in the fall. Now, do we have a deal?"

"Have you met her?" Jill asked.

"Who?" Nora was puzzled.

"Daddy's little bimbo," Jill replied.

"No, I haven't, and to be honest I don't know anything about her. I assume she works with your father in some capacity," Nora said.

"I hate her!" Jill said. "I never even want to meet her! I don't have to, do I?"

"You are of age, Jill. That decision is yours, but you might want to meet her at least once for Daddy's sake. If you don't, he'll say I'm turning you against him. I really don't need that right now."

"I can't believe how good you're being about this," Jill remarked. "What are you going to do now? I mean after the divorce. Both J. J. and I will be away. You'll be all alone. I hate to even think of it."

"Well, don't, then, honey," Nora said. "I'm going to learn how to operate a computer, and then I'm going to check over at the community college to see if they have a course or a seminar about getting into the work force for the first time for old broads."

"Ma! You are not an old broad," Jill said, but she was laughing. "Does this mean Daddy isn't paying you alimony? I can't believe it!"

"Jill, we haven't settled anything yet, but I don't want to take money from your father any longer than I have to take it. I want to be useful in another capacity from the one in which I have been. I married your father right out of college. I'm a dinosaur in this day and age. A woman who never worked. It's past time, and I'm kind of excited thinking about it."

"And you might meet another man," Jill said slyly.

"I don't think so," Nora replied.

"Oh, Ma, do you still love Daddy that much?" Jill asked.

"I'm afraid I don't love your father at all, honey," Nora responded. "I probably haven't for some time. I just didn't realize it. I went about doing the same things year after year. I wasn't unhappy, but neither was I happy. I want an opportunity to live on my own now, but I'll always be here for you and J. J. to come home to, Jill."

"I gotta go now, Ma," Jill said. "I've got a class. I love you!"

"And I love you, Jill. I'll see you for your brother's graduation, okay?"

"Yeah. Bye, Ma!"

"Bye, sweetie!" And the phone clicked off. Nora set it down. She looked out the kitchen windows into her backyard. The pool was open. The bright scarlet rhododendrons were in full bloom, as were the pink azaleas. The lawn was a deep green, but it needed mowing. She'd have J. J. do it before the weekend. The lawn always grew so quickly in the spring.

And then suddenly Nora began to consider if this was the last spring she would sit here and look out at her backyard. She had designed the layout of the garden herself. Worked with Mr. Handlemann to oversee the plantings all those years ago. It was so perfect, and she wasn't ready yet to give this all up to strangers. Whatever happens, she thought grimly, I am going to keep this house. Jeff is not going to sell it so he can buy his damned co-op for some other woman! Let him take a mortgage. If he wants to play, he's got to pay. I deserve my home. All he did was pay a mortgage. He never told me, but his mother did. He didn't save the money for the down payment. His father gave him the ten percent, and my father gave him the other ten percent. I made this house what it is. It's mine! I won't let him take it from me! And then she began to cry. She wept herself into a small headache before her tears finally subsided. Nora got up and, walking into the powder room, grabbed a handful of tissues and blew her nose. Then she washed her face. J. J. would be home from school soon, and she didn't want him to catch her crying.

I need Kyle, she thought again. How am I going to access The Channel if my son is upstairs doing his homework? But if someone walked into the den while I was in The Channel, what would they see? She had absolutely no idea. She had to take the chance, and it had to be tonight. Then she laughed softly. The Channel was like some sort of drug, and she was hooked. She went back into the kitchen, called Suburban Cable, and ordered The Channel for this evening. She could go on it anytime. She'd wait until J. J. was fast asleep, and she'd keep the sound on mute. And having made that decision, she felt better. A whole lot better. She let herself think about Kyle's hard young body. His big tireless dick. The mouth that kissed so well, sucking on her lips, her nipples, and her clit. She could almost taste him in her mouth, and felt herself suddenly wet with need. The sound of J. J.'s car screeching into the driveway drew her swiftly from her reverie.

She got up, and with a familiarity borne of habit, she opened the fridge and pulled out a soda, setting it on the table. Then, going to a pantry cabinet, she got out a bag of his favorite cheese crunchies. She smiled, remembering that as kids, her children had had to eat those damned cheese things in the kitchen, and then wash their hands before going anywhere else in the house. She had learned that after finding yellow cheesy fingerprints on the living room couch.

"Hey!" J. J. came into the kitchen, his eyes lighting up at the sight of the cheese crunchies and soda. Pulling the bag open, he stuffed some in his mouth, then opened the can, drinking some of it down immediately.

"Hey," Nora said back at him. "Sit down. We have to talk."

"What's up, Ma?" he asked her.

"Rick came by earlier. I gave him a sandwich, and we talked. Daddy's lawyer is a tough guy, and it looks pretty bad right now, but Rick says it's just negotiating tactics."

"How bad? And Ma, remember I'm eighteen now. You don't

have to soften it for me like you do with Jill," J. J. told his mother.

"You may not be able to go to college this year," Nora began. "Dad says he's through paying. He paid Jill's first year at Duke Law, but after that, she's got to get aid. He says he won't pay for your first year at State, and it's too late for us to go for aid. Grandma's already shelled out fifteen thousand dollars to help us. I just don't know if I can ask her for more, and you can't pitch a tent on campus."

"What happened to my college fund? The one he was always shoving in our faces every Christmas morning, and bragging about?" J. J. wondered.

"Those papers he asked you to sign a couple of months ago, right after your eighteenth birthday?"

"Yeah, something about taxes," J. J. said.

"That's where the money went," Nora said.

"You mean he stole our college funds?" J. J. was outraged.

"Well, honey, it was his money, after all," Nora began.

"Oh, crap, Ma! Don't defend him. Please don't defend him! Every efffing Christmas for as long as I can remember he was waving the year-end statement at us, and saying how we'd never have to leave college with a lot of debt. That his father did it for him, and he was doing it for us. What a scam! Where's the money gone?"

"I don't know," Nora lied. "Maybe it's just one of those legal negotiating tactics that Rick says we're going to see a lot of, honey."

"I'm going to lose my soccer scholarship if I don't go this year. They're not going to hold a sports scholarship until I can come."

"Well, he has paid your sister's first year at law school," Nora reminded her son.

"Yeah, he would. Jill was always his favorite," J. J. said almost bitterly. "And think of the bragging rights he's got. 'My daughter is at Duke Law.' He's probably yapped about it so much already that he couldn't not pay. He knows Jill will get the moneys she needs for her other two years. Besides, it actually isn't costing him any more than if she'd done her undergrad work in four years instead of three. He's always been a cheapskate, Ma, and you know it. Damn! What the hell am I going to do?"

"J. J., you wanted the truth, and I've told you the truth," Nora said. "We will find a way, I promise you. But there's more, honey. My car's lease is almost up, and I can't afford to buy it. It has to go back to the dealership. Your car is about to become the family car. I'm sorry. Daddy won't buy the car for me, and he won't pay for car insurance either. Rick is seeking insurance we can afford."

J. J. looked up at her. His face was that of the Jeff she had once known. "Ma, why is he doing this to you? To us? What did we do wrong?" His voice was strained.

"Honey, I don't know. You know there's another woman involved. I think your father wants everything to be perfect for them. The problem is he can't make it perfect without a lot of money. He wants to sell the house. He's taken the college funds for himself. He's jettisoning his old life to make a new life. He doesn't know what else to do, I'm afraid. But J. J., I don't want you to worry. I'll do the worrying for this family. You need to concentrate on your exams. I will not let your father sell this house from under us. It is my house. Our home. He's not going to get it. Okay?" She tipped his face up to hers, looking directly into his blue eyes. "Okay?" she repeated.

He gave her a weak smile. "Okay," he said. "But I think Dad's a real shit, Ma, and don't yell at me for using that language."

"Not this time," Nora told him. "I am forced to agree with your rather astute assessment, my son." She gave him a small smile.

J. J. grinned back. "I don't mind if I have to stay home. You need someone to look after you," he told her.

"You are going to college, young man," Nora said firmly.

"And I'm going to learn how to operate a computer, and take a course in how to get a job so I can support myself, and you. It's an adventure, J. J., and I'm actually looking forward to it."

"You are the greatest, Ma," he replied. "I would have thought that you would have gone to pieces over this, but you haven't. You're real strong. You even seem happier, and you're even starting to look different. Prettier."

"Thanks, babe," she said. "Now go study, and I'll start dinner." His words surprised her. After he had disappeared from the kitchen, she walked into the hall and looked at herself in the mirror. Was she beginning to lose weight? And her face seemed to have lost those stress lines she had been wearing for months. Nothing like a whole lot of loving to make a woman feel better, Nora thought mischievously. She could hardly wait to get to The Channel. She returned to the kitchen and began getting the supper ready for the two of them.

Afterwards she curled up in the den with a magazine, waiting, waiting for her son to go to bed. Just before midnight he came down, got himself a glass of milk, and said, "I'm going to hit the sack now, Ma. You really should go to bed yourself."

"Good article," she told him, waving the magazine. "I'll be up eventually." She heard his footsteps retreating back upstairs. She waited another hour just to be certain. Then she crept upstairs, and peeped in his room. J. J. lay deep in sleep. Taking the empty milk glass, she slipped from the bedroom, closing the door softly behind her. Hurrying back downstairs, she put the glass in the dishwasher, and then almost ran into the den to turn on the television, her eager fingers punching in sixty-nine. And there was her apartment on the screen. Nora placed her hand flat against the screen, and to her vast relief was immediately in the living room.

"Kyle!" she called. "Are you here?"

He came through the open bedroom door, and Nora flew into his arms. He kissed her hungrily. "God, Nora, I missed you! You said you'd come last night."

"I couldn't. J. J. is home at night now. Kyle, if he came into the den now, what would he see?" she asked.

"I guess what's here," he told her. "I don't really know."

"Then I can't stay," Nora said. "I can't take the chance of his seeing this."

"Don't go," he begged her. "I need you, baby."

She could see the thick ridge beneath his black silk boxers. "I need you too," she said. "But it's too dangerous, Kyle."

"Look," he began reasonably, "from the other side you can just see the living room. If we went into the bedroom and closed the door, if anyone came into your den, all they would see is the living room. And if the kid's asleep, Nora, we have time. Is he a sound sleeper? Does he wake up in the night?"

"J. J.?" She laughed. "No. When he socks, he's good for at least six hours."

"Then we can take an hour for ourselves, can't we?" he tempted. "I've got some very nice champagne on ice in the bedroom, and I've been eating raw oysters all evening waiting for you." He pulled the sash of her robe open, and began to play with her breasts. "It would be a shame to let this go to waste," he told her, pulling his penis from his shorts. "I want to do you, Nora. I need it. You need it too."

She swallowed hard. She did need it. All afternoon she had been thinking about screwing him. "You're certain if we close the bedroom door, we'll be safe?"

"Pretty certain," he told her, pushing her through the bedroom door, and kicking it shut behind him. He took her head between his hands and kissed her again. "Just an hour, Nora. Then I will let you go."

She shrugged the silk robe off and reached down to fondle him with both hands. Reaching beneath, she cuddled his balls in her palm. They were cool to the touch. She tickled them lightly with her fingers.

He slid to his knees, and began to kiss and suckle on her

breasts. He blew soft little puffs of air onto her flesh. His tongue lapped at her torso. Then his hands slipped around to hold her firmly by her thighs. His tongue poked between her nether lips, seeking her clit, and when he found it he began to tease at it with quick jabs.

"Yes! Yes! Yes!" Nora said breathlessly, feeling the heat begin to rise up within her. "Oh, Kyle, that's so nice, but I really need to be fucked, darling. I've been dreaming about it all day."

He stopped and stood up. "A little more foreplay, Nora. It's nice, and it will make what comes even better."

He lay atop her on the bed for several long minutes, kissing her face, his arms wrapped around her. His body against hers was wonderful. Then at a whispered command Nora drew her left leg up and Kyle pushed his penis into her wet vagina. He fucked her slowly, stroke after stroke after stroke, until she was almost ready to scream. He stopped and murmured another command in her ear, and his tongue licked it for emphasis. Nora raised her right leg, but she did not wrap her limbs about him. She just brought them up. He remained buried within her, and then he began to slowly move on her once more, bringing her almost to the point of orgasm, but stopping again. He whispered again into her ear. Nora raised her legs up farther, rolling backward to raise her hips, allowing him the deepest penetration yet.

She could feel him inside of her. Hard. Oh, God, so hard. She squeezed him with her vaginal muscles, making him moan. Then he began to pump her, and Nora's head began to spin with the pure, hot pleasure he was giving her. She screamed as her own lust burgeoned and then burst in a mutual orgasm, Kyle coming in fierce hot spurts, and her own juices drenching his penis. "Oh, God, that was perfect!" she gasped.

"You think?" he groaned, falling back.

Nora was immediately atop him. "Yes!" she said. "I wish I'd known sex was so good before this. Think of all the fun I've missed. I'll bet Jeff never had it this good. He sure didn't give it to me like you do, Mr. Gorgeous."

He grinned up at her. "Remember, I'm everything you ever wanted, Nora. That's the way it works here in The Channel."

"I wish I could stay here," she said. "Oh, not forever. Just for a little while to get away from everything unpleasant that's going on in my life right now."

Kyle looked thoughtful. "I never heard of anyone taking their vacation here, but I suppose you could ask the administrator, Mr. Nicholas."

Nora rolled off of her lover and, propping herself up on an elbow, looked down at him. "The administrator? You have an administrator? What does he do?" She was surprised. There was someone who ran The Channel? Of course there had to be someone in charge. Was he here, or was he there?

"Mr. Nicholas is in charge of The Channel," Kyle said. "I really don't know what he does, but I suppose someone had to create all of this, and all of us."

"And I can see him?" Fascinating, Nora thought.

"Sure! I can make you an appointment, but let's make it when you don't have to worry about your kid. You don't want to rush an appointment with Mr. Nicholas," Kyle told her.

"Have you ever met him?" Nora asked her lover.

He nodded. "You'd like him. Everyone does."

"Other people from my reality have talked to him?"

"Yeah. Some people who visit The Channel are content to just enjoy their fantasies, like your girlfriends Carla and Tiffany. Others are curious, and want to know how it all works, so they go to see Mr. Nicholas."

"You know Carla and Tiffany?" Interesting.

"I know of them, but no," Kyle told her. "I don't know them. I don't fit into their fantasies like I fit into yours, Nora."

"How do you know of them?" Curiouser and curiouser.

"Because I know everything about you, darling. Remember,

I'm a part of you," Kyle told her, and then he pulled her down and kissed her.

Nora sighed. "I have to go," she said softly. "I'm so afraid that J. J. will wake up and come looking for me, and find his mother starring in a porn movie." She drew away from Kyle. "Tell me, what should I wear to see Mr. Nicholas?"

"You've got a closet full of nice things, Nora. Open it, and look," he told her.

She got up, and walking across the bedroom floor to the mirrored walls, behind which was a closet, she pushed open one of the doors. Inside was an entire wardrobe of clothing. It was all beautiful. All expensive. And all in the colors she loved. She turned. "Mine?" she asked Kyle.

"All yours," he said. "Like?"

She pulled out a silk wool suit in palest heather mauve. "Oh, yes, I like very much." She put the suit back.

"The Channel offers you everything you want, Nora," he told her.

"That suit sure didn't come from Talbots, like most of my stuff," she noted.

"Your wardrobe here is a bit more elegant, more upmarket," he said.

Nora bent and, picking up her shorty robe, slipped it on. "I do have to go," she said to him.

"When will you be back?" he asked her.

Nora shook her head. "I don't know. With J. J. in the house, I have to be careful."

"I'll be waiting," he promised her.

"Really?"

He nodded.

"How do I get back before closing time?" she wondered aloud. She hadn't even considered that when she made her plans to come tonight.

"Just touch the screen of the plasma telly in the living

room. When you turn it on you'll see your den. Good night, Nora, my love."

She blew him a kiss, and hurried back into the living room to turn on the television. When the screen lit she could see her den, in the dimness. Reluctantly she reached out and put her hand flat against the screen. She didn't want to go back, but she had to if she was going to beat Jeff. And no matter how the cards were stacked against her, Nora had already decided her husband wasn't going to get his way this time.

CHAPTER FIVE

Nora heard nothing from her husband after he had asked her for a divorce. His attorney, Raoul Kramer, had called Rick and said they would all get together after J. J.'s graduation. "No need spoiling the kid's big day," he said.

"It's already spoiled, but maybe a few days will give Jeff a little more perspective," Rick replied. "He can't just dump the woman he's been married to for over twenty-five years without something."

"Sure he can," Kramer laughed. "I'll call you in two weeks, Johnson." And he hung up.

"You looked pissed," his partner, Joe Pietro d'Angelo, said, coming into Rick's office. "Let me guess. The Buckley divorce."

"Joe, we gotta do something. Jeff and his lawyer won't budge. What the hell is going to happen to Nora, and her kids?"

"What did Kramer want?"

"They don't want to discuss anything until after J. J.'s graduation," Rick said.

"Okay, no problem," Joe told him. "They're hoping by putting it off you'll ease up on some of your demands. This is a game, Rick. They won't back down. We won't back down. Jeff Buckley has more to lose than Nora does."

"How do you see that?" Rick asked.

Joe chuckled. "Look, he's divorcing the long-suffering wife for the younger trophy wife. They want to make a nice nest. He's obviously found something, and that's why he wants to sell the house. The kids' college money isn't enough. He wants to be debt free. No mortgage. He paid off the Ansley Court house a couple of years ago. If he sells it, it's all profit except for the agent's commission. And I'll bet he tries to sell it without an agent. No judge is going to let him disenfranchise Nora and her kids. We take it to a judge, and the judge is going to rule Nora stays in the house until they reach a fair settlement. We can hold them off that way, and Raoul Kramer knows it. They want a fast settlement, and we're not going to give it to them unless Jeff gets reasonable."

"Nora wants the house," Rick said.

"I don't think we can get it for her," Joe told his partner. "The best we're going to do is half the value of the house because her father put down half the down payment. And that's the absolute best. Kramer is going to claim she never paid a penny of the mortgage. We're going to have to counterclaim that while she never put money into the house, she did put sweat equity based on her track record as a wife. Nora has always been frugal with Jeff's money. Tiff says she's been wearing the same stuff from Talbots for years. She never buys anything for herself. In other words, her good habits have helped Jeff build the wealth he now wants to squander on a younger new wife."

"God, you're good!" Rick grinned.

Joe grinned back. "I learned a lot at that big practice I worked for in town when I was a callow youth. People with money get real possessive in a situation like this. What do you think Nora will do when this is all over?"

"She's planning to go to the community college to learn computer skills and take a course on how to get a job," Rick said.

"Won't be easy at her age, and with no previous experience,"

Joe noted, "but if Nora's careful, she'll manage. Has she got an aptitude for anything in particular?"

"You got me," Rick said. "I wonder if Jeff will show up at the graduation. Maureen is friends with J. J.'s girlfriend, Lily Graham. She told Carla that J. J. doesn't want his dad there. That he's really mad at him, especially since he won't pay J. J.'s board at State."

"Yeah," Joe said, "that's something we've got to do for Nora. Tiff was talking to me about it. The kid's got a soccer scholarship for tuition. Why don't the rest of us kick in for his dorm and meal plan? It's only about fifteen hundred apiece. The kid's got a summer job, and he's already lined up an on-campus job. That'll take care of everything else. I'd feel lousy if he lost that scholarship because his father is a horny prick."

"It'll have to come through the girls. I'll talk to Carl Ulrich, and you speak to Sam Seligmann," Rick suggested. "God, I hope Jeff doesn't show up at graduation."

"He's got to be asked, or Kramer will say we're turning the kid against his dad. Judges don't like parents who play divide and conquer," Joe noted.

"I'll check with Carla, but knowing Nora, she'll ask him, because she's just that decent, even if it's wasted on Jeff," Rick answered.

And of course Nora did make certain that her husband was asked to their son's graduation. She had stood over J. J. as he addressed the invitation to his graduation to his father's office, since they had no idea where he was living. After receiving no response, Nora called her husband's office two days before the graduation, but Jeff, according to Carol, his longtime assistant, was unavailable to speak with her.

"I just wanted to know if he's coming to J. J.'s graduation, Carol," Nora said. "We sent his invitation to the office. Maybe it didn't arrive? But graduation is in two days. This weekend."

"Oh, he got the invitation, Mrs. Buckley," Carol said. "I

opened it, and gave it to him myself. I can't imagine J. J. graduating already. I came to work for Mr. Buckley the summer just
before J. J. started kindergarten. It doesn't seem possible that
much time has passed. I'm sure he'll be there in spite of everything."

Nora laughed. "I don't want to put you on the spot, Carol,
but satisfy my curiosity. Just a yes or no will do. Does she work
in the office?"

There was a long pause, and then Carol said, "Yes." She lowered her voice. "I'm so sorry, Mrs. Buckley!"

"Thank you," Nora responded. "Tell Jeff I called, and I'd like
to know one way or the other if he is or isn't coming."

"Of course, Mrs. Buckley. Good-bye."

"Good-bye, Carol," Nora said.

"I hope he doesn't come," Jill Buckley said. She had just arrived home that afternoon. "J. J. doesn't want him there, and for
once I agree with my brother."

"He's your father," Nora said quietly.

"He's a creep," Jill replied. "Dumping you for another woman
is bad enough, Ma, but trying to make you a homeless bag
woman stinks."

"It's a negotiating tactic, Jill. Nothing more. You'll learn that
in law school. Do you have your summer course set up?"

"Yeah. If my college didn't require those damned gym courses,
I could have been through now," Jill grumbled irritably. "At least
it doesn't screw up my waitress job."

"If you had taken those gym courses in your first two years instead of waiting until the last minute, you wouldn't have had to
take them this year, and miss the other course you needed and will
now have to take this summer," Nora reminded her daughter.

"I hate that phys-ed stuff. I'm not an athlete like J. J.," Jill
replied.

"Honey, don't you miss not having a graduation?" Nora
asked.

"Nah. Lot of bother, Ma. I just want to go to law school, and get on with my life," Jill responded. "And I've got to start thinking of an internship for next summer."

Nora shook her head. "You're your father's daughter," she said.

"Don't say that!" Jill cried. "I'm nothing like him! I don't want to be like him!"

"Honey, I only meant you were organized, and ambitious," Nora soothed. She hated seeing her children so angry with their father. This problem wasn't really theirs. It was hers and Jeff's. Jill had always adored her father. "You have to be nice to your dad, Jill, when he comes. I don't want him taking away your law school tuition this year. There is no way you could go to Duke without him this year, and he seems to be in an odd mood. Remember that."

"Probably his teenybopper girlfriend has him on drugs. Drugs give you mood swings," Jill said nastily.

"Jill! I have no idea how old or how young this woman is. Don't say things like that," Nora scolded.

"Ma, you know she's got to be younger. When a man has enough money, and is happy in his job, the only thing he wants is red-hot sex. I learned that in psych. I don't think you and Dad were having red-hot sex, if you were having sex at all."

"Enough!" Nora said sharply. "Your father wants a divorce. I'm happy to give him one. Our only disagreement is money. Let it go, Jill. I don't want to hear any more about this. Dad and I will both be happier apart."

And it couldn't all come soon enough, Nora thought to herself. She hadn't seen her husband in several weeks, and to her surprise she wasn't unhappy. In fact she was downright happy, and she was looking forward to starting her own life anew. Rick assured her that they would get a decent settlement out of Jeff eventually. He explained why Jeff couldn't sell the house from under her, but he didn't have the heart to tell her that in the end the house would be sold. That news would come later when there was no other choice. For now it was a huge burden off of her shoulders, as was the financial problem of J. J.'s college tuition.

Carla had come to her with a check for six thousand dollars, and when Nora had demurred, Carla had quietly explained that it wasn't right for J. J. to lose his sports scholarship, and that it was a graduation gift to him from his neighbors on Ansley Court, who had watched him grow up with their kids. It would pay for his dorm room and his meal plan. Nora cried. There was no way she could deny her son this chance. And he was going to write thank-you notes to them all, or she'd kill him!

On graduation morning J. J. donned his kelly green gown and cap. The school's colors were kelly green and white. Maureen Johnson was wearing a white cap and gown, like all the other girls graduating that day. The two families met on the lawns outside. Pictures were taken. Margo Edwards had come up from South Carolina in her gentleman friend Taylor's private plane. They had flown in early this morning, and would be leaving almost immediately after graduation.

"We have a dance tonight at the club, darling," Margo told her daughter. "You know, Nora, you are looking better now than you have in years. You've lost weight, and you have a positive glow about you. If this is what getting rid of Jeff has done for you, you should have done it sooner," she laughed.

Nora laughed too. "Thanks, Mom," she said. And then wondered what his mother would think if she told her about The Channel, and that she was having the best sex of her life with an imaginary lover.

Since Nora had to turn in her car to the dealer, they squeezed into J. J.'s and Jill's two little cars.

"You really should have told me, darling," Margo said. "You can't be without a car. How are you going to get around?"

"I'm taking J. J.'s car for now. I'll drop him at work and pick him up every day. That way I'll have the car for errands, and he's not taking it to college anyway this year. He's got it exclusively Friday nights until Sunday church. It won't be so bad, Mom," Nora said. "Besides, I've got to pay the insurance now."

"Jeff is a monster!" Margo said, and she turned to her escort. "This is a perfect example of his perfidy, Taylor. Didn't I tell you?"

"Now, honey, don't you go getting yourself all upset," Taylor Bradford said. "I think your Nora will just be fine, won't you, girly?"

"Yes, I will," Nora agreed sweetly, and she winked at him.

They were all laughing as they parked and got out of the car. J. J. and Maureen ran off to join their classmates. Nora and her family walked to the soccer field, where chairs had been set up for the graduation. The day was sunny, with a light breeze. It was perfect June weather.

"Who is that?" Carla asked as a sleek dark gray limousine pulled into the parking lot. "Oh, Jesus, Nora! It's Jeff, and he's brought the Jennifer with him."

"I cannot believe the effrontery of that man!" Margo gasped.

Nora stared. Well, there was the answer to her question. The next Mrs. Buckley was not a great beauty, but she was a very striking young woman. Tall. Blond. Willowy.

Nora instantly regretted her mauve-and-green floral dress. While it certainly fit her better than it had in a long while, it wasn't the kind of dress in which you wanted to meet your successor. It screamed ordinary. The Jennifer was dressed in a pale gray silk suit with a fitted jacket. She was wearing a pair of the highest sling-back heels Nora had ever seen. They were straight out of Carrie's closet on *Sex and the City*. Her blond hair was pulled back neatly.

"Let's get out of here," Carla hissed. "I don't want to be introduced now."

"Agreed," Nora said. "God, I look so fat in this dress, and she looks like she lives on lettuce leaves."

"You do not look fat in that dress!" Margo said loyally. "You look lovely."

Oh God, Nora thought, lovely? She didn't want to look lovely. She wanted to look smashing and sexy. She wanted to look like she looked in The Channel. Oh, Kyle! She hadn't seen him since Jill got home. Jill was a night owl, and there was no chance to sneak into The Channel with Jill home. But right now she wanted to look like she did with Kyle, and she wanted to have him on her arm. Wouldn't that surprise old Jeff?

They found an open row, and crowded in. The Seligmanns, the Pietro d'Angelos, and the Ulriches were already waiting for them. Just enough chairs, including Margo and Taylor. No room for Jeff and his Jennifer. Too bad.

"Jeff just arrived in a big limo with his Jennifer," Carla hissed to the others.

"Such a nerve," Rina said. "I wouldn't want a nerve like that in my tooth."

"Do you think they'll come back to the house for the party?" Tiffany asked.

"It's his son's graduation," Nora whispered at them. "I'm sure he'll come back, and please, for the love of God, no confrontations. I've got enough trouble, and the lawyers start talking again on Monday. We don't want Jeff feeling hostile."

"I can't talk to him, Ma," Jill said. "That woman with him isn't much older than I am. It's embarrassing."

"No, Jill, what's embarrassing is wearing a seven-year-old flowered dress when your husband's next wife-to-be looks like she stepped out of *Vogue*. So shut up, and be nice to your father," Nora snapped irritably. "This situation isn't about you. Got it?"

"Good for you, girly," Taylor Bradford murmured, and he patted her hand.

The graduation ceremony began. It was like every graduation day. *Pomp and Circumstance*. Welcome to Parents and Guests. A small speech by the principal. The Salutatorian's

Speech. The Valedictorian's Speech. The Awards. The Confer-
ring of the Diplomas. The Dismissal, when all the mortarboards
went flying in the air to the happy shouts of the graduating
class. And it was over.

J. J. headed toward his family. "I saw him," he said to his
mother.

"Be nice. Remember what we talked about," she warned him.

And then Jeffrey Buckley and his companion were upon them.
"Congratulations, son," he said. "I'd like to introduce you to my
friend, Heidi Millar."

The girl quickly held out her hand. "Your dad speaks highly
of you, J. J.," she said.

To Nora's relief, J. J. shook the young woman's hand. "Thank
you," was all he said.

"Nora, Heidi Millar," Jeff said.

"You'll come back to the house, of course," Nora responded.
"We're having a small celebration before J. J. goes off with his
friends." She quickly turned away, as did the others.

"Of course," he said jovially.

"I can't believe you asked him to come here with his . . . his
woman!" Jill raged at Nora in the car.

"I had no choice, Jill. Now behave yourself," Nora snapped.

"Grandma!" Jill turned to Margo.

"No, Jill, your mother did exactly the right thing. Your father
isn't divorcing you, darling. He's divorcing your mother. Now behave. Taylor and I can only spend another hour with you before
we leave, and I want to have nice memories of my grandson's
high school graduation."

Jill slouched down in the car, scowling. "I'll speak to Daddy,
but I absolutely will not talk with that woman," she said.

Nora's hands clutched the wheel of the car. If Jill started a
brouhaha, she was going to kill her. She angled her way from
the parking lot and headed off home. She had to get there before
Jeff, and in her rearview mirror she could see the limo making its

attempt to leave. She pressed down on the gas pedal and stared ahead.

Rina and Joanne were at the house ahead of her. They were already putting the sandwiches out on the silver trays. Tiffany was putting the finishing touches on the sheet cake. She was their cake decorator. No one else ever bothered to do a cake once they learned how clever Tiff was. The rectangular pastry was bedecked with a soccer field design complete with goal, and a figure kicking a ball between the posts. Tiffany was just finishing up the writing. "Congratulations, Jeff" was emblazoned across the cake.

The women hurried out to the brick terrace off the den, where a table had been set up, covered with a lovely white linen cloth edged in delicate lace. There were heavy paper plates with a graduation motif, cups, and silverware on the table. The cake was set in the center with plates of small sandwiches surrounding it. Nora had used a mix of her good china, her silver, and paper goods. Margo and Taylor came from the kitchen, each carrying two pitchers of lemonade mixed with iced tea. Nora liked the way Taylor Bradford seemed to fit right in with them. Trust Margo to have found the right man whether she married him or not.

Then Jeff arrived with Heidi, behaving very much like the lord of the manor. He seated his companion by the pool, and hurried over to the table to fetch her refreshment.

"Where are the glasses?" he wanted to know.

"We're using paper cups," Nora replied quietly.

"You know I don't like paper," he said irritably. "Go and get me two glasses."

"You haven't been gone so long that you've forgotten where the glasses are, Jeff," Nora said dryly. "If you want glasses, go and get them yourself. My days of servitude are over. Please try and be pleasant for J. J. sake."

"What the hell has gotten into you, Nora?" he demanded.

She smiled brightly at him. "I have guests to attend to, Jeff." And she walked away. Inside she was shaking with her anger. How dare he bring her replacement into her house, and behave as if everything in it, including Nora, were at his pleasure.

It was a brief party, because J. J. desperately wanted to join his friends. Maureen would be having the big party tonight, but Nora knew there were other parties going on even now that the two kids wanted to go to. She got J. J. to come and make a ceremonial cut of his cake. Tiffany came then to slice up the cake for the guests.

"The girls and I want to go now," J. J. said to his mother.

"Go on, but say good-bye to your father first," Nora advised her son.

Reluctantly J. J. walked over to where his father sat with his girlfriend. "I'm going now, Dad," he said.

"Sit down for a minute and visit with us," Jeff said.

"Mo and Lily are waiting for me, Dad," J. J. said.

"Sit down!" Jeff snapped. "You haven't said a word to Heidi."

"What do you want me to say, Dad? You're dumping my mother. You've taken away my college funds. What am I supposed to say? Thank you?"

"Heidi is going to be your stepmother, J. J.," Jeff said.

"So?"

"I want you to know her, and like her," his father responded.

"Look, Dad, I don't want to know her, and I'll never like her. Got it?" J. J. told his father. "I'm eighteen now. I won't have to come to you every other weekend like some of my friends do with their parents. It's over between us. You gave me life, but not much more. You never came to my games, or the plays I was in, or the mountain house." He turned to Heidi Millar. "I hope you aren't planning on kids, ma'am. He's a lousy father."

Heidi Millar's cold gray eyes looked directly at J. J. "I don't think you have the right to speak to your father like that. You obviously have no idea what a wonderful and talented man he is. You're angry because he won't pay for your schooling. Why should he pay for a boy who obviously has no respect for him? You, your sister, and your mother have lived off of Jeff's hard work and generosity long enough. It's past time you took care of yourselves."

J. J. stood up. "So long, Dad," he said.

Jeff stood up too, holding out his hand to his son. J. J. looked at the hand, laughed, and then turned away. Jeff Buckley's face grew florid with his anger at the snub. "Your mother," he snarled, "is obviously working very hard to turn you against me. It won't help her to do it at all."

J. J. turned, his fists clenched, to glare at his father, and it was then that Taylor Bradford stepped into the fray. He put his arm about the boy, murmuring as he did, "The man ain't worth it, son. Go on with those two pretty girls waiting for you," and he gently pushed J. J. in the direction of Lily and Mo. Then he turned back to Jeff Buckley. "I think you've just about worn out your welcome here today, sir. Why don't you take the young lady and head back to town?"

"Who the hell are you?" Jeff demanded to know.

"Taylor Bradford of Bradford, South Carolina, sir. I'm planning on being Margo's husband one of these days real soon. So as the patriarch of this family, I'm telling you to git."

"Taylor Bradford of Bradford Industries?" Heidi said, and when he nodded she continued eagerly, smiling her best smile at him. "We've been trying to get your business, Mr. Bradford, for our agency, Buckley, Coutts and Wickham."

"I don't think I'd count on my business now, missy," the older man said. "Your driver's waiting."

"I haven't seen my daughter yet," Jeff said stubbornly.

"You can say your heys on the way out." Taylor Bradford smiled.

Heidi Millar stood up. "Come on, Jeff. This is already old,

and I'm bored." She took his arm and they moved off, but Jeff
guided them to Nora, determined to have his say before he left.

Nora was sitting with her mother and daughter when Jeff approached. She stood, smiling weakly. "Going so soon?"

"You're going to be sorry, Nora, for turning my son against
me," he growled at her. "I'm not going to forget this, and come
Monday you're going to wish you hadn't done it, you embittered
bitch."

The look of surprise on Nora's face was instant. "I didn't turn
J. J. against you. What happened?"

"He was rude to me, and Heidi," Jeff said angrily.

"He was incredibly awful to his father," Heidi Millar added.
"He said the most terrible things. It's no wonder Jeff is washing
his hands of him!"

"My brother is a good kid," Jill said, jumping up to defend
her sibling. "He's hurt because of what's happened. You can't
blame him."

"He's a nasty little brat," Heidi responded.

"Do you hate me, Jilly?" her father asked.

"Of course not, Daddy, and neither does J. J. I'm just upset
that you are being so unfair to Mom. How is she supposed to live
if you won't pay her alimony, at least for a little while? And
where is she supposed to live if you sell our house?"

"Jill!" Nora put a hand on her daughter's arm, in a warning
gesture.

"Your mother has a college degree. Let her get a job like
everyone else these days," Jeff said, ignoring his daughter's query
about the house.

"You just better be careful, Jill," Heidi said. "If your father
hadn't already paid your tuition at Duke this year, you wouldn't
be going. And it's the last time he's going to pay for you. I hope
you understand that."

"Get out!" Nora said. Her eyes were filled with tears, which
were beginning to spill down her cheeks. "Get out, Jeff, and

please, don't come back. And take that girl with you. I wanted you to come to J. J.'s graduation today. You're his father. But you've spoiled the day for us all. I hope you're satisfied."

"You've gotten old and bitter, Nora," he said cruelly.

"Jeff, you wanted a divorce. I said you could have one. But just bear this in mind—I will not let you have my house. Do you understand me? You will never have this house! If you want to start again, then do it all the way. Take a mortgage like all young couples do," Nora sneered at him, the tears still pouring down her cheeks.

"You will get nothing from me, bitch! Nothing!" And then he spun about and dragged Heidi with him as he headed for the limo.

Nora was shaking with anger now, but she couldn't stop crying. Taylor Bradford pushed a paper cup into her hand. Nora drank, and then began to cough. "It's whiskey!" she gasped.

"Yep," he agreed. "Nothing like a little drink to calm the nerves, honey."

Nora began to laugh, and looking at her mother, she said, "If you don't marry him eventually, Ma, I will." Then she drank down the rest of the potent liquid in the paper cup. And she did feel better. "Nobody leaves here till those damned sandwiches are all eaten," she said. And the tension broken, her friends began to eat and talk again.

Margo put an arm around her daughter. "That was hard," she said, "but you did just fine. I never thought I'd see the day when you stood up to Jeff Buckley."

"A lot of things are changing, Ma," Nora admitted.

"We're going to have to go soon," Margo said.

"I know. You've got a dance at the club," Nora answered. "I like Taylor. I wouldn't mind if you married him."

"We'll see," Margo replied.

"He's very rich, isn't he? I mean, you flew up in his private plane," Nora said.

"He flies the plane himself," Margo told her, "although at his age he has another pilot with us, and yes, dear, he's very rich."

"Wow! Mom, you really surprise me," Nora told her parent with a smile.

Margo laughed. "Thank you," she said. And then she grew serious. "I would have never thought you would be so good about what's happening, Nora. I'm proud of you, darling, and until you get on your feet I will help."

"I'll pay you back one day, Ma," Nora promised.

"Honey, you're going to inherit it anyway," Margo said. "You need it now, and frankly it gives me pleasure to see you make Jeff Buckley's life a little difficult."

"I want the house, Ma! I don't care about anything else, but I want the house," Nora told her mother.

"I'm sure Rick will do his best for you, darling," Margo assured her.

"Time to go, honeybunch." Taylor Bradford had come to where they were seated. "Car is here, and Hal has the plane ready. We got a nice tailwind, and should be home in no time at all so you can get yourself all gussied up for the dance tonight."

The two women stood up, and Nora put her arms about Taylor Bradford, giving him a big hug. "Thank you for bringing Mom, Taylor. You're welcome in my house anytime." Then she stood on her toes and kissed his ruddy cheek.

"I got two sons, girly," he said. "Wouldn't mind having a daughter like you at all. Even at this late date." And he kissed her cheek heartily.

"Good-bye, darling." Margo kissed Nora, and gave her a quick hug. "Tell J. J. to look in the graduation card I gave him." She turned and kissed Jill. "You did very well under the circumstances, darling. Grandma was proud."

"I wanted to smack him," Jill admitted.

"So did I," Margo replied.

"Then we both did very well," Jill chuckled.

The guests were gone at last. Carla stayed to help Nora clean up. Jill had gone upstairs to pack. She was taking an early-evening flight back to her college.

"The Channel tonight, you lucky girl." Carla grinned at Nora.

"I don't know," Nora said. "What if J. J. comes home? What does it look like to people on this side of reality when we're on the other?"

Carla shrugged. "I have no idea. But J. J. won't be home until dawn. Our party starts at nine, and when it finally ends they're all going up to the mountain house for a long weekend. No chaperones." She waggled her eyebrows at Nora.

"I had forgotten that they were going up," she said. "Yeah, maybe I could get The Channel tonight. I haven't been able to get there with Jill home."

"Call now," Carla encouraged her. "I'll finish the cleanup. Just a little cake to put away anyhow. I've packed two sandwiches for Jill to have on the plane."

"You are an angel," Nora said, picking up the telephone handset.

J. J. came home to change for Maureen Johnson's party. He had been at his girlfriend Lily's party. Jill was just going out the door to her waiting Cassandra cab. He hugged her. "So long, big sis. When will I see you again? Before I'm off to State?"

"Not till Christmas, kiddo," Jill told him. "I've got just enough time between finishing my course and orientation at Duke to pack up and get there."

"Where will you live?" he asked, walking with her to the cab.

"Duke hooked me up with two other girls, and we've rented a house," Jill said. "I've got the money from working and saving almost everything Daddy sent me. No more where that came from. Miss Icy Eyes is going to get it all." She gave him a quick kiss. "Don't screw up, J. J. It will be tempting to party, party, party, but that first semester is important. I've been there. Besides, the whole neighborhood helped get you there. You don't want to disappoint them." She got into the cab. "So long!" She blew him a kiss as the cab revved up and sped off.

"No pressure," J. J. mumbled to himself as he went into the house. "I'm home," he called to his mother.

"I'm upstairs," Nora said, and heard him taking the steps two at a time. He came into his room. "I packed a few things for you for the mountain house," she said. "Why don't you take them over and put them in Mo's car? Or are you riding in Lily's?"

"Lily," he answered, "but Mo'll take my stuff up, and if I toss it in her trunk now, I won't forget. Toothbrush, razor, etc.?"

"Yes," she said.

He sat down on the edge of the bed. "You don't mind being alone this weekend? We probably won't be back till sometime on Monday."

"Actually I'm looking forward to a little peace and quiet," Nora told him. "I've never minded being alone, and I'm going to be in a few weeks when you head off to State. And you're going earlier than most kids because you're on a team, honey."

"Ma, maybe I ought to put off college for a year. Until this thing with Dad gets straightened out," J. J. said.

"You can't do anything to help, honey, and you'll lose your scholarship if you don't go now. It's alright, J. J. Now shower and change before you go, and don't forget your duffel. I'll put it downstairs by the door."

She left him, thinking he was a sweet kid, and so protective of her. She ought to feel guilty for wanting him gone, out of the house, but she didn't. She was through being superwife and supermom. She wanted to be that woman who lived in The Channel. She wanted to be fucked in every way imaginable by Kyle, and Rolf, and whomever else she could think up. She wanted to be licked, and she wanted to suck cock until she was mindless. And she was no longer shocked by these thoughts.

Smelling of soap, shampoo, and aftershave, J. J. kissed his

mom before he left for his party. With a grin at her, he picked up his duffel. "Have a good weekend, Ma," he said as he headed out the door.

"You too, honey," Nora told him, watching as he made his way across the lawn, where even now a crowd of kids was gathering. She shut the door, and threw the bolt. She checked the central AC, and set the thermostat at seventy-two degrees. She went into the kitchen and shoved a small ham-and-cheese into the microwave. When it was done she sat down at her kitchen table, and looked out into her beautiful backyard, and ate her sandwich and drank her lemonade/iced tea mix. As she always did, she put her dishes in the dishwasher and cleaned up the counters. Returning upstairs, she showered and got into a clean nightshirt. Then she went downstairs to the den. It was still not quite eight o'clock. Nora sat down in her recliner, and considered. It was still light. Maybe she should wait until after nine. No. The den faced the back of the house. No one was going to see her. The doors and windows were locked. The clock struck eight, and Nora eagerly punched in The Channel. The television clicked on. The dark screen lightened, and there was her apartment. Eagerly Nora reached out and put her palm flat against the screen.

She was here at last! She sighed with relief. Where was Kyle? And then she saw a note propped up on the coffee table. She walked over to it, and read, "Wasn't certain when you would get back. Dial 1, and I'll be right there. Kyle."

Nora picked up her telephone, and pressed one. An automated voice greeted her. "Your message has been received. Kyle will be with you shortly." Then the phone clicked off. Nora walked into the bedroom and shrugged off her shorty robe. She was bored with it now. She opened the closet its full width and stared at the clothing. On one end was a line of slinky negligees in silk and satin, with lace, in luscious colors. She debated which one she would wear, trying to decide between a lavender silk and a pale green silk with lace.

As she stood deep in thought, she was suddenly grabbed from behind, a blindfold tied over her eyes. Her wrists were bound with silk. She was shoved facedown on the bed, her legs pushed apart. She felt a single finger pushing between her ass cheeks. She could feel it touching her anus. Her breath was coming in short pants as she struggled not to panic. No word was spoken by her attacker. The finger rubbed her. It was slick with oil. She couldn't help herself. She squeezed the finger with her butt muscles. The finger pressed against her extraordinarily sensitive flesh. She squealed, but the finger went no farther. It just continued to rub at her until she was wiggling with rising excitement. Her ravisher's other hand slipped beneath her, and another finger found its way to her clitoris. Both fingers rubbed, and stroked, and pressed at her flesh, until she thought she would go mad. Unable to contain herself she hissed, "Do it, damnit!"

The finger between her ass cheeks pushed into her anus just a single joint's length.

"More!" she pleaded.

The finger sheathed itself fully, and she moaned. "Yes!" Her sphincter muscle tightened about the digit, making it almost impossible for him to withdraw it, but he finally managed to do so, smacking her butt as he got free.

"Do not move," Kyle's deep rough voice growled in her ear. "If you try to get away, I'll catch you, and you won't get fucked for a month."

She heard him go into the bathroom, the water running in the sink, and then finally he was back. She could smell the soap. He had washed his hands.

"Now, Nora, get your butt up," he ordered, and he shoved a pillow beneath her belly.

She felt him behind her, but he entered her vagina, much to her relief, and as he pushed forward he made contact with the spot she had never believed existed. The legendary G-spot. Slowly, slowly, very slowly he rubbed it with his hot penis. Nora thought she was going to explode with the incredible sensations that began to sweep over her. "Oh, my God!" she gasped. "Oh, my God!"

He laughed in her ear. "Found it, didn't I?" he gloated. "Now, baby, I'm going to fuck you until you come, and come and come! Do you know how much I've missed you? I've had a hard-on for almost a week now." He pressed down with his penis on that sensitive spot, and Nora thought she would dissolve in a puddle of lust. Nothing had prepared her for this.

"I couldn't come," she said. "My daughter was home, and she's up half the night."

"Couldn't come?" he teased. "Well, baby, you're going to come now, and a lot later too." He thrust hard now.

"Oh, please, yes, Kyle!" she begged him. "Do it to me, darling! Do it to me!" The slightest movement of his dick and the sensations were overwhelming her. One orgasm after the other came until she was weak. Finally he let his load explode into her, and collapsed atop her for a few minutes. "Untie me," she finally said, and he did. Nora removed the blindfold. "That was very exciting," she said with understatement. "Can we play that game with Rolf one day?"

He grinned weakly at her. "Anything you want, my lady."

"I didn't know I wanted that," she said, referring to their encounter.

"You had a bad day," he said. "I thought it would help."

Nora rolled over, and lay with her head on his chest. "It did, Kyle. I needed to be taken and satisfied like that." She kissed his nipples, licking at them provocatively. "How did you know I'd had a bad day?"

"I always know how it is with you. It's my job, Nora." He put his arm about her.

"You do your job well, darling," she told him.

"I spoke to Mr. Nicholas," he said to her.

"Mr. Nicholas?"

"The administrator of The Channel. He says you may have an appointment with him anytime you want. He says he's looking forward to meeting you."

"Oh." She had forgotten.

"Don't you want to stay in The Channel, Nora? Have you changed your mind now, darling?" Kyle wondered.

"No, but I'm not ready yet. I have to get my son off to college. I have to see what kind of a deal the lawyers can work out between Jeff and me. I can't take my vacation yet. It was sweet of you to speak with Mr. Nicholas, Kyle."

"You really ought to see him soon, Nora. You don't know when you'll need to escape from your reality, and you need to know what will happen if you do, don't you?" Kyle pressured her gently.

"You could be right," Nora considered. "If I need to make a quick getaway, it would help to have his approval, wouldn't it? Can we arrange it now?"

"Why not?" he said, and he reached for the phone. "Mr. Nicholas's office," he said, and then, "Good evening, sir. Nora Buckley is ready to make her appointment with you. Yes, of course." And he put the phone back in its stand.

"Well?" Nora said anxiously.

"I have to call back in a few minutes. His assistants are all on a break right now. He can't make any appointments without them, because he's never certain of his schedule." Kyle laughed. "You'd think someone that important would have all the information he needed at his fingertips. I'll tell you what, Nora. Go shower and get the smell of sex off of you. I'll pick an outfit for you to wear."

Nora got up and went into the bathroom, where she showered, and then reentering the bedroom, she said, "What have you chosen for me?"

He held it out. "Simple and elegant," he told her.

Nora looked at the dress. It was a wrap style, a dark green silk with a deep V neckline and long fitted sleeves. "It's lovely," she said. Lovely, but not like the damned floral print she had worn today to her son's graduation.

"But first these," he said, laying the dress on the bed and picking up a green lace garter belt. He hooked it around her, and then ordered her to sit while he rolled the sheerest nude stockings she had ever seen in all of her life up her legs, then hooked them neatly to the belt. "No bra," he said. "Your tits are too good."

"Panties?"

"Nope," he told her. "Too much trouble getting off when you get back, and I'll be waiting for you. The kid is out, and we've got the whole night ahead of us, Nora."

She stepped into the dress, while Kyle pulled it up and zipped it. Then kneeling down, he slipped sling-back heels on her slender feet. When he stood again, he put her back from him and whistled. Then he pulled the mirrored doors shut, and said, "What do you think?"

Nora stared. She looked absolutely marvelous. Far better than Heidi Millar, and here in The Channel she was probably Heidi's age. "Give me a brush. I need to do something with my hair," she said. "I'll put it up."

"No, down," he disagreed.

"I'll look like a tart out of a 1940s movie," she protested.

"We'll compromise," he said, brushing her long red gold hair out. Then he picked up a large tortoiseshell barrette, and gathering her hair into a single thick strand, he fastened the clasp. "Elegant. Goes with the dress. Doesn't look like a schoolmarm."

"I am hardly schoolmarmish in this dress with no undergarments," Nora laughed.

Kyle took a bottle from the dressing table. Uncorking it, he dabbed a little perfume in her cleavage. The phone rang, and he picked it up, putting down the scent bottle. "Mrs. Buckley's penthouse," he said. "Yes. Of course. I'll send her right down.

Thank you, Margaret." He put the handset down, and turned to Nora. "Mr. Nicholas will see you now."

"Will you come with me?" she asked, suddenly nervous. She had never left her fantasy apartment other than to go back to her reality.

"I'm not invited," Kyle said. "You'll be alright, Nora, and I'll be waiting for you to get back. Remember, we have a couple of hours left." His hand went beneath her elbow, and he led her to a double door of heavy bronze. It was an elevator. Rolf came this way. Kyle pressed the button, and the doors opened soundlessly.

The elevator was of polished pecan wood. There was a mirror in its rear, beneath which was a small red leather bench. A little crystal chandelier was fitted into its ceiling. He ushered her in and, leaning over, pressed a button. "It's okay," he said as the doors closed softly. She couldn't feel any movement, and yet she knew the elevator was going down. For a moment she grew claustrophobic, and then she took a deep breath. It was all an adventure, and she suddenly realized she could hardly wait to see what came next. The elevator stopped suddenly, and its doors opened. Nora stared at what was in front of her.

CHAPTER SIX

She wasn't certain exactly what she had expected, but certainly not this. Stepping from the elevator, she found herself in a big room with a pale creamy carpet so plush she wasn't certain she could stand up in her high-heeled shoes. The lower half of the walls was paneled in oak. The upper half was wallpapered in a large elegant floral pattern in quiet tones of greens and coral on a cream-colored background. The ceiling was oak coffered, and the lighting was subdued. There was a couch covered in a pale gold silk brocade, a row of matching single chairs, and a mahogany coffee table on one side of the room. On the other, there were two beautiful wood desks with matching computer workstations, where two women of indeterminate age worked. They did not look up as the elevator opened and Nora entered the room.

A third woman, however, dressed in a nicely tailored wool tweed suit in shades of gray and lavender came forward, smiling. Her hair was salt-and-pepper in color, cut short, and styled beautifully. "Mrs. Buckley?" She held out her hand to shake Nora's hand. " I'm Margaret, Mr. Nicholas's personal assistant. Come this way, please. He's waiting for you." She turned and moved down the room toward a set of carved and paneled mahogany doors at the other end of the room.

Nora followed, amazed that she could actually walk in her stylish sling-backs. There was an empty desk next to those doors, opposite the other two. As she moved by those desks, neither of the women seated bothered to look up. They seemed to be very busy with whatever it was that they were doing. What were they doing? Nora wondered a little nervously.

Margaret knocked on one of the carved doors and, opening it immediately, ushered Nora inside. "Mr. Nicholas, Mrs. Buckley is here." Then she turned and retreated through the doors, closing them behind her.

Once more Nora was surprised. She had thought Mr. Nicholas would be French or Italian perhaps. She pictured a man in his early forties, suave and sophisticated, tall and well tailored, with dark hair and a lean body. The man who now came smilingly forward, his well-manicured hand outstretched in greeting, was nothing at all like that, except perhaps for his well-tailored dark pin-striped suit. He was short. Perhaps five feet and seven inches. He was in his late fifties, or possibly early sixties. His hair was wavy and gray, and obviously styled. His feet, she noticed, were small and he wore beautifully polished dark leather shoes. Her father had always worn shoes like that.

"My dear Mrs. Buckley, how very nice to meet you," he said. His voice was cultured, with just the slightest hint of a British accent. "May I call you Nora?" He took her hand and, tucking it in his arm, led her to a mulberry-colored velvet brocade couch that was set before a blazing fire. On the butler's tray before the couch was a silver tea tray. "I thought you might be ready for a small nibble, my dear."

"Thank you," Nora managed to say.

"Green or black?" he asked her.

"Green would be lovely," Nora responded. "Would you like me to pour?"

"No, no, my dear, I shall do it."

He picked up a delicate china cup and saucer in one hand, and a silver teapot in the other. Nora watched, fascinated, as the pale green gold tea poured from the silver spout into the round cup. She reached out to take it from him. He then poured himself a cup of tea from the other pot.

"Milk? Sugar? Lemon?" he inquired politely.

"Lemon, please," Nora said, reaching out to take a tiny silver fork to snare the round, and put it in her tea.

"At this time of night I far prefer cambric tea," Mr. Nicholas said, liberally adding sugar and milk to his cup. He smiled at her, and nodded to another plate on the tea tray. "Biscuit?"

Nora reached for a chocolate biscotto. "Thank you," she said. "I love these, but they are so expensive. It's a lovely treat." She took a bite, crunched it down, and then sipped at the tea, which had the faint aroma of peach.

They sat in silence for a short while, drinking their tea and eating the cookies on the plate. It was a bit, Nora considered, like the Mad Hatter's tea party. She had to swallow back a giggle at one point. Finally her companion spoke.

"Kyle tells me you have some questions regarding The Channel," Mr. Nicholas said, engaging her with his dark eyes. His eyes were mesmerizing.

"I would like to know," Nora said, coming right to the point, "if it would be possible for me to remain in The Channel for a short time."

"Why?" he asked her.

"I am in the midst of a rather nasty divorce," Nora began, but he stopped her, waving his hand.

"I am aware of that, my dear. My question was, why do you want to remain within The Channel for a time?" he said.

"I have never been happier than when I am here," Nora said. "I just want to get away from my reality for a little while. Not forever. Just for a little while."

"Anything is possible here," Mr. Nicholas began. "Yes, you could remain with us for a time."

"How would my absence be explained in my reality?" Nora wanted to know.

He smiled a brief cool smile. "You would appear to be unconscious," he answered her.

"They would move me if I were unconscious," Nora said. "How would I return to my own reality if that happened?"

"When you wished to leave us you would indicate your desire to do so, and you would wake up wherever you were, my dear. There is really no mystery to it." He took a deep sip of his sugared tea. "The use of the television is a technology you understand, but it is not really necessary to The Channel."

"If my son came home, and found me in front of the television, what would he see on the television?" Nora asked Mr. Nicholas.

"Of course you would not want J. J. to see you amusing yourself with Kyle, I understand, my dear. These are private pleasures you enjoy, and not for general consumption. Your son would see what appeared to be an unavailable channel, as if you had punched in the wrong station. The zigzagged screen," he explained.

Nora did not bother to ask him how he knew her son's name. He would have said what Kyle said, she suspected. "Is The Channel available everywhere?" she queried him.

"We are given different names in different locations, but yes. We can be accessed all over the world in one way or another," Mr. Nicholas told her as his dark eyes danced with amusement. "Do you know when you would like to join us?" he said to her. "Now that I know your wishes, we need no further notice. You may come when you choose to come, my dear."

"Not yet," Nora said. "I just wanted to know if it were possible, and I may never remain longer than an evening."

"Ah, but I think you will," Mr. Nicholas told her. "Kyle is very charming, and so much nicer than what you have been used to, my dear. Since you have not changed him, I can assume he is performing his duties in a satisfactory manner. Have you grown bored with Rolf? You have not used him recently."

Nora felt a blush heating her cheek. "Rolf is delightful," she said coolly, "but Kyle needed more of my time. Rolf will return to join us soon."

"How intuitive you are," Mr. Nicholas noted, "to understand Kyle's needs as well as your own. He will serve you well under those circumstances. Have I answered all your questions, my dear?"

"Not all, but all I mean to ask you for now," Nora said. Should she be afraid of this man? And yet he was very charming, cultured, and mannerly. There was nothing to be afraid of from Mr. Nicholas.

"One final thing, my dear," he said to her. "If I do you the favor of allowing you to remain within The Channel at your pleasure, is it not reasonable of me to assume that you would owe me a favor one day? Would you agree?" The dark eyes looked directly into her gray green ones.

"Of course," Nora agreed even as a small shiver touched her spine.

He smiled, and then he arose. "Then our business is concluded for now, my dear. I shall look forward to seeing you again one day. Our tea party has been a delightful interlude for me. Shall I call Margaret to escort you to the elevator?"

"I can find my own way," Nora said. She held out her hand to bid him good-bye.

But instead of shaking her hand this time he took it in his small soft hand and, raising it to his lips, kissed it. "It has been a pleasure, Nora. Good-bye."

"Good-bye," she said, feeling a burning sensation where his mouth had touched the back of her hand. She hurried to the door and, opening it, went into the outer office. "Good-bye, Margaret," she told Mr. Nicholas's assistant, and the woman smiled and nodded a farewell. Nora almost ran to the elevator. It opened at once, and stepping in, she saw there was only one button to press. She pushed it with her finger, and the doors closed, and the sensation of rising filled her. When the elevator finally stopped and the doors opened again, she stepped out into her penthouse.

Outside the large windows, the cityscape glowed with a clear night. She drew a deep breath and turned, startled to find Kyle there. "Oh! You frightened me!" she said.

"I'm sorry," he apologized. "You look pale, Red Rover. Come and sit down, and tell me about your visit with Mr. Nicholas." He drew her to the couch, and pulled her down into his arms. "You're shivering."

"Who is he?" Nora asked Kyle. "Who is Mr. Nicholas?"

"I don't understand," Kyle replied. "Mr. Nicholas is Mr. Nicholas."

Nora bit her lip. "He is so urbane. He treats this as if it were a normal occurrence, and damnit, The Channel isn't exactly your everyday recreation."

"Do you really want to question the very thing that brings you so much pleasure, Red Rover?" he asked her gently. "Ask yourself what your life would be without me, without The Channel? When you return to your own reality, Nora, don't you feel stronger for having been here?"

"Yes!" she said. "Yes, my life has been so much better since I found The Channel," Nora agreed.

"Then don't question how this has come to be, Red Rover. I'm here—The Channel is here—just for your enjoyment. No more second-guessing, okay?"

"Okay," Nora agreed. "Now, kiss me, slave!" She raised her face to him.

His lips brushed hers tenderly.

"Take off your shorts," she commanded, and she helped him remove the single garment, twisting her body so that she might begin to kiss and lick at him. He stretched his length, his heels pressing into the carpet. Nora's tongue lapped at the flesh of his chest. She would lick, and then she would blow, and then she would tease him with her hair. Inch by inch she covered his torso with her homage, moving slowly, slowly until she buried her face in his dark pubic hair, breathing in the scent of him, kissing his mound. Her hand wrapped about his penis. Her tongue swiveled about its head several times. She licked at it. Then she put the tip in her mouth, and sucked on it. "Mmmmm," she said, and drew him deeper into her mouth and throat.

His big hand began to caress her bottom, smoothing around the pale flesh. Her mouth was driving him wild. She would draw on his knob until he was at the point of explosion, and then stop, letting him throb within the cavity of her mouth unfulfilled. Then when the tension had eased, at last she would begin again, teasing him to the point where he thought he would burst, only to stop. His hand wrapped itself in her hair, and he pulled her head up. "It's time for madame's riding lesson," he told her. His dick was sticking straight up. "Get on, Red, or else!"

"Or else what?" she taunted him, and then she shrieked, as he pulled her over his knees and smacked her butt hard several times.

"Get on," he said again, pulling her over, pushing up her skirt, and lowering her onto his cock. "Ahhh," he breathed as he slid inside her hot silken vagina. "Now, that's better. "Now I think we'll go for a trot, a canter, and a gallop, mistress."

Nora began to ride him. Slowly at first, then increasing her tempo until he began to moan. His eyes were closed, and the look on his handsome face was utter bliss. "Good horsey," she teased, and her fingers dug into his shoulders. His hands wrapped themselves about her waist.

"Lean back so I can go deeper," he told her.

She arched her body, leaning backward, and felt his dick slide deeper into her fevered maw. She squeezed him with her vaginal muscles, and he groaned low. "Oh, very good horsey," she told him. "Ohh, that's nice, darling."

Suddenly to Nora's surprise Kyle released his hold on her waist, and sliding his palms beneath her buttocks, he slowly stood up, still impaled within her. She wrapped her arms about his neck so she wouldn't fall as he carried her to the end of the couch and pulled his swollen penis out of her body. Before she could ask he was turning her facedown and laying her across the wide rolled arm of the couch. He pushed her legs apart, and she felt his cock pushing between the cheeks of her ass. "Kyle!" she gasped.

"You can do this, Nora," he told her. "I won't force anything, but I knew you were ready earlier. Just trust me. I'll stop if you say the word." He put the tip of his penis directly in the center of her anus. "Just feel it there, Red. Aren't you just a little bit curious? When I put my finger in before, you squeezed it tight. Let's just try." He pushed her hair aside, and tenderly kissed the nape of her neck.

"You'll stop if I say no?" she asked nervously.

"I promise," he told her, pushing her dress up.

"It feels so big," she said.

"It is big, and it's going to feel really, really good," he whispered hotly, and he gently pushed his penis against the tight little hole. "Just the tip, baby. I'll just put the tip in at first." He could feel her muscles beginning to relax, and he moved carefully, telling her, "You control me, Nora. Push back, baby."

She could feel him, but she wasn't in the least afraid of this so-called sexual taboo. She had always been curious, but she had never dared tell Jeff. After all, a man who would call his wife a slut because she wanted a little spanking would have gone berserk at the suggestion of anal sex. "Ohh!" Suddenly she felt the tip of his penis push through. It was a unique sensation, but he hadn't hurt her.

"Is it okay?" he asked.

In reply she pushed back on his cock carefully. The feeling of fullness was incredible. She gasped softly. "My God, Kyle!" She was coming, and she couldn't help it. She wasn't certain she liked it, but she had wanted to try.

"I'm all the way in," he groaned. He didn't move at all. Just stood encased within her denseness. The sensation for him was wonderful. She was so tight.

"I know." She squeezed him with her rectal muscles, and with a sob he came. She could feel the spurts of his juices, and finally he shuddered, finished.

It was then he withdrew slowly and carefully from her, pulling her up, and holding her tightly in his embrace. "You are the most incredible woman," he told her.

"Another adventure," Nora laughed weakly. "I think I need a drink."

"Me too. Can you pour us one while I go wash off Big Dan?"

"I'm still hot," she told him.

"Me too," he said, and she looked down to see his penis still hard.

"Go wash. I'll pour us something, and meet you in bed," Nora said.

There was champagne open on the bar. She poured them two flutes, and took them into the bedroom. She could hear him showering as she set the narrow goblets down, and pulled her dress off. He came out of the bathroom, a towel wrapped about his loins, and looked at her, naked but for the garter belt and stockings.

"Don't take those off," he said. "I love fucking a woman in a garter belt, Red."

She handed him one of the champagne flutes. "Here's to garter belts," she toasted him with a grin.

"Garter belts!" He raised his flute at her, and drank the champagne down in a single gulp.

They put the goblets down, and sliding to her knees, Nora took him in her mouth again. Her fingers dug into his buttocks. The smell of soap on his skin was intoxicating. Within the briefest time he was ready again, and they fell on the bed. He pushed her legs up, and thrust himself into her warmth with a sigh. He moved on her slowly, slowly as they enjoyed this nearness, and when he found himself beginning to get bored he pushed her legs straight up, and drove deeper into her, thrusting and withdrawing, thrusting and withdrawing until she was sobbing softly.

Why had she never had sex like this before The Channel? Nora wondered. Every movement he made she felt acutely. When he raised her legs all the way up, leaning against them, his dick had gone deeper than she had ever felt. She could sense the impending explosion coming. "Yes!" she sobbed, and then it happened, and they came together in a wild burst of lust. She actually swooned with her pleasure, and when she revived she curled up against him, and he tenderly enfolded her in his embrace.

"Will it always be like this?" she asked him.

"Until you tire of me," he said softly.

"I'm not going to tire of you," she reassured him.

"Good," he told her. "I don't want to lose you, Red."

"You're jealous of Rolf, aren't you?" she asked him.

"I don't like it when you do other men, Red."

"But I may want to now and again," she warned him. "I've led a very circumspect life up until now, darling. But you'll always be here for me, and I'll always want you more than I want any of the others."

"Are you going to remain in The Channel?" he wondered.

"Not tonight, Kyle. I'm saving that for another time. Maybe I never will. I don't know. The Channel has become my refuge, I think, but I'm not ready yet to disappear from my own reality. Mr. Nicholas says it will appear as if I am unconscious when I do. I'm not sure I want to frighten my family like that."

"What if I said I wanted you here with me always?" he tempted her.

"I don't know," Nora answered. "If we were together all the

time, would we grow bored with one another, Kyle? I don't think I'd like to spend my life in this apartment, as wonderful as it is. If I could be in my reality like I am in The Channel. If you could be with me there instead of here. It would be perfect, I think, darling."

"Your husband wouldn't like it if you looked like this and had me as a lover. He might even consider coming back to you. Is that what you want, Nora?" He was angry, and definitely jealous.

Nora pulled out of his embrace, and looked down into his face. "No, Kyle, there are no circumstances under which I would want Jeff back. He's a pig. You are the man for me. You're tender and gentle. You're thoughtful of me. And, my darling Mr. Gorgeous, you aren't bad on the eyes. And the best thing is that as long as we are here, we'll always be the same, right?"

He smiled up at her. "Right, Red!"

She smiled back. The phone rang then, and they heard the wake-up call. "I might as well go now," Nora said. "We've certainly had a busy evening, haven't we?" She got up from their bed.

"Tomorrow?" he asked.

"Yes," she promised. "J. J. won't be home until Monday late." Then turning, she walked back into the living room, and placed her hand on the television screen. The now familiar pop sounded, and she was back in her recliner. Reaching for the channel changer, she clicked the set off, and standing up, she went upstairs to her bedroom. She needed a shower, and she was exhausted. Kyle was a tireless lover. Going into her bathroom, she pulled off her nightshirt, and then she stared shocked. She was wearing a green lace garter belt, and sheer stockings. This had certainly never happened before. Nora shivered. Well, if she had ever needed any proof that The Channel was real, this sure as hell was it. She couldn't wait to tell Carla. She undid the garter belt, and laid it aside, rolling the stockings off her feet. Showering quickly, she fell into bed.

She awoke early the following afternoon and, reaching for the phone, called her best friend. "Come over," she said. "I have something to show you."

"Be there within the hour. We're just up after the party. Kids left at sunrise for the mountains. I'm bushed. God, they danced till dawn, and the music! Thank God we're all friends, or someone would have called the cops for sure."

"Funny," Nora laughed, "I never heard a thing."

"Ohh, I know what you were doing," Carla singsonged. "See you shortly."

Nora dressed, and as she did, she felt a slight soreness in her ass. I can't believe I did that, she thought, but it was really exciting. I'm not sure I'll do it again. She pulled on her shorts and a T. Going down to the kitchen, she considered making coffee, but she didn't want coffee. She wanted iced tea. There was some of that mixture left from yesterday. She was still tired. Yesterday had been a big day, and then last night's activities had added to it all. Pouring herself a glass of the cold tea/lemonade mix, she went out onto the terrace by the pool, and sat down.

It was a beautiful late June day. The sky was clear, and the sun hot on her shoulders. There was a faint breeze. The water in the pool lapped against the steps. She had roses in bloom—reds and pinks and whites in one corner of the yard, yellows and peach and apricot in another corner. She got up, then sat back down on the top step of the pool, and dangled her feet in the water. It was so quiet. So peaceful. How she loved it, and she wanted it always to be this way. And it would be. She wasn't going to let Jeff take her home away from her. She heard the gate creak, and turned.

"Hey," Carla said, coming into the yard. "Whatcha drinking?"

"The stuff from yesterday. I'm pooped, and I always get extra thirsty when I'm tired like this. Go help yourself if you want some."

"What I want is to know what happened. You sounded really spooked when you called, Nora."

"Did you ever bring back something from your visits in The Channel?" Nora asked her best friend.

"Something? What do you mean?" Carla said.

Nora got up. "Come into the house." She led the way, going upstairs, Carla following. In her bedroom she picked up the garter belt, and the stockings. "I came home last night in these," Nora told Carla.

"Holy crap!" Carla breathed. "You don't own anything like this."

"Nora Buckley, this reality, doesn't. But Nora Buckley of The Channel does, and I was wearing them last night when I woke up."

"Pretty snazzy." Carla grinned. "Just what is your fantasy?"

"Penthouse apartment, Mr. Gorgeous, and a masseur named Rolf," Nora replied with a half smile.

"What's Mr. Gorgeous's name?" Carla pried.

"Kyle," Nora told her.

"And he likes you in green lace garter belts," Carla said.

"It matched my wrap dress," Nora said. "I could hardly visit Mr. Nicholas unless I was properly dressed."

"Boy, two guys don't satisfy you, and you got three? You're almost as bad as I am," Carla chuckled. "Every time I recruit a new crew, I screw 'em all before we set sail."

"Mr. Nicholas is the administrator of The Channel," Nora told her friend. "I wanted to meet him because there were things I needed to know, questions that only he could answer. I could hardly go to his office looking like a tart in my blue silk shorty robe," Nora said.

"There's someone who actually runs The Channel?" Carla asked, sounding surprised. "And you met him? And he has an office? What's he like?"

"Sure, someone runs it, and yes, I met him, and his office is out of *Architectural Digest,* old-money edition, and he . . ." She stopped for a moment. "He's nothing like I thought he would be.

I was thinking Louis Jourdan, or Ricardo Montalban. In fact on reflection he reminds me of that nineteen-forties-movie character actor, Claude Rains. He has two secretaries and an assistant named Margaret, and we had tea before a fireplace, with chocolate biscotti."

"No way!" Carla exclaimed.

"Way!" Nora said, laughing. "It was almost bizarre except it was so damned civilized. The tea was that really good gunpowder green, and the biscotti were heaven."

"What did you want to know from him?" Carla said, curious.

"I'll tell you that another time. Just tell me, babe, did you ever come home with a souvenir from The Channel?"

"Other than a hickey?" Carla replied with a grin. "Nah. And I know none of the others have either. They'd freak if they did, and tell. And I'm not certain this isn't creeping me out, Nora."

"It's creeping me out a little too," Nora admitted. "It's like one of those too-good-to-be-true scenarios you read about."

"Hey, we get charged for it on our cable bills," Carla said. "So did this Mr. Nicholas answer all of your questions?"

"I suppose he did, but in a very roundabout way," Nora responded.

"You going to keep going to The Channel?" Carla's dark eyes were curious.

"It's like potato chips," Nora said. "You just can't eat one. Yeah, it helps me not to collapse with fear over this whole situation, especially now that I've met my replacement. She no beauty, but she's pretty, isn't she?"

"She's young," Carla answered. "I figured about thirty, thirty-one. And she dresses well, and she's got a good body. I'll bet she goes to the gym every day. She hasn't had any kids, although maybe she'll have one once they're married. These second wives always like to have one kid to take the attention away from the first wife's kids. They never really feel safe as long as the first wife and her kids are hovering in the background," Carla said.

"Where do you get all this information?" Nora demanded to know.

"Oprah. Dr. Phil. Jerry, and Jenny," Carla said. "And every damned women's magazine has articles on your situation. You aren't the first woman to be dumped by her husband for a younger woman. You won't be the last."

"As long as I get my house," Nora replied.

"Listen, hon, I wouldn't count on keeping the house," Carla said, sitting down on Nora's bed. "Rick says they're going to really have to do a number to even get you half its value in cash. And really, Nora, what the hell do you want this big place for anyway? The kids are practically gone, and you aren't going to have the money to keep it up. It's a lot of work, and we're not getting any younger, babe."

"I'm not letting Jeff take my house," Nora said stubbornly.

"Look, there's a great new condo community opening up right on the old Carstairs estate on the bay. Half the value of this house would buy you a nice two-bedroom, and you would always have room for the kids."

"No," Nora said. "The house is mine, and I'm not letting him have it, Carla. He can have everything else. The kids can take loans for the rest of their schooling. He can cut me off without a penny, but the house is mine."

Carla sighed. There was no point arguing further with Nora. Something was happening to her, and it had begun with her first visit to The Channel. Nora was suddenly exhibiting a strong will, and she was getting thin too. But none of that meant anything because the best Rick's law firm was going to do, the absolute best, was to get Nora the cash value of half of the house's selling price. And that would be a real battle with Jeff's world-class divorce attorney.

Nora spent another incredible sex-filled night in The Channel with Kyle. She wasn't certain when she would be able to get back. J. J. returned home after his mountain sojourn, and immediately started his summer job. He would be heading off to State in mid-August. Sports teams reported early, and he was a member of State's junior varsity, thanks to his scholarship. On one hand Nora dreaded his leaving. J. J. was good company, and he made her laugh. But on the other hand she could barely wait for him to be gone. She needed Kyle, and the passion that they shared between them. It had become more than just mindless sexual games. He was openly and obviously in love with her, and Nora was certain she was beginning to feel the same way.

Her days were filled with all the things a mother does for a son going off to college. She made lists, and bought items she would never have bought for herself, but that she knew he would need and appreciate, like a sandwich maker and a small coffeepot. She and Carla shopped together because Maureen would be going two and a half weeks after J. J. They bought sheets, pillowcases, towels, washcloths, and down comforters. Margo's generous graduation gift to her only grandson had allowed him to buy a nice laptop, and the rooms in State's dorms all had Internet access cable connections. Oh, brave new world, Nora thought, remembering how up-to-date she had been in her freshman year with a small electric typewriter. And as the day came closer for J. J.'s departure, Nora began to pack her son's possessions, glad she was alone and could sniffle over the very worn Clifford the Big Red Dog stuffed toy that J. J. had always loved.

Those were the good days. There were bad days too, like the day she and her attorneys met with Jeff and his attorneys. Her husband, certain of victory, was pompous and unyielding. Nora was certain he had expected her to weep and go to pieces. Instead she had attacked him verbally and told him he would get their house over her dead body. She accused him of stealing the kids' college funds, and when Raoul Kramer had protested, Nora had attacked him too.

"If those accounts didn't belong to the children, why did he show them to the kids every goddamned Christmas morning and tell them that those accounts were their college funds! Jill went through her undergrad studies in three years on the interest from her account. Do you know what your client did, Mr. Kramer? He fraudulently stole those accounts last spring. He went to the kids and had them sign papers telling them it was for tax purposes. What he obviously did was get them to sign paperwork taking their names off those accounts so he could have the money to spend elsewhere. He refused to pay our son's freshman year at State. J. J. has a sports scholarship, but it was our neighbors who gave him the money for his dorm room and meal plan!"

"Jill's tuition at Duke Law is paid," Jeff put in.

"For this year only, because you had to pay it early," Nora snapped. "You've told her you won't pay the other two years, you miserable bastard! You have disenfranchised your own children so you can marry a girl young enough to be your daughter. I don't care that you want to divorce me, and that hurts, doesn't it, Jeff? I'm supposed to be weeping and begging, but I'm not, and I never will. I don't want a penny from you, but the house is mine. If you attempt to take it from me, so you and your trophy wife can begin anew debt free, I will find some way to make you sorry, you can be certain of that." She glared hard at him.

"What the hell has come over you, Nora?" he demanded. "You've changed."

"Gee, have I?" she said sarcastically. "You have been screwing everything that moved but me for years. Now you want a divorce. You don't want to meet your parental obligations. You want to put me out on the street, and make me homeless, and I'm not supposed to stand up to you? Get real!"

"You can get a job," he snapped. "Other women do."

"I have a degree in English literature, Jeff. No teaching credits. No work experience. I don't know one end of a computer from another. What the hell am I supposed to do to support myself? I need to take some classes to get me up to speed, and I'm not going to do it living in a homeless shelter. Besides, Egret Pointe doesn't have a homeless shelter."

Raoul Kramer sighed, and said, "I think I need to take my client back to town and talk to him again. Let's meet again in ten days?" He stood up.

"Look, Heidi and I have been accepted by the co-op board, Kramer. We need to close on our apartment," Jeff told his attorney.

"I'll get you a bridge loan," Kramer said in a hard, tight voice. "This matter is not going to be settled as quickly as I anticipated."

"You said it would be a matter of days." Jeff's voice was strident. "You said it was a no-brainer. Everything was mine. She didn't have a leg to stand on, damnit!" His face was red, and Nora noticed in that moment how much he'd aged.

"That was before I knew her father gave you half of the down payment for your house, Jeff. That was before I knew those accounts were in your kids' names, and you conned them out of them. She's right. It's fraud. Now, I'm certain Mrs. Buckley doesn't wish to encourage your son and daughter to press charges. I'm certain if we reconsider your position, we can come to an agreement that will be satisfactory to us all. Let's go." He turned to Rick. "I'll have Bev call your girl to set up another meeting." He closed his black Italian leather briefcase with a snap, and turned toward the door.

"You've turned into a real bitch," Jeff snarled at Nora.

"Only two good things came out of our marriage, Jeff, J. J. and Jill," Nora told him. "I feel sorry for Heidi. She'll learn soon enough what a jerk you really are."

Jeff Buckley stormed past his attorney and stalked out of the room. Raoul Kramer followed at a discreet pace.

"I'm glad I'm not riding back to the city with him," Rick said with a grin. "Well, I think that went rather well, considering. I think we can get you a half interest in the house, and some alimony until you're able to get a job that will support you. I had already told Kramer about the accounts, but I don't think he gave it much credence until you blew your top at Jeff, Nora."

"This isn't fair," Nora muttered.

"No, it isn't, but the law isn't always about what's right, or what's fair. It's about the law," Rick told her.

"Let the house be appraised. I'll buy his half from him," Nora said.

"Honey, you couldn't get a mortgage," Rick said. "You don't have any credit. Your one credit card is in his name. The phone is in his name. The electricity. The water. The gas. And you don't have a job, nor the hope of one for a while. I'm sorry, Nora. Those are the facts."

"I don't care what I have to do," Nora said, and now her voice was shaking. "I . . . I'm not going to let him sell my home!" Then she turned, and left Rick Johnson's office.

She didn't tell J. J. of her meeting. No need for him to worry. He was heading off to State next week. She had intended on driving him, but the school was sending a bus all over the vicinity to pick up the new players of the various campus sports on scholarship. This way, it was reasoned, they could begin to get to know one another on their ride up to school. In a way she was glad. She wouldn't have a long lonely ride home. She had bought J. J. one of those prepaid cell phones with three hundred minutes on it.

"Don't use up all your minutes calling Lily," she warned him. "I want to hear from you, and know you're alright. Those minutes should last you until Homecoming Weekend. I'll buy you more minutes then, okay?"

His main concern was that she be alright, but Nora assured her son she would be fine. He was to study hard and play well. "He says he's selling the house," J. J. told his mother. "He can't do that, can he, Ma?"

"I don't want you to worry, J. J.," Nora said. "We're not losing our home. I will not allow that to happen. When did you talk to your father?"

"He called the other day when you and Carla were out shopping. I had just got home from work. I wouldn't have talked to him otherwise. Do you know what he had the gall to say to me, Ma, just before he hung up? Heidi says hi. Like I care!"

Nora laughed at her son's outrage. "I hope you said hi back," she teased.

"In your dreams, Ma!" he chuckled.

And then it was J. J. day to leave her, and she drove down to the Egret Pointe village green, where the bus was going to meet the football, soccer, tennis, swimming, and lacrosse players going to State. There were half a dozen boys standing there and three girls. The big bus pulled up, and the driver got out, opening the baggage compartments. Luggage was stowed, and the kids began to board. Nora hugged her son, and J. J. hugged her back.

"Be good," she whispered in his ear.

"Yeah." His voice was a little shaky.

"Call me when you get settled," Nora told him, pretending she hadn't noticed.

"Yeah, okay." He hugged her again and then, turning abruptly away, got on the bus. He found a window seat, and knocked on the window at her.

Nora saw him and smiled bravely. The door closed. The driver released his brakes with a hiss, and the bus began to pull away. Nora waved, feeling the tears pushing forward. Several other mothers were already crying, and being comforted by their husbands. The bus was gone. She walked to J. J.'s jalopy and got in. She had no one to comfort her. Not here. But she had already ordered The Channel for this evening. She hadn't seen Kyle in several days now, and their last meetings had been hurried ones because Nora was so nervous about anyone, especially J. J., learning her secret. Now, however, she would be alone in her house. Alone to live out her wildest fantasies with her lover. And no one would ever know. It was her secret. Hers, and the secret of all the other women, whoever they might be, outside of Ansley Court.

She thought about the meeting she had had with Mr. Nicholas earlier this summer. When this mess with Jeff was settled, she was going to tell everyone she was going away for a few days, everyone but Carla, and then she was going to take a delicious vacation in The Channel. She would close the den door tightly, and Carla would come and feed the cats twice a day. She thought about waking up next to Kyle, and maybe even Rolf too, in that great big bed, in that sensuous room. Rolfie would massage her every day. She would have a facial, manicure, pedicure. She would demand to be treated like a queen, and they would do it because it was The Channel, where all your fantasies came true.

Nora laughed aloud as she drove along back to her house. And jerky old Jeff back in the city, forced to pay the interest on a bridge loan so Heidikins could have her co-op. She suspected Heidi wasn't stupid enough to let Jeff put just his name on the deed of ownership. Jeff couldn't possibly imagine what a wonderful time his soon-to-be-discarded wife was having getting her brains fucked out by two very virile and handsome young men. Nora was still laughing as she pulled into her drive. Tonight couldn't come soon enough.

CHAPTER SEVEN

The autumn came, and Carla remarked that she thought Nora was really losing a lot of weight. "Haven't you noticed? Your clothes are hanging on you. Are you eating enough, sweetie?"

"I'm fine," Nora reassured her friend, "but I miss our coffee hours, and I miss all the kids on the court. It'll really be empty next year when the twins are gone, and Tiff is already working in Joe and Rick's office. She goes to class a couple of mornings a week, and then works the afternoons. Even you're gone during the days now."

"Yeah, I was really lucky being able to switch to the seven-a.m.-to-three-p.m. shift from nights," Carla said. "I can be home now in plenty of time to fix a nice dinner for Rick, and then when he goes to sleep before nine"—she grinned—"I can spend an hour or two playing in The Channel."

"I wonder if the others are playing too?" Nora said softly.

"Rina is back full-time with social services. They need case workers desperately, especially experienced ones like Rina. And Joanne is subbing this year for one of the fourth-grade teachers who's out on maternity leave."

"When did that happen?" Nora asked.

"The sub they had got preggers too, and without benefit of

clergy. The school board wasn't too thrilled, but it's a difficult pregnancy and so she quit. They called in Joanne," Carla explained.

"Fourth grade," Nora said softly. "I remember fourth grade."

"Yeah, the year when all nice little kids turn into know-it-all, smart-mouthed preteens," Carla replied. "I don't envy Joanne one bit. How are your classes coming? You never did tell me what you decided to take."

"Introduction to Computers, Introduction to Business Management, Beginning Marketing, and a course called How to Get a Job in Today's Market. That one only meets once a week, but it's fascinating, and it's scary. I wish I was more interested in teaching, but I'm just not," Nora said.

"Doing any Channel surfing?" Carla said with a grin.

"Every night," Nora replied. "I don't know what I'd do without Kyle and Rolf."

"My God, Nora, no wonder you look so drawn!" Carla exclaimed. "You've got a full course load, and you're partying all night. When the hell do you sleep? Not to mention get your homework done." Her brown eyes showed concern.

"My schedule is set up so I only have classes three days a week. I go nine to noon two days, and nine to one on Wednesdays. I come home and do the course work and the reading. I'm asleep by five thirty most nights, up at nine, and into The Channel for some fun. I'm limiting my time there on school nights. I'm home by one a.m., and then up at seven thirty on school days. I've never been happier," Nora said with a smile. "Jeff isn't as happy," she laughed. "You're right, though. My clothes are hanging on me these days. I'll have to do some alterations. I just don't have the funds for new stuff, but I'm going to splurge and get my hair colored. Jeff wouldn't let me, but nothing ages a woman more than too much weight and faded hair."

"Are you dieting?" Carla asked.

"Nah," Nora said.

"What did you eat for breakfast this morning?" Carla demanded to know.

"I grabbed a yogurt and cup of coffee before I left," Nora replied.

"And lunch? What did you eat for lunch?" Carla persisted.

Nora thought a moment. "I forgot lunch," she said.

"It looks like you're forgetting lunch a lot these days," Carla told her, and going to Nora's fridge, she opened it to peer inside. "Good grief!" she exclaimed. "There's nothing in here."

"Yes, there is too," Nora responded.

"Half a cooked chicken, and you didn't cook it. It's one of those rotisserie birds from the market," Carla said. "A bowl of salad greens. Yogurt, a couple of bottles of flavored soda water, cheddar cheese, and some two percent milk. Nora, you aren't cooking for yourself! No butter? No bread?" She pulled open the top freezer. There was a package of Stouffer's macaroni and cheese, a bag of frozen green beans, and two packages of frozen chopped spinach. "No ice cream?" Carla shook her head. "Honey, you aren't taking care of yourself," she fretted. "You're going to get sick."

"I don't know how to cook for one," Nora muttered. "Besides, I take a multivitamin pill every day, Carla. I'm hardly skin and bones right now."

"You were a size sixteen, and I would put money on it that you've lost at least two dress sizes," Carla said, her sharp eye examining her best friend.

"I used to be a size eight," Nora said.

"Older women who lose too much weight always look their age, or older if they don't have the dollars to do face work, and you don't, sweetie. And even those women who do, hell, you can tell. I don't care how good the doctor is—those done-over faces on older gals always end up looking like an Egyptian death mask. There comes a time when a woman should age gracefully."

"I am aging gracefully," Nora laughed, "but losing a little

weight will be good for my heart and blood pressure. Look at Margo. My mother is in her early seventies, and still a size six. And she doesn't look her age at all."

"Come to dinner tonight," Carla said.

"I've got a test tomorrow. I can't," Nora responded. "I'm not even going to go play tonight."

"I'm having my famous manicotti with meat sauce, and that garlic bread you love so much," Carla tempted.

Nora laughed again. "Bring me over some later, and I'll freeze it for another night."

Carla sighed. "When are you seeing Rick again?" she asked.

"Friday, after school," Nora answered. "Then I'm heading up to State for Parents Weekend. J. J. asked me to come."

"We're going too," Carla said. "Ride with us?"

"I will," Nora said. "I hate making that drive alone. Where are you staying?"

"The Fairfax Inn," Carla responded.

"Me too! That's great." Nora smiled. "It'll be fun."

"Okay, you're off the hook for tonight. I'll bring you some manicotti to freeze."

But after meeting with her lawyers on Friday afternoon, Nora didn't know if she wanted to go anywhere. She felt sick with their news. More than anything, she just wanted to find a hole, crawl into it, and die.

"What do you mean, I can't get the house?" she demanded of Rick. "It's the only thing I want from him. Nothing else."

Rick sighed. "It's been a long shot all along, Nora. Joe and I told you that right from the beginning. The house has always been in just his name, and that gives him the advantage over you. However, when he nicked the kids' college money he made a mistake, and that's been our club. It's a little club, but we've gotten you a really incredible settlement under the circumstances. The house has no mortgage, and you're going to get forty percent of the sales price. That ain't hay in this market, given the neighborhood we're in," Rick explained. "You should see close to four hundred thousand dollars, Nora. And you're going to get a thousand dollars a month in alimony for five years. J. J.'s scholarship is good for four years, and we've got Jeff to pay for J. J.'s dorm room. However, if the kid goes off campus, he's out of luck, and he'll have to buy his own meal ticket, but he'll manage it."

"What about Jill's tuition at Duke?" Nora wanted to know.

Rick shook his head. "Jeff loves having a daughter in law school at Duke, but he won't pay for it. He paid for her undergrad work, and this first year at Duke. No court will think him unfair to ask that she get scholarship money for her last two years. Jill is bright, and she's resourceful, Nora. She'll manage it, and we'll see she does, I promise you. What are friends for?"

Nora felt the tears, but she blinked them back. "A car?" she asked hopefully.

Rick shook his head. "Sorry," he told her.

"What if I bought out his interest in the house?" she said.

"Nora, you couldn't afford it, and you couldn't get a mortgage in your name. You have no credit. Everything—the phone, the electricity, the water company, the car, the credit card you had—it's all been in Jeff's name. I told you this before. That's something you've got to do. Begin to establish your own credit. I've gotten the bank to agree to give you a credit card in your own name, but it only has a twelve-hundred-dollar credit line, I'm afraid." He reached into his desk and pulled out an envelope. "Here," he said.

She took the envelope, heart sinking. She knew that Margo was very well-fixed, but she couldn't ask her mother for six hundred thousand dollars to buy the house. Her mother lived comfortably on her interest income and her late husband's Social Security. She would have to sell something to help Nora, and that would drastically cut her income. I can't do it, Nora thought. She loves being independent, and I can't make her pinch pennies. It isn't fair. But what wasn't fair was Jeff taking the house. "There's no way of stopping him from selling?" she asked.

"If you got lucky, and he died screwing Heidi before the divorce, then you would get everything," Rick said, "but we can't count on that happening, Nora. But he's not going to put the house on the market until next April first, so you've got at least until then, and while the house will sell quickly, by the time the details are settled it will be June or July. Almost a year," he finished, looking uncomfortable. Carla was really going to give him grief about this, but what could he do? They were dealing with the law.

"Don't tell Carla yet, Rick. I don't want to spoil our weekend. I don't feel much like going right now," Nora admitted, "but J. J. would be so disappointed."

He looked relieved. "Yeah," he agreed. "If we tell Carla, she'll go on about it all weekend, and no one will have a good time. What do you want to say?"

"Let's give her something or she'll be suspicious," Nora told him. "We'll tell her about the five years of alimony, and J. J.'s dorm room. You can say you and Joe are working on the rest, okay?"

"You're a good friend, Nora Buckley," he told her.

"So are you and Carla," she responded.

The leaves were turning as they drove to the state university at Whitford. At the Fairfax Inn they discovered that Nora's reservation in the name of Mrs. Jeffrey Buckley was now in the name of Mr. and Mrs. Jeffrey Buckley.

"There's an error," she said. "My husband and I are in the midst of a divorce. Here's my reservation number. See? Three-six-nine-one-one." She held out the postcard to the clerk. "And you will note it is addressed to *Mrs.*, not *Mr. and Mrs.*"

"There's obviously been an error," the desk clerk said, "and Mr. and Mrs. Buckley checked in a half an hour ago." He looked uncomfortable.

"That would be my husband and his girlfriend," Nora replied sweetly. "Well, give me another room, then."

"I can't." The clerk looked agonized now. "We're full. It's Parents' Weekend, madame."

"I know, and I'm here to visit my son, who is one of the junior varsity soccer stars." She smiled a dangerous smile. "You have a choice, young man. Either give me another room, or remove my husband and his little playmate from my room."

"Is there a problem here, Roberts? We're stacking up with check-ins," asked an officious man in a dark blazer with a name tag on his lapel that read C. ELDERS, ASSISTANT MANAGER.

Before the poor besieged clerk might answer, Nora said coolly, "The reservation I made has been given to my husband and his girlfriend. Roberts says there are no other rooms. I have my confirmation, and I will wager that no confirmation number was checked when Jeff arrived. I want my room. And I want it now."

"We can give you a room in the annex, madame. We do keep a few vacant for emergencies," C. Elders said. He glared at the check-in clerk.

"But I don't want to be in the annex," Nora replied, and she gave the man a steely smile. "I want my reservation that is next door to my friends. Put Mr. Buckley and his tartlet in the annex."

"Madame, we are doing our best," the assistant manager sputtered.

"I am Mrs. Buckley's attorney," Rick broke in, "and I should hate to see this incident become any more public than your inefficiency is making it. Mrs. Buckley will wait in our room while you remove Mr. Buckley and his friend from her room. Is that clear, Mr. Elders?"

"Yes, sir," the assistant manager said, and then he turned to the hapless check-in clerk. "See to it, Roberts! Immediately!"

Nora and Carla looked at each other and swallowed back their laughter.

"Doncha just love him when he get tough?" Carla said, grinning.

"He's quite amazing," Nora agreed. "It's a whole 'nother side of Richard Johnson, and I have to say I like it."

They went upstairs, and Nora listened with a large grin on her face as she heard Jeff bitching when he and Heidi were moved out of the room next door.

"Does this other room have a fireplace?" Jeff demanded to know. "I want to speak with the manager!"

"I'm sorry, sir. The manager isn't here this weekend, but you can speak with Mr. Elders, his assistant," the bellhop said.

"I've already spoken with that moron," Jeff almost shouted. "How the hell could this kind of a mix-up occur?"

"I don't know, sir," the bellhop said, and they heard the elevator doors closing.

The trio burst into laughter.

"He'll figure it out soon enough," Nora said with a chuckle.

Shortly afterwards there came a knock on the door, and Mr. Elders himself was outside it. "I've had the bellhop bring up your luggage, Mrs. Buckley. The room has been cleaned, and is ready for you. I apologize for the distress this mix-up has caused you. May I escort you?"

"Thank you," Nora said quietly. Then she turned to her friends. "What time are we meeting the kids?" she asked.

"Six. Downstairs. We've got a reservation in the Colonial Dining Room for dinner," Carla said.

"I'll see you there," Nora told her, and followed the now-unctuous Mr. Elders.

When he had left her Nora looked about the room. It was beautifully done with a tester bed and faux Chippendale furniture. On the table by the fireplace were a small basket of fruit and a box of chocolates. She pulled the card from between an apple and a pear. "Thank you for your patience. C. Elders," the card read. Nora tossed it into the fire, and picking up the telephone, asked the answering operator, "Do you get The Channel?"

"Yes, madam," the operator said. "Would you like to order it?"

"Yes. This is Mrs. Buckley in room 320."

"No problem, Mrs. Buckley. It will be available after ten p.m."

Well, Mr. Nicholas had said The Channel was available just about everywhere. Nora grinned to herself.

J. J. met her two hours later in the lobby. He hugged her hard, and then said, "Dad's here with Heidi. I told him he didn't have to come, that you were coming. He just called me this morning to tell me. I didn't have the time to call you, and I was afraid you wouldn't come if you knew he was here."

"It's okay, honey," Nora assured him, and then she told him about the botch with the room reservations.

J. J. laughed. "Does he know he got kicked out for you?" he wondered.

"I suspect they just told him it was a mix-up because of the nature of the weekend. I was in Carla and Rick's room when they moved him out. He wasn't being very gracious," Nora chuckled.

It would be difficult seeing Jeff, especially knowing what she knew now about the house, Nora thought, but she didn't share her news with J. J. She had promised herself when this all began that she wouldn't build a wall between father and son. Not that Jeff had been a great dad. He hadn't. But he was still J. J.'s male parent. She set her mind on having a good weekend with her child.

And it was good. They all had dinner together that night. The Johnsons, with Maureen, Nora and J. J. They had breakfast the next morning at the inn's wonderful and justly famous buffet. Jeff and Heidi were there. Nora sent her son to sit with them, although he objected. For me, she had told him. At least Jeff couldn't claim she was keeping their son from him.

They went to the football game together, and State won. Nora showed her son the different dorms she had lived in when she was at State. But things had changed a lot over the years since she had graduated. J. J. showed her his dorm, where the soccer team resided. But Pagano's was still there, and they had pizza for dinner that night—Rick, Carla, Maureen, J. J., and Nora.

"And this time I can legally order a pitcher of real beer," Nora said, laughing. "It was only three-point-two percent back when I was here."

On Sunday the soccer teams played. While the varsity lost, the junior varsity won. J. J. was elated that his mother had been there to see him play, and win. They had Sunday dinner at the inn. Then they bid their kids good-bye, and drove home, arriving in Egret Pointe in a dusky mid-October twilight.

"I'll bring over the manicotti," Carla said. "I froze it for you. You can have it for supper tomorrow night."

And when she came with a dish big enough to feed a family, tucking it into Nora's fridge, Nora told her all of her Friday meeting with Rick. Carla sat down, and burst into tears. "No," she said. "You can't move. You can't! I know I said you would be better off without this big house, but I never meant it."

"I don't have a choice," Nora told her friend.

"There has to be a way," Carla wailed. "I'm going to tell Rick he has to find a way, Nora. You can't lose the house."

"Honey, Rick has done his best. I don't want to lose the house, but at least J. J. gets his college money, and Jeff has got to ante up for me for the next five years. That will give me plenty of time to get on my feet."

"A thousand a month isn't much," Carla said. "And where are you going to live? If you spend the money you get on a condo, you won't have a helluva lot left for investments for your old age."

"I'll inherit something from Margo one day," Nora replied.

"What if she gets a catastrophic illness, and runs through the money?" Carla said. "You need the house to be safe. The taxes aren't too bad, but they will go up when the name is changed on the deed. You can still manage."

"Maybe Jeff will die in the sack with Heidi before the divorce," Nora teased her friend. "Then it's all mine."

"From your lips to God's ear," Carla replied fiercely. "Oh, God! I can't bear to think that you won't be next door this time next year." And she cried a little more.

I can't bear it either, Nora thought, comforting her best friend. I'm not going to go. There has to be another way. There has to be!

Rick had said that Raoul Kramer would have the papers for her to sign in a few days. "Get me a few more weeks before I have to sign," she instructed him.

"How?" He knew she was stalling to avoid the inevitable.

"Ask for more alimony! Try for Jill's tuition again. And then say I'll sign after the New Year. I don't want to spoil the kids' holidays. They'll both be home, and I don't want them to know that it's the last Christmas they'll celebrate in this house. Jeff has got to understand that, hard-hearted bastard that he is! Both Jill and J. J. have lived every Christmas of their lives in this house. Please, Rick. Appeal to Kramer, and let him convince Jeff."

"I'm not going to haggle with them at this point," Rick said. "They could withdraw the deal, but I'll speak with Kramer. I can vouch that you've always been a woman of your word, Nora, and Jeff knows it too."

"You're certain she'll do it after the New Year?" Raoul Kramer asked Rick Johnson after the call had been made.

"Look, I've known Nora Buckley almost twenty-five years, Kramer. If she says she'll do it, she'll do it. But look at it from her standpoint. She doesn't want her kids to have a miserable time when they come home for Christmas. Is it really that much to ask? He's agreed not to put the house on the market until April first anyway. Signing after the holiday isn't going to change anything, but maybe this little bit of extra time before she signs will let Nora come to terms with her situation. You know she's getting the short end of the stick."

"Usually I like my business," Raoul Kramer said, "but in cases like this I don't. He's a real piece of work, my client, but you never heard me say it. Relax. I'll get Mrs. Buckley her time. But tell her I want you both in my offices at ten a.m. on January second to sign those papers. Deal?"

"Deal," Rick replied. "And, Kramer, thanks. I owe you for this one."

Raoul Kramer laughed. "What the hell could a little country mouse of a lawyer like you do for me?" he asked.

"Hey, you never know," Rick said, feeling better already. "Remember, the turtle won the race over the faster hare."

Raoul Kramer laughed again and hung up.

Jeff, however, wasn't happy. "I wanted this thing tied up fast. You promised me it would be, Kramer. That's why I'm paying you the big bucks. But instead I've ended up paying a bridge loan, and Heidi has me in debt up to my ears furnishing the place!"

"Look, if you hadn't defrauded your kids of the moneys for their college educations, Buckley, it would have been a done deal. I could have gotten you off almost scot-free. But you got greedy before you hired me, so you're paying for that blunder. When the first Mrs. Buckley signs the papers doesn't matter. The timetable we've set up will remain in effect. Let her and let your kids have one last peaceful Christmas in their home. She isn't going to tell them until after she signs the papers on January second. What the hell difference does it make to let her and your kids be happy? You act as if she's done something wrong, and you want to punish her for it, but if the truth be known, she's the innocent party in all of this. If I were her lawyer, I'd have hung you out to dry."

"Jeff"—Heidi Millar put a hand on his arm—"Mr. Kramer is right. Let Nora and the kids have their last moments in the house. The bridge loan payment hasn't come out of your pocket. I've been paying it. You've got just about everything you want. Be gracious in victory. And I'll stop buying stuff for the co-op, I promise." She gave him a little kiss, and smiled winningly.

Raoul Kramer almost laughed. Jeff Buckley had already lost his pants, and he didn't even know it. "Thank you, Ms. Millar," he said.

"Alright," Jeff said grudgingly. "Alright. But no more delays after this one. She had damned well better show up here on January second, and sign on the dotted line, or you're toast, Kramer!"

"Did you ever know your wife not to keep her word, Buckley?" Raoul Kramer asked his client. And when his clients had gone he picked up the telephone and called Rick Johnson. "I'm confirming. He's agreed, and yeah, you really do owe me." Then he hung up and sat back in his chair, considering what a shit Jeffrey Buckley was and knowing Nora Buckley would be relieved to have just a little more time. Poor faded little bitch. She really didn't deserve what was happening to her. Then he shrugged to himself. It was the law. Or at least that's what he told himself a lot lately.

And Nora was relieved when Rick called. "You've got your extension, but nothing else changes. We've got to be in town on the second of January to sign the papers."

"Thanks, Rick," Nora told him.

J. J. came home for Thanksgiving, and they had dinner with the Johnsons. He and Maureen were full of stories of their almost completed first term.

"He's studying," Maureen announced to their assembled parents. "He's in my freshman English class, and the teacher just loves him. Says he doesn't usually get sports jocks to whom he can give good grades."

"Hey, my sister said the first semester was important," J. J. protested.

"When did you ever listen to Jill before?" Maureen countered, and they all laughed.

Nora bought Christmas cards, and signed them "Nora Buckley and family." She had them out December 10. She decorated the house as she always had with lights and garlands of greens with red plastic apples, pinecones, and red plaid ribbon. There was a large real pine wreath on the front door hung just below the polished brass knocker. Carl Ulrich as usual got his painter friend with the small cherry picker to decorate the large concolor fir on Nora's lawn with colored Christmas lights. Since the Buckley house sat at the end of the cul-de-sac, the tree had always been a centerpiece for the street. When it had become too tall for even a person on a ladder to decorate, Carl had called in his buddy to do it.

"I wonder if the new people will let us decorate the tree," Rina said to Joanne.

Carla began to cry, standing out in the street, watching her husband and Carl up in the cherry picker draping lights while Nora directed from below.

"Don't cry, Carla," Tiffany said, putting an arm about the woman. "Everything's going to be alright. I just know it is!"

"Nothing is ever going to be the same again if Nora goes," Carla replied, and thought they said nothing because what could they say? They all knew she was right.

All the kids on Ansley Court came home for the holiday season, and as they always had, they celebrated together. They were at Sam and Rina's for the first night of Hanukkah, watching as their four-year-old grandson lit the first candle. They went to Joe and Tiffany's for Christmas Eve, eating her traditional cheese lasagna and salad before going off to the local Congregational church to sing carols. On Christmas Day they all went to Nora's for a traditional dinner of prime rib, Yorkshire pudding, and all the trimmings. And after dinner they moved to Joanne and Carl's home for a beautiful table of homemade desserts. And finally on New Year's Eve Rick and Carla gave a party for the families on the court.

It wasn't uncomfortable at all for Nora. The kids came briefly, and then went off to their own parties, where they would remain until morning. And Nora had been with her friends so often without Jeff that nothing seemed different this year at all. They ate a wonderful buffet, drank sparingly as people their age did these days, and played board games and cards. They laughed and gossiped, and everyone avoided the fact that this time next year, there would be strangers living in the Buckley house on Ansley Court. Midnight came. They had turned on the television to watch the ball drop in Times Square in New York. They sang "Auld Lang Syne" off-key, kissed each other, and then they had all gone off home again. New Year's was for kids.

Jill had flown back to North Carolina on the twenty-ninth. She had met a young man at Duke, a teaching associate in the doctoral program, and they planned to spend New Year's Eve together. Nora had driven her daughter to the airport, and while they were waiting for Jill's flight to be called, she had told her daughter of the settlement agreement she would sign on the second of January. "You are not to tell your brother," Nora warned Jill. "I'll tell him before he goes back. He and Maureen are taking the bus back up to State on the first, rather than waiting until the last minute. They both have papers due and the dorms are open on the first."

"It all stinks," Jill said bitterly. "How could he throw you out of the house?"

"Let this be a lesson to you, honey. Get as much as you can in your name before and after you marry. Don't be a trusting little dope like I was," Nora said.

"You weren't a trusting dope, Ma. You were innocent," Jill replied.

"Same thing, honey, where money and property are concerned," Nora laughed.

Her daughter's flight was called. Jill and her mother embraced, and Nora hugged her daughter perhaps a little harder than she usually did.

"What's that for?" Jill demanded, suspicious.

"I just love you," Nora responded, "and I don't know when I'm going to see you again. Can't a mother hug her grown kid?"

"I'll come home whenever you need me," Jill said. "Don't be a martyr, Ma. Call me, okay?" Then she turned and was gone.

"I will!" Nora called after her daughter.

Now New Year's Eve was over, and returning to her house, Nora went upstairs and packed up her son's belongings for his return to college. She had promised him she would do it if he would remain at Lily's house overnight and not try to drive home. "Too many drunks out tonight. Come home by eight, and I'll have breakfast for you before you take off. I'll even do your packing. Stick out all the stuff you want, okay?"

"Ma, you're the greatest!" he'd told her.

Nora smiled, remembering the words. She looked at all the stuff J. J. had put out on his bed, and wondered how it was all going to fit in his two duffels. Then she laughed. Wasn't she the world-champion packer? She was. When she had finished, she considered going to The Channel, but decided against it. If she lay down now, she could grab a nice nap before she had to get up, and fix her son a terrific going-back-to-college breakfast. She set her alarm for seven a.m. That would give her an hour.

J. J. stamped into the house at eight fifteen, looking slightly bleary-eyed. "I'll sleep on the bus ride up," he told her in answer to her raised eyebrow.

"Sit down," she told him, and then began bringing out the food she had prepared.

"Oh, Ma! Wow!" He gazed at the platter of fluffy scrambled eggs with both bacon and his favorite sausage links. "French-bread French toast!" He began filling his plate after grabbing first at the tall glass of cranberry juice and swallowing it half down.

Nora refilled it and sat down to join him. She smiled, pleased as he shoveled the eggs into his mouth, his eyes lighting up.

"You put cheese in them!" he exclaimed.

"You like them that way," she replied, helping herself to a teaspoon of eggs, two sausage links, and a piece of French toast. "There's soft butter and maple syrup for the French toast, J. J. Eat, and then we'll talk. I've got stuff to tell you before you take off."

"What's up?" he asked her.

"Eat first—talk later." She smiled, hoping he'd assume she was going to give him the usual back-to-school speech. When they had finished Nora suggested that they sit in the den where the fire was going.

"Yeah, the house has been a little cold, I've noticed. Have you had the furnace checked, Ma?" he wondered.

"I've had to keep the thermostat at sixty-eight during the day, and sixty-five at night," Nora told her son. "Your father isn't paying for the oil anymore, and I have to watch my pennies. You should have told me you were cold, J. J."

"I just wore more clothes"—he grinned—"but Jill sure bitched. She's gotten used to a North Carolina climate, I'm made of sterner stuff, Ma. Now, what up? You saw my first-semester grades. I've done great, and I promise I'll keep up the good work. Honest! I'm not even going to consider pledging a frat until next year. I know I'm a legacy at Dad's old house, but that's the one I'm not interested in, seeing how Dad turned out."

There was no easy way to do this, Nora thought bleakly. "The divorce settlement has been agreed upon in principle," she began. "I'm signing the papers tomorrow, J. J. Your dad is going to give me alimony for the next five years. Not much, but I'll be job hunting by spring, and so I'll manage. In five years' time I should be able to do without any help from anyone, don't you think?" She smiled at him. "And, honey, we've gotten your dad to pay for your dorm room until you graduate. You'll have to pay for your own meal plan, and if you want to move off of campus, he won't pay, but since you're on the soccer team, and on scholarship, I think you'll want to stay in the dorms."

"The house?" J. J. demanded to know. "He's selling it, isn't he?"

"Yes," Nora admitted. "I just don't have any option there. But Rick got me forty percent of the sales price. There's no mortgage on it, and Rick says I'll probably end up with almost four hundred thousand, honey. It's not bad. Really."

"When do we have to be out?" J. J. asked her.

"The house goes on the market April first," Nora said, "but Rick says I'll probably have at least two months after a sale before it closes, to move. Jill has said she'll come and help me pack, and you'll be here too."

"Where are we going to live?" he said low.

"I don't know yet, honey, but I'll tell you what. When you come home for your spring break, we'll go looking together, okay? It won't matter to Jill. She's hardly home at all anymore. It'll be fun. Just you and me. I know after next summer you'll probably be staying up at State, or going somewhere else for a job or an internship, but you'll always have a room at your ma's place. Wherever it is." She put her arm about him, and gave him a hard hug.

"I hate him!" J. J. said fiercely.

"No, honey, feel sorry for him," Nora told her son. "He's growing old, and he can't face it. It's unlikely Heidi is going to stay with him till death do them part. Your father is going to end up alone one day in spite of everything he has done and everything he has. But we'll always have each other, J. J."

"I'm glad I didn't go to see him while I've been home," J. J. said. "He called and asked Jill and me to go. She went 'cause she thought she might convince him to pay for her other two years at Duke Law. She was really pissed when she got back."

"Because he wouldn't," Nora said softly. "I did try for her too, you know."

"Serves her right," J. J. muttered, "kissing up to Dad and his bitch."

"Honey!" Nora chided her son gently.

"Well, it does," J. J. said angrily. "Why the hell is Dad treating you like this? All you ever did was be exactly what he wanted you to be, and do everything he wanted you to do. I can still remember those parties you used to hostess for Dad's clients and partners when Jill and I were little. They all loved them. They all thought you were great. What happened, Ma? Why doesn't he think you're great anymore?"

"His needs have changed, honey." Nora tried to explain it to her son, although she wasn't certain she really understood it herself. Jeff was having one whale of a midlife crisis. "I don't fit the profile anymore of what he needs, or thinks he needs, now. Heidi does. I'm learning it isn't unusual for men his age to do this. Particularly men in positions of importance or power within their career arenas. Suddenly the wife who provided the backup and support while they were climbing the ladder of success is no longer the wife they want. They want someone young and intelligent because they think it makes them look younger and smarter."

"I'll never be like Dad," J. J. said stonily. "When I marry it's going to be forever."

"I hope it is, honey," Nora told him. "It used to be like that." She stood up. "You had better get your shower. Your bags are all packed. I'm taking you and Maureen to the bus in just an hour."

J. J. arose, and putting his arms about his mother, he hugged her hard, planting a kiss on her cheek. "I'll always love you best, Ma," he said.

"Best of your parents is flattering, honey," she said, "but love the girl you marry one day best of all, and above all other women. That's the way it should be. And if it is that way, then your wife and I will always be friends and never jealous of one another."

Releasing her, he ran off to take his shower, returning forty minutes later smelling of soap, shampoo, and too much aftershave. He was wearing his best worn jeans, a flannel shirt with an Irish sweater over it, and his favorite leather work boots. His hair was wet.

"You can't go out with wet hair," she scolded him. "Use the dryer in my bathroom. You've got time before we have to go."

Grumbling, he returned back upstairs, and when he came

down again his hair was dry, and slicked back with some kind of goop he used. "Better?" he demanded to know.

"Better," she said, resigned as she watched him slap his favorite baseball cap, brim backward, on his head. She couldn't convince him that he would ruin his hair with that damned cap on his head all the time. She picked up the car keys from the bowl on the hall table. "Let's ride, Clyde," she said with a small smile.

He picked up his two duffels. "You get everything in here, Ma?" he asked.

"Everything you left out, and some other stuff you forgot," she told him as they walked to the car in the driveway. She popped the trunk, and he tossed his bags inside.

Joe came staggering across the street with Maureen's matching luggage, his daughter followed pulling another suitcase on wheels, and Carla carried a shopping bag that Nora knew had sandwiches, chips, goodies, and juice boxes for the long bus ride. The luggage was all loaded up. Hugs and kisses all around, and Nora got into the car and drove her son and neighbor's daughter to the bus station. Reaching their destination, J. J. and Maureen were out of the car quickly, waving and calling to two other kids they knew, who were obviously returning to State today as well. Then he unloaded the trunk.

"You don't have to wait, Ma," J. J. said. He wasn't embarrassed yet, but he was going to be if she didn't take the hint and go.

How long until she saw him again? Nora wondered, struggling with herself not to cry. "Give me a hug and a kiss, honey," she said, and he did.

"Bye, Ma. I'll call you tonight, okay?"

"Call early," Nora said. "I'm going to bed right away. Tomorrow is going to be a bitch of a day for me. Before eight, okay?"

"Sure," he said, and turning away, he joined his friends as they gathered up all their luggage and began loading it on the waiting bus.

"Bye, Mrs. Buckley," Maureen said, giving her a quick kiss. "Thanks for driving me down here."

"Have a good term, Mo," Nora told the girl. Then she got into the car and drove away. She tucked the car carefully into the garage when she got home. The house was cold when she entered it. She kicked the thermostat up to seventy-two degrees. Screw the cost. It was only for a few hours. It was just a little after 11 a.m. Nora went into the living room. The ornament box was waiting for her. She had pulled it out early this morning. She looked a final time at the tree. It wasn't the biggest she had ever had, but it had been a pretty tree. She removed the many ornaments efficiently, replacing them in their slots in the special box she had bought years ago for just this purpose. When the ornaments were all stowed, she drew off the strands of tiny colored lights, wrapping each strand neatly and placing them in a row on the top shelf of the box. Finished, she closed down the lid of the box. The tree still smelled fragrantly rich with its piney scent.

Nora picked up a telephone handset and called Rick Johnson. "I'm ready now," she said when Carla answered.

"We'll be right over, sweetie," Carla replied. "I'm only half finished."

"I got going early," Nora answered, and hung up the phone.

They were at her house a few minutes later. Together the three of them took the tree from its holder and jostled it out the front door to the curb, where the town would be picking it up on Tuesday next.

"Thanks," Nora told them, turning to go back into her house.

"I'll pick you up at eight a.m. tomorrow," Rick reminded her.

"I'll be ready," Nora said, but she didn't turn to face him.

"Nora, wait a minute," Carla said, catching up with her friend, and walking with her back to her house. "Look, I know tomorrow's going to be a bitch. I have to work, but I'll be home by three thirty, and I'll come over, okay?"

Nora debated a moment, and then said, "Listen, Carla, whatever happens, I don't want you to worry about me, alright? I'll be fine."

"Sure you will," Carla said halfheartedly.

"No, Carla, you don't understand. I'm not going to sign those papers tomorrow. Jeff isn't going to get my house." She put her fingers over Carla's mouth even as her best friend was opening it to speak. "Carla, whatever you see, whatever they tell you, I will be alright. I'm going away. That's why I spoke with Mr. Nicholas all those months ago. I needed to know if I could use The Channel as a refuge, and he said I could. If I don't sign those papers tomorrow, then Jeff is stuck until I do."

"But what good will that really do?" Carla whispered.

"Look, how long do you think Heidi will wait around, especially if because he can't sell the house, he has to get rid of her co-op?"

"But Jeff owns the house," Carla reminded Nora.

"Yes, he does, but I know Jeff far better than Heidi does. How he appears to the public, to his partners, his clients, is far more important to Jeff than anything else."

"Are you trying to break them up so he'll come back to you?" Carla asked, surprised that Nora would even consider such a thing.

Nora shook her head. "I don't want him back," she said, "but yes, if I can break them up, then there is no need to sell the house. At that point, Rick might even be able to convince Jeff to give me the house in exchange for relief of all his other obligations toward me and the kids. Look, Rick says she's been paying the bridge loan. With the way good real estate is going in town, he can sell the co-op for a profit, pay her back, and still come out of it smelling like a rose. He could even have enough to buy himself a small place. Yes, Jill will have to get herself through her last two years of law school, but she'll do it. And I'll have to help J. J. get a student loan so he has a dorm room, but it's possible. I'm taking a gamble, I know, but I just can't let Jeff sell the house!"

"What will happen to you?" Carla asked.

"It will look like I'm unconscious, Mr. Nicholas said," Nora replied.

"And you believe him?" Carla wasn't certain about any of this.

"Yes, I do believe him," Nora said.

"They'll put you in the hospital at first," Carla told her.

"I know."

"How long are you going to stay unconscious?" Carla queried her friend.

"As long as it takes, but knowing that my dear husband has absolutely no patience, I expect a few weeks, a few months at the most," Nora told her companion. "Listen, sweetie, I'm going to be fine. You should see my apartment. It's right out of *Architectural Digest*. And I've told you about Kyle, and Rolf. Incredible! I have absolutely everything I want there. While I'm going to look like I'm at death's door, I'm going to be having a helluva good time, and the best nonstop sex I've ever known. It's going to be alright, and I already know how this is going to mess up Jeff's life and screw with his mind. I'll bet you the first thing he says is that I did it deliberately."

Carla laughed aloud. "You're right!" she said.

"You can't tell anyone, Carla. Not Rick because he wouldn't believe you, and he'd think you were losing it. Not Rina, Tiff, or Joanne. Give them hope as a nurse, and don't let them be too upset, but you can't tell them what I've done."

"How will you know what's happening in this reality?" Carla asked.

"I don't need to. I know Jeff. And I'll contact you in a few weeks to see how it's all going, okay?"

"How will you contact me?" Carla asked.

"I'm not certain yet, but I think if you want me in your fantasy, I can be there. I'll ask Kyle, and if he doesn't know, Mr. Nicholas's door is always open to me, I'm told. But honestly, I think you just have to put me in your fantasy. I can be a barmaid at one of your island inns, or maybe another female pirate captain you know. You work it out." She gave Carla a hug. "I'm freezing. I've got to go in now."

"Be careful," Carla said. "God, I wish you didn't have to do this!"

"So do I," Nora responded, "but if I don't, by this time tomorrow, I'll have signed my house away and be on my way to a final divorce. I don't give a crap about Jeff, but I'm not letting my house go. Wait a couple of weeks before you contact me unless Jeff cracks sooner, but I don't think he will."

"Okay," Carla said, and then she turned away before she started to cry. She heard the front door of the Buckley house close behind her, and the lock turn with a loud click. Nora's plan scared the hell out of her, but what else could Nora do? Jeff had driven her into a very tight corner. Nora was far braver than she herself was, and Carla would never even have considered that until recently. And what about Jill and J. J.? Nora wouldn't have told them. How could she? Jill, in particular, would have thought her mother crazy. We're all going to have to be there for them, Carla thought to herself.

Nora watched her best friend walking slowing across the street from the bay window of the living room, where the Christmas tree had recently stood. There were needles all over the floor. She got out the vacuum and cleaned them up. Then she took the ornament box back upstairs and stored it in the attic. If she was going away, her house was going to be in perfect condition when they found her unconscious body. She had always had a thing about being in an accident, and strangers coming into her house and finding an unmade bed, or dishes in the sink. It was similar to your mother's warning you to always wear clean underwear.

Back down in the kitchen, she put all the dishes from breakfast in the dishwasher and mopped the counters. There was just enough room for her supper plate. It was after four now, and the sunset was visible through the kitchen windows. Nora sat down, and called Margo to wish her a happy new year.

"What are you doing?" Margo asked her daughter.

"I've just got the tree out, and everything cleaned up," Nora answered.

"Where are the kids?"

"Jill went back a few days ago. She's met someone, and they wanted to spend New Year's Eve together. I got J. J. off on the noon bus."

"Tomorrow's the day, right?" Margo asked.

"Yep," Nora said shortly.

"Come down and stay with me," Margo said. "South Carolina coastal winters are really lovely. The winter jasmine is already starting to bloom. We could house hunt for you. It's really so much cheaper down here. You wouldn't have to give up any of your furniture. Taylor is building a lovely development just a few miles from here. You could customize it to suit you at this stage."

"Thanks, Ma, but I'm not ready to make that kind of a commitment yet," Nora said. Nor ever, she thought silently.

"Look, honey, you really have nothing to do now. Come down," Margo persisted.

"Ma, I've got another semester of classes to take, and then I've got to job hunt. The thousand dollars a month Jeff is going to be doling out to me isn't going to make it. I can't be a lady of leisure like you can," Nora told her mother.

"They still have midwinter breaks, don't they?" Margo said dryly. "I'll send you a ticket. I'll send you two, and J. J. can come with you."

"He's already mentioned something about going skiing with Lily and her family," Nora said.

"Then I'll just send one ticket. Come on, darling, you need a break. The last six months have been horrendous for you. Besides, I miss you. And Taylor does too," Margo coaxed in her best tones.

"Still set on not remarrying?" Nora teased her mother.

"I'm rethinking my priorities," Margo admitted. "Taylor is a lot of fun, and right now he does seem to be pretty maintenance-free. We're going to be cruising in the Bahamas in March on his yacht. Now, say you'll come," Margo pleaded, not being pulled from her determination.

"Okay, I'll come," Nora said. Might as well tell her mother she'd come even if there was little chance she would. It made Margo happy, and Nora wanted to leave her happy. They spoke for another few minutes, and then Nora said, "I want to call Jill, Ma. I'll talk to you in a few days."

Jill sounded sleepy. She was up, but it had obviously been a very late night for her, and Nora heard the voice of a man in the background. She smiled. This was serious. Jill never let anyone stay over, and her roommates hadn't returned yet, so that male voice had to belong to her friend.

"Will you be alright tomorrow, Ma?" Jill sounded genuinely worried.

"Fine," Nora responded. "Your grandmother has me coming down in midwinter break to South Carolina. She wants me to look at places to live. Taylor is building a new development. I told her I'd come, but no new house."

"Ma, it wouldn't be a bad idea. The Carolinas are so much cheaper, even now. And I'm here."

"Your brother isn't, and J. J. needs his mother for a while longer," Nora said. "He has to go to State. I can't afford to send him anywhere else. Thank God he got the scholarship for soccer."

"Okay, but you should think about it," Jill pressed.

They spoke for a few more minutes, and then no sooner had she hung up than the phone rang. It was J. J. They were back. The dorm was warmer than the house. The trip was fine, and he'd call tomorrow after she got back from town.

"You don't have to, honey," she said. "I'm going to be fine. I'm resigned to this now. Not happy, but resigned."

"If you need me, Ma, at any time, I'll come home," he told her.

"You damned well better stay in school, J. J.," she scolded. "I love you, honey, but no way will I ever need to lean on you."

"Okay, Ma, I get it. I am woman, hear me roar," he kidded.

"You got it, boyo!"

"I gotta run," he said.

"Got a life now, do you?" she teased back. "Okay, honey, bye, now."

"Bye, Ma. I love you!" And then he was gone.

It was done. She had said her good-byes for now to everyone she loved. She fixed herself supper, consisting of cold ham and macaroni and cheese. Her mother always said eating pork on the new year brought luck. I'm going to need luck, Nora considered. She got up, put her dishes in the dishwasher, turned it on, and put food in the cats' bowls, filling their water dish and crunchies container. She had called Suburban Cable while J. J. had been in the shower this morning. Now it was her turn to shower. She went upstairs, bathed, and washed her hair, drying it with the dryer her son had left on her sink counter this morning. She got into the clean new flannel nightgown that Jill had given her for Christmas. It was soft pink, and had lace at the wrists and a small ruffle at the neck. She slipped her feet into the new pink suede slippers lined with lamb's wool that J. J. had given her. After brushing her hair, she drew it back and fastened it neatly with an elastic band. She headed downstairs and fixed herself a cup of tea, put the last of Carla's Christmas cookies on a china plate, and carried them into the den. She had lost a lot of weight during the last six months, but Carla's cookies had always been irresistible, and it was the end of the holidays, Nora reasoned. She turned on *Jeopardy!* and got a lot of the answers right. Next came *Wheel of Fortune* but she was never any good at solving the puzzles until it became so obvious the village idiot could figure it out. She tipped the teacup over into the saucer, and regretfully left the last cookie on the plate. It made a nice effect. The clock on the fireplace mantel struck eight o'clock.

For a moment Nora debated one last time if she was doing the right thing. What if Mr. Nicholas had lied, and she couldn't get back? Then she decided that if Jeff was going to get the house, the reality of The Channel was a far better world for her than the one she was now in. Reaching out, Nora pressed her palm against the television screen, feeling the now-familiar pop within her body. She was there, and she meant to stay until she could force Jeff to give up his selfish quest for the house.

"Honey," she said, calling out for Kyle, "I'm home!"

CHAPTER EIGHT

"What the hell do you mean, she can't sign the papers today?" Jeff Buckley's face was beet red with his anger. "I warned you that the bitch would try something cute if you didn't make her sign last autumn. What are you going to do about this, Kramer? I've paid you a fortune so far, and I'm still married to Nora."

Raoul Kramer looked at his client with what he hoped was an emotionless face. He didn't like Jeff Buckley, and the more he knew him, the less he liked him. He had taken his case as a favor to Jeff's senior partner, with whom he had roomed at college. It should have been a quiet divorce. His voice was cool as he spoke. "Your wife is in the hospital, Buckley. She is unconscious. Her attorney found her this morning when he went to pick her up, so they could drive into the city together."

"Is she going to die?" If she died, everything would be his.

"They don't know yet. They don't even know what's the matter. You would have to speak with Rick Johnson, her attorney. You know him. You were neighbors," the lawyer said.

"So what happens now?" Jeff asked. "Can I get the divorce?"

"Not until she regains consciousness or dies," Raoul Kramer

said. "The judge ordered that we had to have a settlement before she would hear the case in its entirety."

"Get another judge, then," Jeff said.

"Not possible. You haven't got the grounds for it. No judge will grant you a divorce from Mrs. Buckley without that settlement being signed. You're stuck for the time being, I'm afraid. Besides, how would it look if you divorced her now?"

"She isn't on my health insurance anymore. How long will the hospital keep her under those circumstances?" Jeff wanted to know.

"You took her off your health insurance?" Kramer was astounded. "That was part of the agreement. You have to pay her health insurance along with the alimony for five years. When the hell did you do that?"

"Months ago. I asked my assistant Carol to arrange it," Jeff said nervously. "Is this going to cost me?"

"Oh, yeah," Raoul Kramer said. "It's going to cost you bigtime. You take the kids off too?" But he knew the answer to that even as he spoke.

"Yeah, but they never get sick. And I never knew Nora to get sick in all the years we were married. Isn't there some law or something that says I can refuse to pay for her care?" Jeff asked.

Raoul Kramer picked up his phone and punched in a number.

"Who are you calling?" Jeff wanted to know.

"Your assistant. Carol? Raoul Kramer. Did you remove Mrs. Buckley and the kids from Jeff's health insurance? I see. Yes. You're a smart lady. If you ever get tired of working for your boss, call me." He laughed. "Thanks." And put his phone down. "You owe Carol a big one, Buckley. When she read the draft of the settlement for you, she saw that Mrs. Buckley would get health insurance for five years. She arranged it, and in doing so has saved your ass. For God's sake, don't do anything else without checking with me first."

"So it isn't going to cost me?" Jeff wanted reassurance.

"You're home free," Raoul Kramer replied.

"But I can't get the divorce until Nora either wakes up or croaks, right?"

"Right," Kramer said. What a moron this guy was. He expected the ultrarich, whom he usually acted for, to be tight with a dollar, but this guy was just a dumb boomer who had made more money than his father and thought he was rich. "I would suggest you go out to Egret Pointe and get Nora's prognosis from her doctors. Let me know how she's doing, and we'll go from there." His tone was dismissive, and even Jeff got the point.

He stood up. "Yeah. I'll go see what's happening." While driving out to Egret Pointe, Jeff Buckley wondered if Nora would live or die. Kramer was right. The divorce had to be put on hold until they knew. How would it look to his conservative partners at the agency if he divorced his sick wife? More important, how would it look to their clients? There was so much to consider, not to mention Heidi. Heidi was not going to be happy about this delay. There had already been too many delays. He put himself out on a limb with that damned co-op in order to make her happy and to keep her from leaving him. He couldn't bear it if she left him. Heidi was the best damned sex he had ever had. She knew how to thrill a man and keep him coming back for more. He couldn't lose her.

Because Nora had not really been a part of his life in the city, he had been able to keep his divorce discreet, more or less. His partners, older men married for years, hadn't been happy, but he had brought them around, selling them a bill of goods that salved their consciences, making him the victim in the matter. But they wanted everything to be circumspect, controlled, and careful. It was to be quick with no, or at least minimal, gossip involved. There were their clients to consider. It was the youngest of the senior partners, Mr. Archibald Wickham, who had suggested Raoul Kramer. And he had spoken to Raoul himself before sending Jeff to see him.

And he'd done a good job, Jeff had to admit, even if he hated giving up a penny to Nora. Heidi was right. Nora had been living off of him for twenty-six years. In the beginning she had been just the wife he wanted. She was just like his mother: docile, quiet-spoken and frugal. She had made a beautiful home, and kept it nicely. She had produced two children, a daughter and a son. They were intelligent and well-mannered. But as the years had passed he realized that Nora wasn't at all what he wanted. She bored him. And in bed she had not been inspiring at all. How could a woman be so damned dull? he wondered. And now the old cow had thrown a monkey wrench in his plans by getting sick. If she didn't recover from whatever it was that she had, he was going to be stuck with her for the rest of his life. Would he lose Heidi? But maybe Nora would die.

He was so deep in thought that he almost missed the parkway turnoff to Egret Pointe, but he managed it, his brakes squealing just slightly as he cornered the turn. The hospital was nearby. He hadn't been to Egret Pointe General since J. J. was born. He swung into the lot and parked his sports car. He found a Pink Lady manning the desk.

"I am Jeff Buckley. My wife, Nora, was brought in this morning."

"Buckley. Buckley," the Pink Lady repeated, going down the list. "Ah, here it is. Buckley. She's in the ICU, but no visitors, Mr. Buckley. Still, if you're her hubby, I suppose no one would mind. Three West is the ICU. Take this card." She handed him an index card with the words ICU VISITOR stamped on it in black. The edges of the card were frayed.

"Thank you," he said, giving her his best smile.

The elevator opened on the third floor. Immediately in front of him was a sign with arrows pointing in various directions. THREE WEST was the heading. CCU was to the left, and ICU was to the right. Jeff turned right, and hurried through a pair of swinging doors.

"Jeff!" He turned to see a small lounge. Rick and Carla were in it. He turned again, and went in to greet them. Carla just glared, but said nothing. "What happened to her?" Jeff asked.

"They don't know," Rick said quietly. "I was to pick her up this morning to drive into town to Kramer's office. When she didn't show up, I called first but didn't get any answer, so I went over. I rang the bell. I knocked. I called her. Nothing. So I went back home and got a spare key. We all have keys for the other houses on the court," Rick explained, knowing Jeff wouldn't have known that. "I let myself into the house. Both cats shot by me. We'll have to get them in later. I called her name, but the place was as silent as a tomb. So I started searching the house. I went upstairs first, and when I couldn't find her, I came back down to look around there. I found her in the den.

"She was in her chair, in front of the television. It was still on, but no picture. She must have ordered a movie, and whatever happened to her happened while she was watching it. Her teacup was tipped over. There was no sign of forced entry, or violence. I called emergency, and they brought her to the hospital," Rick concluded.

"Did she try to commit suicide?" Jeff asked. "Did you see any pills?"

"You know Nora doesn't take anything stronger than aspirin," Carla finally spoke up, "or maybe you don't. You've never been around much. Besides, Nora wouldn't kill herself over you." The last word was said in a scornful tone.

"What do the doctors say?" Jeff wanted to know.

"We're waiting for Dr. Rhone now," Rick answered. "He's the ER guy."

"I'll wait with you," Jeff said.

Carla made a rather rude noise but said nothing more for the time being.

The doctor arrived. He looked to Rick and spoke, but Rick

quickly introduced Jeff to the physician, who said, "I didn't realize Mrs. Buckley's husband was still alive."

Carla laughed aloud.

"We're in the process of a divorce," Jeff said. "Rick is my wife's attorney, and should be told anything that concerns her health. I'll be driving back into town shortly. I just came out when I heard the news."

"Oh," Dr. Rhone said. "Well, the preliminary tox reports are in. There is nothing in her system that would indicate she took any harmful substance. Not even an aspirin. She doesn't appear to have had a stroke, although those are difficult to pinpoint actually, so it might be she stroked out, but the MRI shows nothing. Other than that, I have no answers. Her vitals are good. But Dr. Sam will know more. He's her regular guy."

"She isn't dying?" Jeff asked.

"Not at all," Dr. Rhone replied. "She's simply unconscious, and we can find no cause yet. But I'm sure we will. And she could wake up at any time. Tell me, Mr. Buckley, has this divorce proceeding been particularly stressful for Mrs. Buckley? Stress is something we're learning more about every day. It seems to be able to do just about anything to a body and mind's well-being."

"You bet, she's been upset," Carla burst forth. "Wouldn't you be if after twenty-six years of devotion and love, you were told you were being replaced by a Heidi, who is young enough to be your daughter?"

"Carla!" Rick pleaded.

Dr. Rhone looked uncomfortable. "About your wife's care, Mr. Buckley," he began. "Since you aren't here, would you like to sign a document delegating your wife's attorney to make any decisions that need to be made?"

"Sure," Jeff said. He turned to Rick. "That's okay with you?"

"Yeah," Rick told him. "I'm here. You're not. What about her health insurance? Has the divorce policy kicked in yet?"

"Call my assistant, Carol. She's got all the particulars, but yes,

Nora is covered," Jeff said. He turned back to the doctor. "Can I see her?"

"Certainly, come with me," Dr. Rhone replied.

Jeff followed the physician into the ICU, where Nora lay quietly in a neatly made hospital bed. He looked down at her. She looked younger than she had last spring. And she had colored her hair. He figured she'd be going fishing for another husband once they were parted. And she was a heck of a lot thinner. There was even a slight smile on her face. She was very still. She actually looked as if she were sleeping, and having a very nice dream while she did. He turned away. Wake up, or die, damnit! the voice in his head said. "Let me sign that paper now so Rick can have the responsibility of her care," Jeff said, and returned to the waiting room.

"I'll have a nurse bring you the papers," Dr. Rhone told him. Then he was gone.

"You're certain you don't mind doing this?" Jeff asked Rick one more time.

"He doesn't mind!" Carla snapped. "Nora and I are best friends. Who else is here who can look after her?" You schmuck, she thought silently.

Jeff signed the papers and handed them back to the waiting nurse. "Look, Carla," he said, but she stopped him with a wave of her hand.

"It isn't the divorce that bothers me, Jeff," she said. "It's what a son of a bitch you have been about it. All she wanted was the house. She deserved it. She wanted nothing else from you. No alimony. Nothing. Just the house."

"I don't want to start with another mortgage at my age," he said.

"Hey, you're starting with another wife. And don't think she won't want at least one kid, Jeff. She will. If you play, honey, you gotta pay. But Nora shouldn't have had to pay for your libido, and your big whopping midlife crisis. Whatever has happened to her is your fault. She's lying there right now because of you. I hope you're satisfied! Now run home to Bambi, or whatever the hell her name is. Just don't let me ever see your face again!" And Carla began to cry.

Jeff Buckley looked distinctly uncomfortable. He had never understood his wife's friendship with Carla, a smart-mouthed city kid—an Italian Catholic, for God's sake. And the others. Rina Seligmann, a Jewish social worker. Joanne, who was the wife of a hardware store owner. Tiffany Pietro d'Angelo, that hot little blonde who had kneed him once when he had come on to her. Good riddance to them all. Rick was comforting his wife. Jeff caught his eye. "Thanks," he said, and then he left. He could hardly wait to get back to town, but telling Heidi wasn't going to be easy.

"Is he gone?" Carla asked, sniffling into her husband's shoulder.

"Yeah. You sure gave it to him," Rick chuckled.

"He's a bastard!" Carla muttered.

"Agreed," Rick said. "I think he was hoping she would die. I really do."

"Nora's not going to die!" Carla said. No, she wasn't. Right now she was having a very good time in The Channel. Carla almost smiled. When Nora got back, she'd tell her how she had told off Jeff. Yet seeing her best friend lying in the ICU bed so still and fragile-looking was not easy. She did look as if she were sick, and it scared Carla just a little bit. Was Nora really alright?

"Let's go home, honey," Rick said. "There isn't anything we can do right now." He put his arm about his wife. They stopped at the nurse's station, and Rick gave the charge nurse his card. It had all his numbers. His office. The house. His cell. His e-mail. "Call me if there's any change," he told her, and she nodded.

Carla called Jill and J. J. that night. Both of them wanted to come home immediately, but Carla told them there was nothing they could do, and warned them that Nora would have a fit if she woke up and her kids weren't in school, where they belonged. "I'll keep you up to speed," she told them both, and they agreed to remain where they were for the interim. Next she called Margo.

"I just talked to her yesterday," Margo said, suddenly sounding very frail. "She didn't try . . ."

"No!" Carla said quickly.

"What about the divorce?" Margo asked.

"Everything is on hold for now."

"I'll come up," Margo said.

"If you want to, and you can stay with us," Carla replied, "but honestly, there's nothing you can do right now, and she could wake up any minute." Carla hated lying to Nora's mother, but she couldn't possibly explain what Nora had done.

"Well," Margo responded slowly, "I'll wait, then. Who's in charge? Not Jeff!"

"No. He signed everything over to Rick. I think he was relieved to do it," Carla explained. "I think he's afraid of the responsibility under the circumstances."

"Thank God!" Margo replied.

That had been the difficult call, but she had gotten through it, Carla thought, relieved. Margo wasn't the kids. Now all we have to do is wait for Jeff to cave like Nora said he would, Carla considered. But it was all very nerve-racking.

Nora lay in her unconscious state for ten days. There was no change. The hospital kept her hydrated, but they did nothing more. Finally Dr. Sam suggested that his patient would have to be moved to a nursing facility.

"Shorecrest is lovely," he told Rick, "and when she awakens she'll need physical therapy certainly. They have several excellent therapists."

Rick agreed. He had checked with Jeff's assistant, Carol, and learned that she had chosen the best health care policy possible. It even included nursing-home care for several months. "That was very thoughtful of you, Carol," Rick had noted.

Carol laughed. "He'll never know. He doesn't bother with stuff like this, and fair is fair. Mrs. B. was always nice to me. And I know where those lovely Christmas gifts with Jeff's card came from every year. I put J. J. on the policy, but I didn't dare add Jill."

"I'll tell her so she can get something for herself if she can afford it," he replied. "Thanks, Carol. If this causes any trouble, let me know."

Carol laughed again. "I already have a job offer from Raoul Kramer," she said.

Rick laughed too, and hung up.

Nora was moved from the hospital into a sunny private room at Shorecrest. The nurses at both the hospital and the nursing facility remarked upon how Nora's mouth was always smiling. Some smiles were broader than others. It was encouraging, but it was eerie too. Carla had noticed it as well, and one day she bent to whisper in Nora's ear, "Don't wear them out, sweetie!"

She couldn't know, but Nora actually heard her. She was sitting atop Kyle's chest while he amused himself with her breasts. His thick cock was buried deep in her wet pussy, and she was burning with her lust. She laughed softly to herself at Carla's words. She needed Rolfie too today. "Rolf!" she called, and he came eagerly into the bedroom. "I need two today, darling," she said. She leaned forward, offering Kyle a nipple, which he quickly took and began to suck on hard.

Rolf was behind her now. "I want to put it in your ass," he whispered hotly in her ear. "You haven't let me do that yet, Nora, and I want to do it so bad." His big hands massaged the cheeks of her bottom. "You have the cutest tush," he said, stroking her.

"I'm not sure," she teased him. Her clit was tingling at the thought of Kyle throbbing in her cunt, and Rolf throbbing in her ass.

"Let him," Kyle murmured. "Together we can give you the climax of your life, Nora. And then send him away, please."

"I'm in charge here," she reminded him, smiling into his handsome face. "I need you both tonight." She could feel Rolf's finger rubbing her anus with sweet-smelling oil. She wiggled provocatively against his finger. His cock began foraging between the twin half spheres of her bottom. "Ohh, do it!" she told him. "Do it now!"

His hands closed about her hips to steady them both. He pushed the head of his penis against the tight little opening. She moaned, and arched her back for him. The sphincter suddenly relaxed, and he was plunging forward. Now Rolf groaned as the tight walls of her flesh tightly encased him. He moved carefully. "Can you find the spot, Kyle?" he asked his male companion.

"I'm close," Kyle replied. "I think it's time to blow madam's mind, Rolfie. Agreed?" He moved within her vagina, and when he heard Nora gasp, surprised, he said, "Got it!" She gasped again. It was a sharp sound that seemed to pull all the breath from her. "Hey, you found it too!"

Nora screamed softly, but it was a sound of ultimate pleasure as the two men encased within her body gently rubbed against her G-spot. She began to climax, and the waves of the most incredible pleasure she had ever experienced rolled over her again and again and again. She could barely breathe. She was afire, and every inch of her felt more alive than she had ever felt before in her life. Nora had never known so intense a sensation. She didn't know if she could stand it another minute. "Stop!" she cried to them, but they didn't.

"Not yet, baby," Rolf husked in her ear.

"Kyle!" Her voice was pleading.

"Just a moment more, Nora," he half sobbed.

"You're killing me!" she gasped.

"Now!" Kyle said fiercely.

And as another wave slammed into her she felt both men coming in hard spurts inside her body. "Ohhh, God!" she moaned as they both carefully withdrew from her, rolling onto either side of her. "That was . . ." She found herself at a loss for words.

Both men laughed weakly.

"Yes, it was," Kyle agreed.

They dozed for some time, regaining their strength, and then when they could stand they adjourned to the bathroom, washing each other in the glass shower that was more than big enough for them all. They climbed into the bathing pool and played like kids, splashing water, and reigniting their passions once again. They lay together on the marble floor by the pool. Rolf thrust his thick dick into Nora over and over again as Kyle knelt over her chest while Nora sucked his big cock until they all came again. They reentered the pool to wash off.

Coming out, Nora said to her lovers, "We'll do something a little different now. I've always wanted to see a guy sucking another guy's dick. And the one getting sucked gets to lick my pussy until we all come again."

"You are full of it tonight," Kyle noted. "I'm not bi, however."

"I am," Rolf said.

"Then that settles it," Nora responded. "On your back, Kyle, my darling. You're going to lick me while Rolfie sucks that big beautiful cock of yours, and I watch to see if he enjoys you or me more." And before Kyle could protest, she was pulling him down, and plunking her cunt over his face. His tongue immediately began to rummage between her labia. "Ohh!" Nora exclaimed, feeling a quick burst of excitement, but her eyes were now on Rolf, sucking Kyle's penis eagerly. Perhaps a bit too eagerly, she thought. "If you make him come, Rolfie, I will take a big strap to your round tight ass, darling. I want all of Kyle's jism for myself."

Rolf looked up, and nodded faintly. His blue eyes were glazed, and his lips were working furiously on the peg of flesh in his mouth.

Kyle's lips and tongue were making her juices begin to boil.

Nora couldn't wait to have him inside her again. She was going to send Rolf away when they were done. She didn't like how eager he was for Kyle's cock. Kyle belonged to her. She could see that Kyle's dick was very hard now. "Stop, Rolf!" she commanded her blond lover, and he obeyed. Nora switched positions, and encased Kyle within her hot body.

"Suck me off, Nora, please," Rolf begged, and she could see he was hard too.

She nodded, and he was standing over Kyle, his penis pushing into her mouth. She sucked on him a few times, and he let his load loose. She swallowed the salty, oily substance eagerly. She had developed a strong taste for cum. And when his dick was flaccid again she said, "Go away now, Rolfie. I won't need you again, this evening."

Obediently he walked out.

Still encased within her, Kyle rolled her over onto her back, and began to fuck her hard. "You can be such a bitch!" he groaned, thrusting, withdrawing, thrusting, withdrawing, thrusting, until they both climaxed.

"I know," Nora admitted. She was happy. Happier than she had ever been in all her life. She almost hoped her plan against her husband didn't work, and she could stay here forever experiencing mindless sexual ecstasy. And just how long had she been here? The view outside of her apartment terrace was always night. She had woken up once after several hours, and nothing had changed at all. It made her just the slightest bit uneasy. Well, Carla would tell her when they met in her fantasy. She wondered, however, exactly how she could appear in her friend's world, but she supposed they would tell her.

"Will you come with me to Carla's fantasy when she calls?" she asked Kyle after their last bout of pleasure.

"Do you want me to, Nora?" He was surprised, but pleased.

"She plays in a pirate's world. Yes, I think I should like a little strong male backup, darling."

"Then I'll come," he agreed.

"How will I know when she wants me, and how will I get there?" Nora wondered aloud, her brow concentrated in thought.

"I haven't the faintest idea," he said. "My purpose is to serve you, Nora. The only problem is that I seem to want more than that."

"What do you want?" she asked, her fingers playing with the nape of his neck.

"Is the sex enough for you, Red Rover? Is that all you really want?" he said softly, and his eyes suddenly met hers.

"What else is there, darling?" Nora replied.

"Don't you want to be loved?"

"You love me very nicely," she laughed lightly.

"No, damnit!" He was suddenly pinioning her, his hands imprisoning her wrists on either side of her head. "Not make love, and you know I didn't mean make love. Love! As in emotionally attached. Nora, you're all alone. Don't you want to be loved? Do you even know what love is?"

"I thought I did once, but obviously I didn't," she told him.

"I love you!" he said almost desperately.

"You do?" She sounded surprised. "Why?"

"There is no real rhyme or reason to love, Red. It happens. From the moment I first saw you, I wanted more from you than just sex," Kyle said. His green eyes were warm as he looked into her face.

"As I recall," Nora reminded him, "when we first met you couldn't keep your hands off of my tits. Did you love them first?"

"You don't trust men, do you?" he sighed.

"Why should I?" she countered.

"After Jeff, I guess you shouldn't, but what about all your friends on Ansley Court? Don't they love their husbands?" Kyle demanded.

"Yes, I think they do," Nora admitted. "I ask myself, what was wrong with me that Jeff could not love me till death do us part? And you know what? There's nothing wrong with me, Kyle. What was wrong was Jeff. I may be good at a lot of things, but I'm obviously not a very good judge of men. He's hurt me, Kyle. I did everything I was supposed to do, and frankly more, but he still didn't love me. But I was too dumb to understand it. I know now that he picked me as his wife because I was the right kind of girl. The kind of a girl a man like him was supposed to marry. I did everything I should, but it still wasn't enough. And our sex life? Only on my back. Eyes shut tight because he didn't want me to look at him. No foreplay. Just hump, hump, hump until he was done. Then he would roll off of me. We would shower and go to bed. The second I got pregnant he wouldn't touch me. And when I had my children it was several months after their births before he could bring himself to have sex with me again. Finally our sex life ceased entirely. When I asked why, Jeff just glared at me and made some remark about inappropriate questions."

"What a fool," Kyle told her, kissing her mouth softly. "He had no idea, did he, about the passion boiling inside of you?"

"He would have been shocked if he did," Nora laughed bitterly.

"I love you," Kyle repeated, kissing her again.

"You want me," Nora responded.

"I have had you. Many times. In many ways. And in an astounding variety of positions, my darling Red. I could almost wish it wasn't so, but I do love you. But you will break my heart to revenge yourself for being hurt, I'm afraid." He rolled onto his back again.

"Will you leave me?" She struggled to keep her voice strong.

"No," he replied bleakly.

"Why not?" His response had reassured her.

"Because I love you," he said simply.

"You're a figment of my imagination brought to life by whatever it is that created The Channel and keeps it going," Nora said cruelly. "I could discard you. I could change you into a brute whose only pleasure is in pain!" she threatened him.

"Yes, you could, but then I wouldn't be the kind of man you really want, or need, Nora. You don't want that kind of man. You want a strong, sensitive man who will love you, my darling."

"I don't need to be taken care of," Nora snapped. "Been there. Did that!"

"No, you don't need a keeper," he agreed. "You need someone to love you as well as make love to you. That's the man I am."

"I have a husband who has screwed practically everything with a pulse, Kyle. Now it's my turn! I only wish he knew," Nora responded angrily.

"Yeah, like that's really going to make you feel better," Kyle said tightly. "And any time you want to, baby, we can invade his dreams and show him how I can fuck you until you are screaming with pleasure. But I wouldn't advise it. He might want you back. Do you want him back?"

"Never! The bastard betrayed me! Made a fool of me! If I could revenge myself in some way on him, I would, Kyle. I swear I would! I hate him for what he's done to me! To our children!" And suddenly Nora began to cry. She wept bitterly in great gulping sobs for several long minutes, unable to stop.

Kyle wrapped his arms about her tightly, holding her against his broad chest, his eyes closed as he experienced her pain for himself. He was the man she really desired for herself even if she hadn't yet reached the realization of that truth yet. She would. His big hand soothed her, stroking her red hair as her sobs began to ease and then fade away. Finally he tipped her face up to him, and started to lick away the tears staining her visage.

"Don't look at me," she hiccuped. "I look awful when I cry."

"You look beautiful, Red. You always look beautiful to me," he told her.

"Shut up! You're going to make me cry again," Nora muttered.

"I would never make you cry, Red," he promised her. "I just want to love you."

"I'm so afraid," she whispered at him.

"Of what?" he gently probed.

"I'm not sure I know how to love, and if I did love you, and you found someone else, I don't think I could bear it, Kyle." Her eyelashes were all spiky from her tears.

"Remember, darling, that I'm your fantasy," he reminded her.

"But it all seems so real to me, Kyle. I don't know how Mr. Nicholas does it, but The Channel has become reality for me," Nora admitted. "If I admit to loving you, you'll get bored with me, and do what Jeff did. You'll look for other women, and leave me."

"I will never leave you as long as you want me, Nora. I swear it!" he said. "I belong to you, Red. I'm yours!"

Before they could pursue the subject further, the telephone rang. Nora picked up the handset. "Hello?"

"This is the concierge, Mrs. Buckley. You have been invited to join another fantasy this evening. You will find the appropriate costumes in your closet. When you're ready just step into the elevator, and push the red button. You can return to your own fantasy by the same means when you wish to return," the faceless voice said.

"I'd like to take Kyle with me," Nora said.

"Of course, Mrs. Buckley. There is a costume for him as well. Enjoy your evening," the concierge said, and hung up.

"Carla's invited me into her fantasy tonight," Nora told him. "You can come too. According to the concierge, appropriate costumes are in the closet." She grinned. The sadness was now gone from her face. "Shall we look?" She got off of the bed and, walking across the room, opened the closet door.

The two costumes had been set on the rod, directly in the center of the closet. For Nora there was a short, ragged-edged black skirt, a red sash, and a low-cut, short-sleeved white blouse. A drawstring bag hung from the hanger with the blouse. Nora pulled the costume out, laid it on the bed, and undoing the bag, dumped its contents in the center of the bed. There were several bangle bracelets, and a pair of large gold hoop earrings. She smiled. Right out of an old Errol Flynn swashbuckler movie. She drew the other costume out, and almost laughed. It consisted of a loincloth, a beautiful gold dog collar studded with pearls and colored gemstones and lined with lamb's wool, and finally a red leather leash.

"Oh, my," Nora said, and she giggled.

"Your friend lacks subtlety," Kyle said, but he was grinning.

"Quick shower," Nora said, "and then off to Pirate World, Mr. Gorgeous."

"You go first," he said.

She cocked her head to one side questioningly.

"If I get in that shower with you, Nora, you know what's going to happen," Kyle said. "I can never get enough of you, Red."

She nodded. "Haven't you had enough this evening?"

"Nope," he told her with a grin.

Nora didn't question him any further. She pinned her long red hair up, and showered alone. When she had finished she came back into the bedroom to dress while he saw to his ablutions. No bra, she thought. Pirate wenches didn't have bras. She pulled the white peasant-style blouse on over her head. The scooped neck was very low-cut, and her tits were practically spilling out of the garment. She took the ragged black skirt and drew it on. It was barely thigh high, but it did cover the places it should cover. Just. A thong was the only kind of underpants she could wear, and she hated thongs. So, no underpants. She picked up the red silk sash and wrapped it about her waist several times, leaving enough of the cloth hanging to give her a dashing look. She slipped the bangles on both of her arms, and affixed the gold hoops into her ears. She was surprised there were no shoes, but The Channel did everything right, so she wasn't concerned.

"Well, that's certainly a come-and-fuck-me-outfit," Kyle growled, coming from the bathroom. Then he grinned. "I like it." He slid his hand beneath her skirt, chuckling.

"Keep away," she warned him, slapping at his big warm hand. Then she sat down at her dressing table and brushed out her hair.

"Put it in a single braid," he said. "It's apt to get rough in your friend's world. You don't need hair in your face obscuring your vision."

"You do it," Nora said. "It'll be easier." She sat quietly as he plaited her hair into a long thick braid, slipping a small elastic band on the end of the hair. "You better hurry and dress, Mr. Gorgeous."

He slipped the loincloth on. It was made of soft, almost leatherlike fabric. The front and back pieces were held together by a thin, delicate chain that lay against his narrow hips. He held out the gold collar to her. "You do this," he said low.

Nora stood up and, standing in front of him, put the collar about his neck. It clicked shut. "Are you comfortable? It isn't too tight, is it?" She snapped the dog chain to the loop on the collar.

"It fits perfectly," he told her, and pulled her against him. His mouth seared hers in a hot kiss, his tongue pushing into her mouth to tease her tongue. When he let her go he said softly, "Remember that I love you, Red, whatever you may think about it."

They walked to the elevator, and when the doors opened up, they stepped in together. The chain from his collar hung loosely in her hand. They pressed the button, and the elevator doors closed. When they opened a few seconds later and they stepped out, they found themselves in a large cave. But the cave's opening was directly ahead of them, and beyond it were a beach and the blue sea. They stepped out into a moonlit night. A long boat was just being pulled up onto the sand, and there were figures climbing out of it.

"Nora!" Carla's voice was calling to her, and a figure broke away from the group and ran toward her. She was dressed in tight black shorts, a white peasant's blouse, and a bright gold sash encircling a very tiny un-Carla-like waist. There was a red bandanna on her head, beneath which a tangle of black curls poured forth. There was a dagger at her waist, and gold hoops danced from her ears. She enveloped Nora in a bear hug. "I've been scared you were lost forever," she said, hugging her best friend. "I mean, you look so fragile and frail in the nursing home, Nora."

"I heard you earlier," Nora said. "When you told me not to wear my boys out."

"You heard me?" Carla squealed.

"In my head. Softly," Nora explained. "Now tell me what's going on."

"I will, but let's go to the Mermaid for a drink." She turned. "All of you go back to the ship. Except Caleb Snow. I've got business, and Morgan's vessel is in the harbor. The last time you met up with his crew, it cost me a fortune to get the governor to let you out after the fight between you. Good thing the governor is open to a bribe."

"Aww, Captain," one of the men began to whine.

Carla's hand went to her waist, and she pulled a small coiled whip off of her sash. Flicking it out, she smiled. "Are you looking for a taste of my whip, Hawkins?"

"No, Captain," the man said, moving back. "We're going!"

"Swim for it," Carla commanded her men. "Caleb and I will need the boat to get back." And she laughed as her men, grumbling, waded back into the sea. "You can never be soft with them," Carla said, turning back to Nora. "Now, to the Mermaid!"

The inn was directly on the beach. They walked past the palm trees, reaching the Mermaid quickly. As they entered, Carla was greeted by many there. She grinned and waved, calling out to those men she knew. The landlord hurried up to her.

"Captain Raven, 'tis good to see you again! Let me show you to a table!" He began to push a path for them through the crowd. "Here's a nice one by the hearth," he said, glaring at the people who were already sitting there. Seeing Carla, they quickly vacated the space. "What will it be, Captain? Grog? Rum?"

"Rum, four of 'em," Carla said, and the landlord scurried away. Carla turned and looked at Kyle. "My, my, Nora, isn't he nice?" She stood in front of him, and slowly slid her hands up his oiled chest.

"This is Kyle," Nora said dryly.

"I want him," Carla said. "Just for a few minutes." She drew her dagger from her sash, and slipping the point carefully into one of the delicate gold links, she snapped the chain on one side of his loincloth. The loincloth dropped away. "I didn't cut you, did I?" she asked sweetly as she began to fondle his penis, cupping his balls in her palm.

"No," he replied. His eyes never left hers. "Your companion doesn't look too pleased, however, Captain."

Carla turned away for a moment. "This is Caleb Snow, my first mate, Nora. You can play with him if you like while I play with your Kyle." She turned back again to Kyle. "I like it from behind," she said wickedly. "In my cunny, not my arse." She pressed herself against him, murmuring as he opened her shorts and pulled them down.

"Do you?" he drawled, his hand sliding between her legs, and grinned at the heat she was already generating there.

Caleb Snow sat down at the table, pulling Nora into his lap. His hand plunged down into her blouse. He fondled her roughly. "You've got nice tits, lass," he said. He was a huge man. He had dwarfed them all, including Kyle, who she knew stood two inches over six feet. His bare chest was like a barrel, and his arms were muscled and brawny. He had auburn hair and a short auburn beard. His eyes were very blue. Pushing her back, he pulled her blouse open, and began to suck on her breasts as he held her firmly. His other hand moved beneath her skirt to finger her clit.

"You're a bold man," Nora said. The mouth on her nipple was tugging hard. The finger beneath her skirt was beginning to send ripples of excited lust through her body. Carla certainly had a fine fantasy lover. She could feel herself getting creamy.

"Faint heart never won fair maiden," he growled at her, dumping her suddenly from his lap. "On your knees, lass. You know what I'll be wanting, and when I tells you to stop, you stop and we'll go for a little ride."

Nora slipped on her knees beneath his spread legs. She took his cock from his britches, and began to lick at it. When it began to show signs of life she took him into her mouth and sucked as hard on him as he had on her nipples. She heard him sigh, and after a few minutes, during which time he burgeoned to the point that her lips were spread so wide her cheeks began to hurt, he groaned at her to cease, pulling her up. She stared down at his penis. It was huge. She had never seen one so big.

"Come on now, lass, and ride a cock horse," he said with a wicked leer.

"You'll split me open with that dick of yours," Nora said, backing away.

"Nah, I won't," he promised, reaching out to quickly grab her. He lifted the startled woman up over the long, thick hard flesh, and lowered her onto his peg. "Open wide now, lass. Legs about me waist."

She was amazed that he didn't kill her, but the monstrous cock slipped easily into her cunt. She felt him stretching the walls of her vagina, but it didn't hurt at all. And then the head of his penis touched that most sensitive spot, and Nora screamed with her rising pleasure. His hands fit themselves neatly around her waist, and he began to jog her up and down on his length all the while singing the children's nursery rhyme:

Ride a cockhorse to Banbury Cross, to see a fine
lady upon her fine horse.
With rings on her fingers, and bells on her toes,
She will make music wherever she goes.

And he laughed a thunderous rumbling laughter as he plunged his cock up and down within her. "You're making grand music, lass!" he told her. "Lean back, and I'll go deeper."

Half conscious with her pleasure, Nora leaned back, his big hands bracing her. She felt him slide deeper and deeper within her. "Oh, my God!" she moaned, and after a few moments she climaxed as a hot wave of delight swept over her.

"Isn't he good?" Carla's voice was penetrating Nora's brain. "So is your Kyle. After I came, the naughty fellow ran right up my arse hole, and gave me quite another thrill. Caleb is too big to ass fuck me. I always have to get one of the other men to do it. How did your Kyle know that I wanted that?"

"He's very intuitive," Nora said, coming to herself again as Caleb lifted her off his lap. "You are a talented man," she said, and kissed his rough cheek. "Move over!" She sat down next to him and took a deep swig of the mug of rum in front of her. "We must have given the innkeeper quite a show, but I didn't notice. Did you?" She fixed her blouse, pulling it back up again and tying the strings.

"I was bent over the table," Carla said. "I never saw a thing," she laughed.

"Well," Nora replied, "now that we've all been properly introduced, let our lads recover, and you tell me what is happening in the other reality. How long have I been gone? How are the kids? Is Jeff beginning to cave?"

"The kids and your mom are fine, but I'm having a helluva time keeping them from a vigil at your bedside. You're at Shorecrest now. You've been gone two months. It's already the end of February."

"Time seems to have no meaning here," Nora remarked. "Jeff?"

"Hard as nails," Carla responded. "He and Heidi are coming to the house on the weekends. He had all your clothing packed up and put in the cellar because they're in the master bedroom."

"He's moved into my house with his girlfriend?" Nora was astounded.

"Just the weekends," Carla assured her. "He says he doesn't want to leave the house untenanted all winter. He's had Kramer go back into court to try and get the judge to let him sell the house come spring as he intended. Kramer told Rick that your forty percent will be put in the bank for you. Rick has spoken to the judge, and she isn't happy with the suggestion, but she also knows Jeff is on the hook for the co-op. Rick says she is sympathetic to you, but she also plays fair. Nora, if you stay here much longer, your health insurance is going to run out for the nursing home. They will have to draw on the moneys you get from the house. You've got to do something now! Oh, yeah, and Heidi isn't happy at all. I ran into her at the wine shop the other day."

Nora was silent for a long few moments, and then she said, "How unhappy is she?"

"I think she's really in love with Jeff, though why I can't imagine. But he's a lot older than she is, and this divorce is starting to stress him now too."

"Then why won't he give in?" Nora said.

"If the judge gives him the go-ahead, you've lost," Carla replied.

"Tell me about Heidi, Carla. What did she say to you? How did she act? And why did she even talk to you?" Nora wondered.

"I think she talked to me because I was a friendly face. I saw her wandering around the wine store, and she looked kinda beat. Our eyes met, and I couldn't help myself. I smiled at her. The next thing I knew she was yakking at me. I listened, and nodded a lot."

"What did she say?" Nora asked, and slapped Caleb Snow's hand off her thigh.

"Oh, how she hates to come out every weekend when everything is so exciting in the city in the winter. And Jeff goes to bed so early out here. She's stuck in the den watching television all night. She is sooooo bored. And he forgets his Viagra every weekend, and she is beginning to think it's deliberate." Carla giggled. "Jeff taking Viagra! It boggles the mind, doesn't it?"

"If she's bored, you should introduce her to The Channel, Carla," Nora said softly.

"Are you crazy?" Carla almost shouted.

"No, I'm not. Hear me out. It isn't Jeff who's beginning to crack over this divorce. It's Heidi. You know I don't care if he marries her or not. I just want my house. But now if the judge rules in his favor regarding the sale, I could lose the house. He's not caving, but Heidi is. That's why he's had Kramer go to the judge. Get Rick to ask the judge to wait another month for me to show signs of recovery. Have Rick say if I haven't woken up by then, he'll agree to the sale of the house as my caretaker.

"Heidi will have to wait another month. The young aren't good at waiting. They always want everything now. Tell Heidi that since she's so bored you'll let her in on a little secret, but Jeff can't know. Explain to her that The Channel is a place where all her fantasies can come true. Tell her you know she won't believe you, but to call Suburban Cable and order it when Jeff goes to bed. Warn her, though, that if Jeff is around, it won't work. And then tell her that if she tries it and doesn't like it, you'll work on Rick to agree to sell the house sooner. That's the bait that will hook our little fish."

"Why do you want her to know about The Channel?" Carla asked, curious.

"Because like the rest of us she'll have great sex here, and when she does, do you really believe she'll want to stay with Jeff? Why would she need him then?" Nora answered her best friend.

"You could be right, but what if you aren't?" Carla played devil's advocate.

"Then I lose," Nora said, "but I have to give it my best shot, Carla. I don't want my kids coming home to some dinky one-bedroom apartment, if I can even afford that. I don't want to leave Egret Pointe. It's my home."

"Okay, I'll do it," Carla said. "It just might work. Jeff hasn't looked too good of late. He's a little paunchy, and you know he never was paunchy. And he's got dark circles under his eyes too. You're getting to him, alright. He just won't give in. Yeah, on reflection I think Heidi is the weak link in this situation. It'll be a few days, though. It's just Wednesday night."

"I've waited this long," Nora said. "I can wait a little while longer."

CHAPTER NINE

"No way!" Heidi Millar said.

"Way!" Carla Johnson told her.

They were standing in a corner of the Egret Pointe Wine Shoppe. All around them were wine-racked shelves holding bottles of everything from Long Island, upstate New York, and California vintages to wines from Chile, Australia, and Germany, as well as the finest French Burgundies, Bordeaux, Merlots, and Chardonnays available. There was a popular California table wine known locally as Two-Buck Chuck, and an Opici California Barbarone that retailed for fifteen dollars a gallon jug. There was something for everyone at the Egret Pointe Wine Shoppe.

"It's not possible," the younger woman said. "You must be hallucinating. What the hell do you people smoke out here?" Her blond hair was darker than it had been in June. She obviously wasn't keeping it up for whatever reason.

"Look, I don't pretend to understand it," Carla said low. "All I know is that it works. The Channel offers you whatever fantasy you want. Just think about it, turn on the television, and it's there. You're there. I am not nuts, and this is the best-kept secret among the women here. We can't all be hallucinating, and incidentally I don't smoke anything. Never started."

Heidi's grey eyes were thoughtful, curious. "What's your fantasy?" she murmured.

"I'm Captain Raven, the pirate queen," Carla responded.

Heidi snickered. She couldn't help it. "You're kidding, right?"

Carla smiled a slow, wicked smile. "Darling," she said, "my first mate has a fourteen-inch dick that's two and a half inches in circumference, and hits my G-spot seven times out of ten. No, I'm not kidding."

"Fourteen inches?" Heidi's voice was awed. "You measured?"

"Yep," Carla drawled. "Look, so you're not into pirate fantasies. I've got one friend who does the penthouse, hot lover, and hot masseur thing. She enjoys threesomes. Another who puts herself in the forefront of carving out the nation of Israel. She made her partner a younger version of her husband. She's not a woman who would ever think of another man. One gal I know likes to do other women. She wouldn't do it in her own reality. The Channel lets you be anything you want to be, and do anything you want to do. Don't you have a fantasy you want to live out? You can't be just about marrying Jeff Buckley, honey. There must be something naughty or wonderful that you want to do, and without him. That's the great thing about The Channel, and that's why no men are aware of it. It's all about women and their desires, their needs. Sort of like a grown-up tree house club. And No Boys Allowed. Except the ones we create in our imaginations."

"And you get it by just calling the cable company and asking for it?" Heidi's look was thoughtful.

"Yeah," Carla said. Easy, now. She's hooked. Reel her in slowly.

"Does it show up on the cable bill? Jeff goes over everything," Heidi explained.

"Shows up as a movie," Carla told her.

"You've been pulling my leg, right?" Heidi said suddenly. "I mean you're Nora's best friend, Jeff says. This is a joke, right? Why would you be nice to me?"

"Listen, honey," Carla told the girl, "no one is mad at you. Jeff and Nora haven't had a marriage in years. One day one of them was going to decide it was divorce time. None of us ever really liked Jeff. We put up with him for Nora's sake on the rare occasions he showed up. Yeah, Nora's my best friend. I don't deny it. But even she doesn't hold you responsible for what's happened, although you really should have kept your mouth shut at J. J.'s graduation party, but that's in the past.

"You're stuck out here every weekend until Jeff puts the house on the market. You're bored. Jeff bring his Viagra this time?" she queried, and wisely refrained from grinning when Heidi shook her head in the negative. "So he's probably going to hit the sack early again tonight. And there you are watching *The District*. Rick will be snoozing early too. Men are like bears in winter. They like to hibernate. As for me, I'll be downstairs in my sewing and crafts room in the cellar. Or at least my body will. The body I possess in The Channel will be getting its little self fucked to pieces by that nice fourteen-inch dick that Caleb Snow possesses, and wields so skillfully."

"I still think you're kidding," Heidi said, but she sounded less convinced than she had earlier.

"Look, call the cable company, and ask for The Channel. If I'm joking, they won't know what you're talking about," Carla said. "But if they tell you you've got it from eight p.m. on, then you know I'm not joking."

"It could be something totally different than you say it is. Pets. Or decorating." Heidi shifted her weight nervously.

"And it could be just what I've told you, which it is. If it isn't, and you're unhappy, I'll talk to Rick about letting Jeff put the house on the market sooner. That's fair, isn't it?" Carla gave her companion a little smile.

"I could say I got it and didn't like it, and you'd never know," Heidi replied.

"I don't believe you'd do that," Carla responded. "I think you'd play fair."

Heidi nodded. "Yes, I would. Besides, I really am curious to see if this channel of yours exists."

"What's your fantasy?" Carla probed gently, casually reaching for a bottle of red wine from Long Island.

"I had a boyfriend in college, and we tried erotic-asphyxiation fucking. It was incredible! I've never had an orgasm like that before or after. Jeff isn't into stuff like that," Heidi said. "I love him, but geez, it's tough to get him to be creative in the sack."

The leopard does not change his spots, Carla thought to herself. "So, there's your chance. The Channel."

"Can I get a guy with a fourteen-inch dick too?" Heidi wondered.

"Just think about it, and he'll be there," Carla assured her.

"How do I get from here to there once I get The Channel?" Heidi asked.

"Just touch the screen when you see your fantasy coming up. You'll figure it out, honey. Let me know how you liked it. I gotta go now. Pizza night, and my pie should be waiting at Tony's."

"What goes with Chinese takeout?" Heidi wondered.

"I'd try a domestic Chardonnay or white zinfandel," Carla suggested. "See ya around, honey." And she was quickly gone to pay for her wine and pick up her pizza.

Heidi Millar purchased the Chardonnay. Jeff didn't like pink wine, although she did prefer a zinfandel herself. She picked up the takeout at Wo Fat's and drove back to Ansley Court. Was Carla Johnson kidding her? How was such a thing as this channel possible? Still, would it hurt to try it? If it existed. And if it didn't, who was going to know? She just would say she didn't do it. Fourteen inches of meat, she thought. Jeff had been so preoccupied lately with the divorce, the house, and how the whole thing was appearing to the partners and the clients that he had really neglected her. They used to have sex every night. Now she was lucky if she could get him to get it up twice a week. She needed a good fuck, and she knew damned well she wasn't going to get it from Jeff tonight, or tomorrow night after they had driven back to the city, or any night soon. So why not try The Channel and hope it really did exist? Fourteen inches. Two and a half inches in circumference. A cock like that shoved up her would really feel good right now. She wanted some hot sex. And she wanted it rough. Thinking about her college boyfriend's hands about her neck squeezing, about her coming and coming, almost made Heidi drive off the road.

"Where have you been?" Jeff demanded in surly tones when she got to the house.

"Out picking us up a bottle of wine," she answered, going into the kitchen and setting down the bags. She could smell the Chinese, and her stomach rumbled in anticipation.

"How long does it take to pick out a bottle of wine in this town?" he demanded.

"Hey, the wine shop here is cool. It's got everything. I found that nice Australian white you like," she wheedled him. She held up the bottle as if it were a trophy, and gave him a quick kiss. "Now stop being so grumpy," she told him.

"What's this?" he demanded to know, holding up a narrow box.

Heidi flushed. "It's an e.p.t. test. Relax, I'm not pregnant. I was late, and I got nervous, but I got my period last week. I had it here so I could check this weekend if nothing happened."

"I told you no more kids!" he shouted, and then he slapped her. "Don't I have enough trouble without that? I don't want any more kids."

Stunned, Heidi's hand went to her face. Her eyes filled with tears. "Well, maybe I want a kid. Just one. Your kids hate me, and besides, they're grown."

"No kids," he told her firmly.

"You didn't have to hit me, Jeff," she quavered.

"Baby, I'm sorry." He gave her a quick hug. "It's this damned house! I hate it! I thought having her clothes packed away would do it, but Nora is everywhere in this house. I can't wait to sell the place, and be done with it."

"We don't have to come out here every weekend," Heidi said. "We're missing all the good parties now, you know. And we were invited to the preview of that new show last night. And there are at least two concerts coming up that I wanted to go to, Jeff."

"I can't leave the house alone on a weekend. It's safe during the week, but on the weekends the kids around here run wild," he told her. "There's nothing else for them to do but break into empty houses, drink the liquor, and trash the place. No, until I sell it, we're coming out on the weekends. Now, could we eat? I'm beat, and I want to go to bed. Jesus, that new toothpaste account is giving me fits. The music for the commercial just isn't right yet, and I can't figure it out."

"You will," Heidi soothed him as she filled their plates with the Chinese takeout. Carla Johnson had damned well better not be kidding about this channel thing. Jeff was beginning to look less and less like Prince Charming. Maybe after she'd had a good fuck she'd feel better. After all he was a partner, and he had bought the co-op, even if she was paying the bridge loan herself. She had made him put the co-op in her name. He really did love her. Well, as much as Jeff could love anything, but then, they made a great team. Creatively they were terrific together. And he usually looked good on her arm. Eye candy, she thought, smiling to herself. Until recently. The divorce was really wearing him out.

When they had finished dinner, Heidi put their dishes in the dishwasher, realizing that it was now full after three weekends. Pouring soap into the soap container, she turned it on. She'd unload it next weekend when they ran out of dishes. Housekeeping was not her forte. It never had been. But judging from Nora Buckley's well-kept, well-stocked kitchen, she was a Martha Stewart. I'll bet she cooks well too, Heidi thought. Jeff didn't seem to mind that Heidi didn't cook. She defrosted, and she reheated, and she ordered out, but cook? Who had time?

"Any dessert?" he asked.

"Fortune and almond cookies," Heidi said.

"Give me two almond cookies, and I'll finish the wine," he told her, pouring the remainder of it into his glass. "I'm going to bed. Sorry to leave you alone, baby, but I know you like *The District*." He put an arm about Heidi and gave her a kiss. "Night."

Heidi finished cleaning up, and then she went upstairs to shower. By the time she was in the black silk nightgown that looked as if it had been painted on her, Jeff was already snoring. Picking up the empty wineglass, she returned downstairs. Going into the den, she picked up the handset of the telephone. For a long moment she hesitated, and then she realized she didn't know the cable company's number. Looking around, she found the cable listing and dialed the number. She asked for The Channel, and other than her slight start when the operator called her Mrs. Buckley, it all went smoothly. Channel sixty-nine. Well, that was subtle, wasn't it? It was after eight o'clock. She turned on the television. The screen was dark, and then it lightened to show her a bedroom, dimly lit, with a large round bed in the center of it. Not at all hesitant, Heidi put her hand on the screen, and to both her surprise and delight, she found herself in that bedroom. Upon closer examination she saw the sheets were red satin. There was a mirrored ceiling above the bed. Heidi giggled. She had always imagined a room like this. There was something a little nasty, a little smutty, and very sordid about a room with a king-sized round bed with a mirror above it and red satin sheets.

"Well, about time you showed up, Heidi," a rough male voice said, and he came from the shadows of the room. He was at least six feet six inches tall with broad shoulders and a wide chest. But his waist was narrow, as were his hips. "I'm Brad and I'm fourteen inches of hot meat." Reaching out, he pulled her into his arms. His hand ripped the front of her nightgown down, and he squeezed her breasts. "Nice, baby. Very nice."

"Hey, easy, big boy," Heidi said. "This is real silk not Lycra."

"Come on, baby, you like to be treated rough, and I know it," he replied, pulling her tightly against him. One hand was around her waist. The other was stroking her butt. "I know what you want," he murmured in her ear, "and I can give it to you. You know I can, don't you, Heidi? In a few minutes I'm going to spread your nice white body on those bloodred sheets. You're going to open real wide for me, aren't you, baby?"

Heidi could feel her excitement rising. Her heart was beating faster, and her clit was beginning to tingle just listening to him. She was already wet. "Yes," she whispered in his ear, and her tongue began to lick it.

"And when I get you like that, baby, I'm going to shove myself right up you and let you feel what a real man feels like. Not like that old-enough-to-be-your-daddy lover you've got, but a real man. You need a real man, baby, doncha?" His hand pushed between her legs, and he thrust three fingers into her vagina, moving them back and forth until she was moaning with undisguised lust. He laughed. "Oh, baby, you are hot to trot tonight, aren't you? It's your first visit to The Channel, and we're going to make it a memorable visit, baby." He withdrew his fingers from her cunt, and shoved them into her mouth. "That's the taste of hot pussy," he told her. "Suck 'em clean now."

Heidi sucked the big fingers, almost swooning with her excitement. He was wearing a black thong, and she could see the great big wad his dick made in the silky fabric. His dirty talk was so naughty, and she loved it. She looked up at him, fingers still in her mouth, and then she slowly pulled his fingers out from between her lips and said, "I'm a bad girl, Brad. What do you do to a bad girl? Huh, Brad? Huh?"

A grin lit his face. "Bad girls get spanked, baby." He held up his hand. "They get spanked with this."

"I'm not afraid of that old hand," she taunted him. Then her voice grew fearful. "But don't take the strap to me, Brad! Please don't!" Her lower lip quivered.

"So, you little bitch, you're not afraid of my hand," he roared. "Then it's the strap for you, girl." It appeared magically in his hand, a broad piece of leather at least six inches in width, the ends split into narrow strips that had been knotted. "Get over there!" he said, pointing to a high upholstered bench. He half dragged her across the room, threw her across the bench roughly, and imprisoned her wrists in two manacles attached to the bench's front legs.

"Ohh, Brad!" Heidi cried, but her eyes were bright with her desire.

"I'll teach you to defy me, you little bitch," he growled, and brought the strap down on her helpless buttocks.

She was almost ashamed at how much she was enjoying this. It was a part of her nature she had always, except on one or two occasions, kept hidden from public scrutiny. But here in The Channel she was able to live out her wildest desires. She squealed and pleaded as he brought the strap down again and again. The tiny knotted strips burned as they bit into her flesh. Some of them even curved under to sting her pussy. Finally she cried out that she would always be good, and he stopped. But then she felt his hands holding her steady, and his big dick pushing slowly into her vagina from the rear. Heidi squealed again, and then came, unable to help herself. But it was just a small climax.

Laughing, Brad released her from the manacles and walked her to the bed, his hand firmly gripping the back of her neck. "You're a little liar," he said. "You don't know how to be good, do you, Heidi? Say it! Say, 'I'm a liar.' "

"No," she said. "I won't!"

He slapped her hard. "Say it!"

"No!" He slapped her again, and this time her head snapped back. "No!"

His hand wrapped about her hair, and he yanked her head back as he began slapping her breasts hard, pinching the nipples. "Say it!"

"No!"

"Say 'I'm a liar,' baby." He reached down, and pinched her clit hard.

"I'm a liar!" she shrieked. God! This was wonderful. She could hardly wait for what was coming next. By some damned magic she didn't understand, he knew exactly what she wanted. "I want to be fucked," she moaned.

"I know," he said, "but first you're going to lick my balls. I like having my balls licked by a pretty girl. And if I like how you do it, then I'll give you what you want, baby. That's fair, isn't it?"

"If this is my fantasy, shouldn't I be in charge?" Heidi demanded to know.

"You don't want to be the boss, baby," Brad mocked her. "Out there in that other world you want to be the boss, but not here. This is where you're going to come so you can be the slave, be mastered, 'cause you need that, Heidi, and you want it. Then you can go back into your reality, and be a perfect bitch and get what you want there, which is power. You went after Jeff Buckley because you thought he could give you the power you sought. He was the perfect target with his big ego and libidinous nature, but you'll never be satisfied with him. If you marry him, he'll keep you on a tight leash like he has kept Nora. I'm the lover you've always wanted, Heidi. I'm in charge here. Do what I told you, you little bitch!" He sprawled on the red satin sheets, his long legs spread wide. "Get going, or I'll send you back right now."

Heidi believed him. She scrambled between his legs, reaching for his penis.

"Don't touch it," he told her. "I'll hold it up for you. You just lick."

"Please," she begged him, "I want to suck it! I want to suck it bad, Brad."

"Lick, bitch, and if I like the way you do it, I'll give you a little taste," he commanded.

She crawled to where his balls, encased in a large hairy sac, lay pendulous between his legs. She licked at him, tentatively at first, and then with more assurance. She could feel the twin balls beneath the fleshy sac rolling around beneath her tongue. She took the sac in her mouth, pushing it about with her tongue. He groaned.

"That's nice, baby, that's nice," he praised her. "Okay, you can suck my dick for a minute or two," he rewarded her.

Carefully she released his balls from her mouth and eagerly replaced them with his engorged penis, moaning with pleasure as he filled her mouth and pushed down into her throat. She was in heaven. But for a little poke he hadn't even really fucked her yet, and it was still the best sex she had ever had. But she needed it all tonight. It had been so long since she had really been satisfied.

Jeff needed Viagara most nights to get it up. She really had to work to keep him going. And he wasn't sexually adventurous at all. She had thought he would be the perfect husband for her. Rich. Powerful. And able to advance her career. It was a compromise she had thought she could make, but now that she had found The Channel she wasn't certain. She was a helluva lot smarter than Jeff, and most of the pitches he'd been taking credit for in the last year were hers. He was running dry creatively. Heidi suddenly realized that she didn't need Jeff Buckley to get ahead. And she didn't need to go down on old men anymore. She knew she was clever enough to work the senior partners. Her mind flew back to Brad.

He was like iron in her mouth. She released him. "I want to be fucked," she said. "Now, Brad! And you know how I want it, don't you? I want it to be the best I've ever had. The absolute best, Brad. Let's use that big piece of meat like it was meant to be used." Heidi lay back, and spread herself open to him.

His face was impassive. He slid an overstuffed bolster beneath her hips to raise her up so he could get in as deep as possible.

"Tie my hands," she said suddenly to him. "Let's make it really exciting."

He took his black silk thong and bound her wrists over her head. "Not too tight?"

"Just right," she told him.

He crawled between her milky thighs, and began to lick her most intimate flesh. His fleshy tongue probed, and pushed. He flicked it back and forth over her clitoris, giving her several small clitoral orgasms. Finally he decided she was wet enough, and he slid between her legs, guiding himself with one hand, balancing on the other. His penis pushed slowly and carefully into her vagina. Inch by inch he moved himself up her love passage, driving deeper and deeper into the hot maw of her.

"Oh! My! God!" Heidi groaned as his huge cock filled her. She could feel herself stretching to accommodate him. "Oh! My! God!" He was going to tear her apart, and he kept plunging deeper, and deeper. This was the emperor of all penises. King Penis. And it was all hers. "Ohhhh!" He was moving on her. Moving back and forth. Faster and faster and faster. He was like a damned machine! It was incredible, but it could be better. "Do it!" Heidi told him. "Do it now! Ahhh!" He had hit her G-spot. "Now! Now!" she insisted.

"Very well, Heidi, my naughty bitch, you shall have your heart's desire," Brad said as he sat atop her, his cock buried deep within her fevered body. He looked down at her. Her eyes were closed with anticipation of the bliss to come. His big hands fastened about her slender throat, and slowly he began to squeeze as he continued to fuck her. His fingers pressed down slowly, letting her experience pleasure such as she had known only once before. Her mouth opened in a silent scream. Her face glowed with unimaginable, incredible passion. And when he saw that she had reached the apex of the experience, he climaxed in a fierce rush.

Heidi was unconscious, and his finger marks were visible around her slender neck. Brad rolled off of her and lay on his back breathing heavily. When he had recovered, he leaned over and untied her hands. She opened her eyes and looked up at him, confused at first, and then remembering.

"That was absolutely the best sex I have ever had," she whispered, her voice a little raspy. "How the hell is this all possible?"

"Do you really care?" he responded. "You just want a big cock, and I've got one. And you need a man who knows how to handle you, baby. I do." He got up, and pulled the black thong on. "I'm going now," he told her.

"But I don't want you to," Heidi whined at him. "I want more cock!"

Reaching out, he wrapped his big hand in her blond hair and yanked her up. "What did I tell you, baby?" He slapped her hard, and her head snapped back. "What did I tell you?" He slapped her again, and glared down into her face.

"You said I need to be mastered," Heidi whimpered.

"And?" His hand tightened in her hair.

"You said I'm the slave here," Heidi half sobbed. He was hurting her, and she found she was aroused by it.

The hand in her hair loosened, and he pulled her into his arms now, giving her a quick kiss of approval, caressing her butt softly. "That's right, baby. I'm the master. And as long as you understand that, we're going to do just fine." He let her go and walked toward the elevator door.

"Brad?"

"Yeah, baby?" The doors opened.

"You'll come back?" Heidi quavered. She couldn't bear it if he didn't come back.

"I'll be here when you come, baby," he told her. He stepped into the elevator.

"Wait! How do I get back?" she asked.

"You're on your way now," he told her as the doors closed.

And Heidi felt herself growing dizzy, and the sensation of falling. Her eyes closed just briefly, and then flew open. She was back in the den of the house in her chair. There was a test pattern on the television. Heidi clicked the channel changer off and got up. My God, she thought, her vagina felt sore as if it had been stretched by something very big. And her neck. She rubbed it. Then the realization began to set in. The Channel was real. Very, very real! Her heart raced with her excitement. I've got to go to bed, she thought silently. This can't be, and once I've had a good sleep it will all fall into place.

In the bedroom Jeff was snoring, but as her weight touched the bed, he awoke and rolled over. "You just coming to bed?" he demanded.

"I fell asleep in front of the television," she lied.

He began to fondle her breasts. "I'm horny," he said. "Let's do it." He pushed her nightgown up and rolled on top of her. He slept naked.

"Jeff!" Heidi protested. "A little foreplay would be nice."

"You're already wet, babe. I think my Heidi is horny too," he chuckled, and shoved his penis into her. Then he began to fuck her quickly, and within a moment he had come. He pulled out. "That was good," he said.

Heidi jumped up. "Good for who?" she hissed at him. "I sure as hell didn't get anything out of it. Wham! Bam! And no thank-you-ma'am! I am bloody tired of this."

He was on his feet. "If you didn't get anything out of it, it's your fault, not mine," he snarled. "Women say I'm good at what I do." He leered at her.

"Women who want something from you, you mean," she snapped back at him. "How many times have I told you a woman needs a little time. Five pokes and you're out, and you think I have had enough time?" She stormed into the bathroom and slammed the door.

Jeff followed her, and when he found the door locked, he put his shoulder against it and pushed it in. "What the hell has gotten into you, Heidi?" he demanded to know.

"I just realized that I don't need you anymore, Jeff," she said coldly.

"What the hell is that supposed to mean? I'm in love with you. I'm divorcing my wife. I went out on a limb to buy that damned co-op for us."

"You made the down payment with your kids' college money, and I've been paying the bridge loan while your divorce has been stalled," she shouted at him. "And for the record, I don't love you! And I'm not going to marry you, Jeff. And I'm going to Mr. Wickham Junior and tell him whose ideas you've been using for the agency's clients, and who has been writing the copy. And when I'm through I'll have a vice presidency, and you will be yesterday's headline story. Now get out of the bathroom so I can shower. There must be a bus that goes back to the city from this place, and I'm going as soon as I can." She gave him a shove, and then another.

Jeff Buckley's temper exploded. "You conniving little bitch!" he yelled at her, and then he began to hit her again and again.

Heidi screamed. When Brad smacked her around he didn't really hurt her, and she had loved it because Brad was her master now. But Jeff was hurting her. She felt a warm trickle of blood coming from her nose. She screamed again and, pushing past him, ran from the bedroom and down the stairs toward the front door. He was right behind her, roaring his outrage. She fumbled with the locks on the front door even as he grabbed her and swung her around to slap her again. Heidi reached out for the antique vase on the hall table and, gripping it in her fingers, slammed it down on Jeff's head. He stumbled back, dazed, and it gave her just enough time to get the door open. Then she ran across the lawn screaming at the top of her lungs.

Within minutes windows were opening in response to her cries for help. Jeff had regained his equilibrium and was trying to drag her back into the house. Heidi fought him like a tigress, and continued to shriek. Sam Seligmann and Rick Johnson, in robes, came from their houses to separate the combatants. Heidi flung her arms about Dr. Seligmann, sobbing. Sam looked somewhat startled as the girl in the black negligee clung to him.

"Don't let him hurt me again," she pleaded, her gray eyes overflowing with tears. "Please don't let him hurt me again."

"It's alright, my dear," Sam said. "Come with me now," and he led her across the cul-de-sac into his house.

"The bitch!" Jeff said angrily. "The duplicitous little bitch!"

"Trouble in paradise?" Rick said softly.

"Drop dead!" Jeff snapped and, turning, went back to his house.

Rick turned, hiding his smile, and saw Carla hurrying across the lawn in the predawn light to the Seligmanns'. He sighed, and followed after her.

Heidi Millar's face was a disaster. One eye was blacked badly, and her nose was still oozing blood as she held a cloth tightly to it. Rina was clucking sympathetically and trying too soothe the semihysterical girl. She waved her husband and Rick out of the kitchen, where they had brought Heidi.

"Go back to bed, both of you," she said. "Carla and I will help here."

The two men left, and they heard Sam climbing the stairs as the front door closed behind Rick.

"What happened?" Carla said, trying to keep the eagerness from her voice.

"Oh, Carla, it's wonderful!" Heidi said. "And then I came back, and Jeff wanted to, well, you know, and it was terrible the way it always is, and I just lost it. I mean, why should I have to put up with him when I've got The Channel?"

"You told her about The Channel?" Rina said, surprised.

Carla smiled, and nodded. "What happened?" she repeated.

"Well, I told him some home truths about how he was creatively dry, and I had been doing the campaigns his partners thought he was doing, and that I was going to tell them, and get a promotion, and that I didn't need him. Then he started beating me. I thought he was going to kill me. I honestly did."

"You have to press charges," Carla said softly. "You can't let him get away with that kind of violence." Her eyes met Rina's over Heidi's head.

"Yes," Rina agreed. "You really must press charges against him, my dear. I always suspected he was violent with Nora, though she would never admit it, poor woman. And Heidi, Jeff is what in my day was referred to as a tomcat, or a hound dawg. He never met a skirt he didn't lift, or try to lift. He wouldn't have been any more faithful to you than he was to Nora. I think you're well out of this. I'll call the police for you."

Heidi thought a moment. That would really screw Jeff with his partners, wouldn't it? She felt a smile, and then winced because it hurt her face. She sighed dramatically. "I guess I will have to press charges so he doesn't do this to any woman again. Do you think if his wife ever wakes up, she'll want him back?"

"NO!" Both Carla and Rina said with a single voice.

"Would you please call the police for me, Carla?" Heidi said.

"Rina will do it," Carla said. "Tell me what happened last night."

"His name is Brad. He's big. All over. And I'm going back," Heidi said. "I can get it in the city, can't I?"

"Sure can," Carla responded with a smile. Nora was going to be so pleased.

And Nora was pleased. She had imagined someone like Caleb Snow because she had known Carla would mention his attributes to Heidi, and Heidi would want someone like Caleb. And the elevator had opened to reveal Brad. She had given him his instructions. And of course he had obeyed her, but only after he had struck a deal with her of payment for his favor. He was a bisexual, and had seen Rolf in the stud pool of The Channel. He wanted the blond Austrian. Nora had agreed. She knew very well that it wouldn't be long before Heidi was enjoying a threesome with both young men.

The elevator doors to the penthouse opened and Brad stepped out.

"Have you entrapped her?" Nora asked him as he entered her domain. "Did you give her everything she wanted? I do want Heidi happy in The Channel. Will she be back soon?" Her questions came quickly.

Brad nodded. "Yes, ma'am, I gave her just what she wanted," he said with a wicked grin. "She'll be back. I left her begging for more. Now, give me what you promised me."

"Rolf," she called, and the young blond arose from the couch and came across the room. "I want you to go with Brad now. You're his."

"Why?" Rolf asked.

"Because you make Kyle jealous, and I don't want him unhappy. Because Brad has done me a favor, and I'm repaying him." She patted his cheek. "You've been such a good boy, but I don't need you anymore."

Rolf shrugged. His eyes were on the bulge in Brad's thong. "Good-bye, Nora," he said, and without another word he followed Brad into the elevator.

When they had gone Kyle came from the bedroom. "What have you done?" he asked her. "And why did you give Rolf away?"

"Carla introduced Heidi to The Channel. I suspect she won't be so interested in Jeff anymore now that she's seen the kind of sex she can have here. And once she dumps him, the question of my getting my house back becomes a moot point. I considered the type of man Heidi would like, using Caleb as a model. A rough, good-looking guy with a great big dick. Brad appeared, and in exchange for Rolf he became Heidi's fantasy. Heidi's a lot more sexually adventurous than my soon-to-be ex. Brad saw to it she had the best time she's had in years. By tomorrow when she wakes up she's going to be rethinking her options. I'd put money on it," Nora gloated.

"Who's going to massage you now, Red?" Kyle asked, smiling.

"You are," she said. "Get the oil out. I want you to spoil me, darling. I am feeling very happy tonight."

"No more other men?" he asked.

"For now. I won't make you any promises, however," she told him.

"You love me," he replied.

"Maybe," Nora responded. "I still don't trust your gender, darling Mr. Gorgeous."

"Then I'll have to spend eternity convincing you," he said softly.

"Eternity is a long time," Nora noted.

"Yes," he agreed, "it is." He took her hand, and led her into the bathroom. "I'm going to give you the best massage of your life, darling," he promised her.

Nora smiled. Variety was nice, but having Kyle so totally devoted to her was even better. And here in The Channel they would always remain the same. And he would always be exactly what she wanted him to be. It was a perfect world. And then the phone rang. "Get it," she ordered him.

Kyle picked up the handset. "Yes?" He listened, and then he said, "She'll be there, Margaret. Give me half an hour. Okay." He set the phone down. "Mr. Nicholas wants to see you, Nora. And I'm to come with you. We'll have to put the massage off until later, Red. I'm sorry."

"Pick something out for me to wear," Nora told him, and he nodded.

When they were both dressed Nora found herself in a pair of butterscotch-colored silk slacks, beneath which she wore a cream-colored silk thong, which emphasized her butt beneath the trousers. Her cream silk shirt had a deep V neck and long sleeves. She had slipped a pair of leather sandals on her feet. Kyle was wearing beige linen pants and a white shirt with the sleeves rolled up. He had oxblood leather penny loafers on his big feet. He styled her hair in a tailored chignon. His dark hair was wet and brushed back. They entered the elevator, and pushed the red button as the doors closed.

When they opened again the pair stepped out into the elegant office. It was quiet but for the two women at their workstations. Margaret was there to greet them. "Come along, you two," she said, moving briskly down the room to the double doors. "They're here, Mr. Nicholas," she said, ushering them into the elegant office.

He came forward, a smile on his face. "Come in! Come in!"

Nora saw there was a bottle of champagne in a bucket on the butler's tray, as well as three slender flutes. She looked at Kyle, but he shrugged and shook his head.

"My dear Nora," Mr. Nicholas said, taking up both her hands in his and kissing them. "I am astounded! And very impressed, my dear. It was a brilliant plan. Flawlessly executed, and I never had the slightest hint of what you were doing. Of what you were capable." He poured the champagne into the flutes, gave Nora one and Kyle one, and took the third for himself. "I salute you, my dear Nora!"

"Mr. Nicholas, I have no idea of what you are talking about," Nora said, confused. "What have I done?" She set the crystal flute of champagne down on the butler's tray.

"My dear girl, please don't be modest. There is no place for modesty in a devious mind such as yours," Mr. Nicholas said, smiling. "Or perhaps there is."

Nora sighed. "I honestly don't know to what you refer," she repeated.

For a moment he looked surprised. Then he set his champagne down. "Did you not arrange to lure Heidi Millar into The Channel, my dear?" he said.

"Well, yes," Nora answered slowly. "I thought if she saw she could have her fantasies without my husband, she would decide she didn't need him. Oh, I want the divorce, but if Jeff didn't have to buy her a co-op, he wouldn't want my house. I even had Carla tell her about Caleb Snow's attributes. Most women are curious to try a penis that size at least once. I thought Heidi is young, and the young women today are so much more liberated sexually, at least in public, than my generation was."

"But it was you who created Brad, my dear, and had him go to her, wasn't it?" Mr. Nicholas said.

Nora nodded. "I thought she would want a fantasy man of her own and then I considered the kind of man Heidi might want based on what I know of her," Nora explained.

Mr. Nicholas smiled, obviously pleased. "And she found her fantasy, thanks to you, my dear. Heidi is a young woman who enjoys erotic-asphyxiation sexual activity."

Nora looked confused.

"Explain it to her, Kyle," the administrator said, and Kyle did.

"Oh!" Nora exclaimed. "That certainly wouldn't be my idea of fun."

Mr. Nicholas laughed in spite of himself. Then he grew a bit more sober. "Do you understand what you have set in motion, Nora? Perhaps you don't, but I see much promise in you, my dear. Let me tell you what has happened in your reality. Heidi returned from a most satisfactory visit to The Channel. She went upstairs to bed, where your husband was now awake, and demanding sex of his paramour. She acquiesced, for if the truth be known, Brad deliberately left her hungry for more of what he had given her earlier. But your husband was swift, and selfish in his needs. He gave no thought to Heidi, and she suddenly rebelled, berating him. There was a physical confrontation. She fled screaming into the cul-de-sac that is Ansley Court, awakening your neighbors, who took her in and advised her to call the police."

Nora's gray green eyes widened.

A small smile touched Mr. Nicholas's lips. "Your friends are encouraging her to press charges, and she will. Now, my dear Nora, you have a most unique opportunity set before you, and how you react will decide your fate."

"I don't understand," she said.

"Let us sit down," Mr. Nicholas replied, and picking up his

champagne, he sipped at it thoughtfully. "Assault and battery are not particularly serious charges in general, but you know your husband, Nora. His public persona is most important to him, and even more important to the advertising firm in which he is a partner. There will be some rather negative publicity with regard to the violence done to Heidi Millar by Jeff Buckley. Messrs. Wickham and Coutts will be more than displeased. You, the long-faithful wife, and Heidi, the naive young woman he romanced and took advantage of, will be the victims of an ambitious, greedy, and sexually rapacious man. Your husband's reputation will be ruined. He is scarcely at an age where he can start all over again, is he?" Mr. Nicholas concluded softly.

Nora nodded slowly.

"You and your children are the sole beneficiaries of your husband's will, my dear." Mr. Nicholas continued. "If he dies, the house is yours. However, he could sell the house to mount the rather expensive defense he might have to mount in an effort to stay out of jail. His resources are stretched right now. "Mr. Nicholas murmured. "Of course the shock of Heidi's betrayal, coupled with the shock of learning that Sleeping Beauty has awakened from her slumber, could kill him, couldn't it?" The administrator smiled at her. "Jeff has always been prone to hypertension."

His dark eyes were cold and fathomless, Nora noted. "I can't take advantage of Jeff," she said.

"Yes, you can," Mr. Nicholas told her. "This is the man who was casting you aside after twenty-six years of faithful devotion, my dear. This is the man who was attempting to put you out of your house, who wanted to impoverish you, and your children, just so he could marry a younger woman. Someone not much older than the daughter you bore him. Doesn't he deserve to die?"

Nora was silent. She had wanted revenge, and now she had her chance. Wouldn't her life, the children's lives be better without

Jeff? J. J. could go to college without having to worry. Jill could have her three years at Duke Law paid for, and not have to take time from her studies by working. And I would have my house, Nora thought.

"Listen to him, Red," Kyle said softly. "You don't have to sacrifice yourself any more, baby. We can be together. He doesn't deserve to live."

"If I agreed," Nora said slowly, "how would it happen? He's a bastard, I know, but I don't want him to suffer."

"And we don't want him to run up too large a legal bill," Mr. Nicholas said with a sly smile. "I think on his second night in jail your husband will suffer an acute coronary. He'll die in his sleep, my dear, dreaming of you as you and Kyle make passionate love."

"He'll know it's me?" Nora asked. She liked that idea very much.

"Yes, he will, because you want him to know," Mr. Nicholas responded.

"Yes, I do!" Nora exclaimed. "I do!"

"Then it shall be as you wish, my dear, and you will not feel guilty at all, I promise you. Your husband is only getting his just deserts," Mr. Nicholas assured her.

It was so simple, Nora considered. And no one would ever know. Then she said, "But I'm in Shorecrest. They won't let me out when I wake up. They'll want to keep me a few days, I'm sure."

Mr. Nicholas thought a long moment. "When you awaken you will be fine. It will be as if you had just been asleep. There will be no weakness or atrophy in your limbs. Everything will be normal. Your pulse. Respiration. Everything. You will insist upon going home. They will insist on keeping you. You will compromise by remaining one night. Then your lawyer will see you are checked out, and you will go home. It is quite simple, my dear."

"Do it!" Nora told him. What was the point in her suffering any longer? She owed herself and her children this opportunity, and she was going to take it.

"You do remember that you owe me a favor, my dear, don't you?"

Nora nodded. "And now I will owe you a bigger one," she said. What could he ask of her? That she be one of The Channel's sex slaves for a time? So be it! She'd do it gladly if Mr. Nicholas could solve her problems. She was so tired of struggling against Jeff Buckley. She just wanted to be free of him.

Mr. Nicholas smiled at her. "I don't want you to worry, my dear, because everything will be taken care of for you. I am happy to see you have not forgotten your obligation to me. Now run along and prepare yourself for your return to your own reality, Nora. The next few days will be busy for you. Be patient. It has been a pleasure having you as a longtime guest here in The Channel."

She and Kyle returned to the penthouse. Nora looked about. Was the sky beginning to lighten beyond her windows, or was it her imagination? "You promised me a massage," she said to Kyle, smiling up at him seductively.

"We haven't got time," he told her, taking her into his arms. "I'll miss you."

"I'll only be gone a little while," she promised him. "And after that, we will be together every night."

"For eternity," he said.

"Yes, for eternity," Nora agreed. "Hold me tight, Kyle!" She was beginning to feel herself slipping away from him. Her head was spinning faster, and faster, and faster. She was suddenly unconscious, and then her eyes flew open. She was lying in a hospital bed in a room with pink walls and a floral border. She didn't move for several minutes, and then she turned her head to her right. She could see the dawn staining the eastern sky, and a winter garden beyond the window. There was red-twigged dogwood, bright among small patches of melting snow.

Nora sat up gingerly. Slowly she swung her feet over the edge of the bed. She wasn't dizzy. In fact she felt damned good. As if she had had a wonderful long rest. She was past questioning what had happened, or if The Channel was real. She had a part to play now, and she had to remember that she was supposed to have absolutely no idea of what had happened to her. A call bell. There must be a call bell. She looked about. There it was. Reaching for it, she pressed it and waited. And while she waited she put her feet on the ground and began to walk around. She wasn't in the least fuzzy in her head, or unsure on her feet. She drew the IV on wheels along with her.

The door to the room opened, and a woman in a uniform stepped through. "Mrs. Buckley!" she exclaimed. She hurried over to Nora and attempted to put an arm about her waist. "You shouldn't be up like this!"

Nora pulled away from the woman. "I am fine," she said, "but you will understand I am somewhat confused. Where am I?"

"Please sit down, Mrs. Buckley," the woman in the uniform said. "You're at Shorecrest."

"The nursing home? What in heaven's name am I doing here?" Nora demanded.

"What do you last remember, Mrs. Buckley?" her companion asked.

Being in the arms of the sexiest man you could ever imagine, Nora silently thought, but then she said, "Ordering a cable movie, and sitting down to watch it," she told the woman.

"You obviously had some sort of seizure, or brain incident," the uniform began.

"How long have I been here?" Nora said.

"You were at the hospital for ten days, and then moved here six weeks ago. What is the last date you remember?"

"It was New Year's Day," Nora said. "What is today's date, please?"

"It's March first, Mrs. Buckley." She took up Nora's wrist in her hand to check her pulse. "I'm Elda James, the night nurse on this wing. Well, your pulse is quite normal. Would you mind sitting back on the bed. I want to check your blood pressure, and the cuff is over there. I'll also unhook you from your IV."

Nora got up and walked across to the bed to sit down. The nurse fastened the blood pressure device about her right arm and quickly pumped it up. When she had her answer, she unfastened it and put it back in the holder. Then she undid the IV.

"What is it?" Nora asked her quietly.

"One fifteen over seventy-five," the nurse said. "Very normal. Normal on the low side." She made a notation on the chart at the foot of Nora's bed. "This is amazing, Mrs. Buckley. You seem to be absolutely fine. When Dr. Seligmann comes in he is going to be very surprised, and delighted. Would you like me to call your husband?"

"No. I'm not certain where he is," Nora answered the nurse. "Let's wait for Dr. Sam, and let him do it."

"Please get back into bed now, Mrs. Buckley. I know you feel fine, but just as a precaution. Are you hungry? The kitchen is just getting going for the day, but I could get you some tea and pound cake from the nurses' room."

"That would be lovely," Nora agreed. A mirror. She needed a mirror. She wanted to see what she looked like now. She watched the nurse bustle out, and then slipped from the bed and went into the bathroom. She stared at her face in the glass. She looked fine. Younger if anything. But her hair had faded. She'd have to have it colored this week. She found a brush in the medicine cabinet, and brushed the hair out. Then she braided it into a single plait. Yes. Her face definitely looked younger. And it was stress free after how many years? She left the bath-room, and climbed back into bed just as Nurse James came back into the room with her tea and a plate with a slice of pound cake on it.

"I didn't want to give you too much," she said. "We've been feeding you with the IV twice a day." She set the plate and mug down on the side table. "I'll have to leave you. I have patients waking up, and rounds to make before the seven a.m. shift comes in. I hope you won't mind."

"What time is it?" Nora asked.

"Almost seven now. I'm kind of behind with you, but oh, Mrs. Buckley, this is really a miracle!" And with a smile she hurried out.

A miracle. Nora wondered if such a word would really apply to what had happened to her. To them all. The kids! She had to call the kids.

She missed Kyle. She missed her apartment. She missed the endless and delicious sensuality she experienced when she was in The Channel. It had become a part of her, and she was irritable now not being a part of it. Can something like The Channel be addictive? But she already knew the answer. The Channel was like a narcotic, which was why once you were introduced you kept going back. And I have lived for weeks in The Channel, Nora considered. I'm suffering withdrawal. But it won't be forever. I just have to get through today and tomorrow.

CHAPTER TEN

D r. Sam Seligmann stepped into Nora's room.

"Sam!" Nora threw back the coverlet and came from the bed.

"Elda stayed to tell me you were awake," he said, "but sweetheart, you've been out like a light for eight weeks. Take it easy. Sit down before you give me a coronary." He almost pushed her into the chair, his fingers reaching for her wrist.

"I'm fine," Nora insisted. "I want to go home, Sam."

"Yep, pulse normal." He took the chart from the foot of the bed and scanned it, shaking his head. "Everything is normal," he said, almost to himself. Then sitting himself in the second club chair, he told her, "All your vitals have been normal since you were brought into the hospital, Nora. But you were unconscious. Actually it was more like you were sleeping. Do you remember anything?" He peered through his glasses at her.

"I remember ordering a cable movie. That's it. Oh, my God! I was supposed to sign the settlement papers. Jeff must be furious."

"He'll live," Sam Seligmann said.

"When can I go home?" Nora demanded. "I feel fine, and I really do want to go home, Sam. And the kids must have been frantic all these weeks. I need to call the kids."

"Frankly I'd keep you under observation for a couple of days," Dr. Seligmann said, "but now that you're conscious, I know your HMO will start screaming because they know that other than being out for these past weeks, you haven't shown any signs of trauma or illness. I'm going to keep you a day, Nora. Just today. You can go home tomorrow, okay? But I don't want you to do anything strenuous for quite a while, sweetheart, and I'm going to check on you myself twice a day."

"You're going to make house calls on me?" Nora grinned. "Why, you old sweetie, you have been worried."

"Don't tell on me." He grinned back, then he grew serious. "Whatever felled you, Nora, I don't want you to relapse by flinging yourself back into your life too quickly."

"I don't have a lot of time, Sam. I'll have to sign that divorce settlement, and that means the house goes on the market April first."

"I'm going to talk to Rick about that," the doctor said. "Under the circumstances we should be able to get an extension. I mean would it kill Jeff to wait till May first?"

"I don't know," Nora replied. "He's been carrying a bridge loan on that co-op he bought. Jeff isn't a man who likes wasting money."

"Listen, Rina says that Carla told her the girlfriend is paying the bridge loan. Your husband isn't out of pocket a penny on this," Sam Seligmann replied. There came a high-pitched sound, and he looked down at the pager on his belt, eyebrows lifting. "Excuse me, Nora, while I make a call." He pulled out his cell and punched in the numbers. "Dr. Seligmann here. Yes. What? You're kidding! I'll be right there." He stood up. "Gotta run. Stay here today. I'll release you tomorrow, and I'll be back later."

He stood up, gave her a kiss on the cheek, and was gone.

Nora smiled to herself. Mr. Nicholas had been right. Everything was going to be just fine. The door opened again, and an aide came in carrying a tray.

"Dr. Sam says you get breakfast, Mrs. Buckley. Glad to see you awake. I'm Chrissy. I went to school with Jill."

Nora smiled. "Of course, I remember you. Cheerleader, right?"

Chrissy nodded. "Yep. Then motherhood too early. I'm going to school now to get my R.N. My mom looks after Jason."

"Dr. Sam sure left in a hurry," Nora probed gently.

"It's something big, but I don't know what," the aide replied. "My brother's an EMT with the cops, and he got called out just after six a.m. Enjoy your breakfast, now."

Sam Seligmann's mind, however, was on the telephone call he had just received from his wife. "Come quick," Rina had said. The cops are all over Ansley Court, Sam. Heidi's pressing charges, and Jeff is raising bloody hell." He reached home in record time to find the street cordoned off. "I'm Dr. Seligmann," he said, holding his ID out for the emergency worker to see. "I live here. Number 200." He was waved through, and parking in his drive, he got out and ran across the street.

"Hey, Dr. Sam," the cop in front of the house said.

"What's happened," Sam Seligmann asked.

"Looks like Mr. Buckley beat up the girlfriend early this morning, although he claims he hardly touched her. She's over at the Johnsons' now. Pretty kid. What she sees in him I don't know, anyway he's barricaded himself in the house. They're trying to talk him out now. You don't know if he has any weapons, do you?"

"No," Sam said. "He's not the type. Who's in charge here?"

"Lieutenant Barker," the cop said. "He's the bald-headed guy over there with the pissed-off look."

"Thanks," Sam replied, and walked over to where the police lieutenant stood. "Lieutenant? I'm Dr. Sam Seligmann, Mr. Buckley's neighbor. Is there some way in which I can help?"

"Can you talk that asshole inside outside, Doc?" Lieutenant Barker asked irritably. "Damn, this is no big frigging deal. The guy beat up his girlfriend. She's pressing charges. I have to arrest him, and now he's adding resisting arrest, and God knows what else, to the charges."

"I have his cell number," Dr. Sam said, trying not to laugh.

"Think he's got it on?" the cop asked.

"He always has it on," Dr. Sam said dryly. "He's an important man in his business." He pulled his own cell from his pocket and punched in the number.

"He's a jerk, as far as I'm concerned," Lieutenant Barker said.

"Jeff? It's Dr. Sam. Will you please come out? No one is going to hurt you, and you're just adding charges to the ones Heidi is filing against you." He listened. "Hang on a minute, and I'll tell him." Turning to the police lieutenant, Dr. Sam said, "He says he's not coming out until he speaks with his lawyer."

"And when the hell is that going to be?" the cop demanded. "You tell him to get his ass out here now. He can call his lawyer from the station."

"Jeff, listen, you can call Kramer from the station. The whole neighborhood is in an uproar, and the local news trucks are already beginning to arrive on the scene. You've taken a simple matter and turned it into a spectacle worthy of P. T. Barnum. For God's sakes, think of your reputation, and that of your firm."

"Ask him if he wants his front door broken down," the cop said.

"Jeff, listen to me. How about if Lieutenant Barker and I come in with a couple patrolmen, okay? I'll go with you to the station house." He listened, and nodded. "Alright, Jeff. Just the lieutenant, two cops, and me. I'll tell him." He ended the call.

"Thanks, Doc," the lieutenant said.

"He says he wants time to get dressed once you're inside," Dr. Sam said.

"No problem. I hope you're not a good friend of this guy. He's a real piece of work, if you don't mind my saying so. Wife in the nursing home unconscious, and he's bringing the girlfriend out from the city to sleep in her bed. A real sweetheart, this guy."

"You won't get any argument from the others here on the court," Dr. Sam said. "It's Nora we all love. Jeff? A real putz."

"Funny how the wife was found like that, isn't it?" the cop noted.

"I'm Nora's doctor, Lieutenant. When she was found, there was absolutely no sign of any injury, internally or externally. She was in a locked house and there was no sign that anyone other than Nora Buckley had been or was in the place."

"What do you think the girl sees in him?" the cop continued, curious, and obviously anxious for a little inside information.

"Money. Power. A stepping-stone for her career," Dr. Sam replied. "Listen, when we get inside, can I talk to Jeff?" His cell rang, playing the theme from the "Peanuts" Christmas special. "Dr. Sam. Okay." He turned to the cop, who was grinning.

"I like 'Peanuts" too," the police lieutenant said.

"Jeff says come in now," Dr. Sam replied. "You didn't answer my question. Can I talk to him?"

They walked to the front door, and it swung open. Jeff Buckley was in pajamas and his robe. He said nothing.

"My men will escort you upstairs to dress, Mr. Buckley. When you come back down, I'm going to read you your rights. Okay?"

Jeff nodded. He was pale, and looked a little flushed to the doctor.

Sam Seligmann reached out and took the man's wrist. "A little fast. Calm down, Jeff. You're only upsetting yourself."

"I left a message on Kramer's voice mail. Why hasn't he gotten back to me?" Jeff said to no one in particular.

"Because he isn't up yet maybe?" the doctor replied. "Get dressed, Jeff. You'll feel better when you do."

"What the hell are my partners going to say about this? That damned little bitch has made one hell of a mess for me," Jeff whined.

"Mr. Buckley, please go upstairs now. Or would you prefer to go to the station in your pajamas? I don't give a damn personally, but either way in ten minutes you're out of here, sir. But I think you would prefer to be seen at your best," the lieutenant noted.

Jeff turned and, escorted by the two patrolmen, went upstairs.

The other two men walked into the living room and sat down.

"You can talk to him when he's dressed, and before we take him out of here," Lieutenant Barker said.

They sat in silence for a few minutes, and then Jeff came back into the room with the two patrolmen. He was dressed in a dark pinstriped suit with a white shirt, and a dark patterned tie. A cashmere coat was over his shoulders. He was every inch the prominent businessman.

"He's ready to go, sir," one of the uniforms said.

The lieutenant stood up, and came over to stand in front of Jeff. "Jeffrey Buckley, I arrest you for the assault and battery, with intent to do harm, of Heidi Millar. You have the right to remain silent. You have the right to an attorney. If you cannot afford one, one will be provided for you. Do you understand these rights as they have been outlined to you?"

"She's make a big thing of this," Jeff said. "If I could just speak to her."

"Sir, do you understand your rights?" the lieutenant persisted. "Please answer yes or no."

"Yes, yes, I understand. Do you think I'm an idiot like the lowlifes you obviously consort with daily? I want to speak with my attorney!" Jeff was beginning to recover from his initial shock.

"I am going to give Dr. Sam a moment to speak with you, Mr. Buckley, and then we are going to leave your house, and you will be driven to the police station."

He stepped from the room to give the two men some privacy.

"You're making a fucking big deal out of nothing. So I slapped the bitch. She had it coming, damnit!" Jeff said angrily. Then he turned to the doctor.

"I came to tell you that your wife woke up this morning. She's fine. I plan on releasing her from Shorecrest tomorrow, and she can come home."

"She's not coming here," Jeff said nastily. "The house is going on the market in another month."

"The house is hers until then, you bastard," the doctor snapped. "And it's my understanding that she never signed the settlement, Jeff. Until she does, you're stuck. Damnit, Nora has recovered from whatever felled her, and instead of being relieved, you're pissed. What the hell is the matter with you? What did that nice woman ever do to you to make you so vindictive against her?"

"She's alive," Jeff responded angrily. "Why couldn't she have died?"

Lt. Barker gripped Jeff by the arm. "Let's go, Mr. Buckley," he said.

Jeff pulled away. "I'm not going anywhere with you until I speak with my attorney," he snarled.

"I told you, after you're booked you get a phone call," Lieutenant Barker said. "I'm trying to do this in a way that won't embarrass you, sir. But if you refuse to cooperate, I'm going to have to cuff you."

"Go to hell!" Jeff yelled, and then to his astonishment he found himself slammed facedown into the couch. His arms were dragged behind him. He tried to struggle, but his efforts were futile. He felt the metal cuffs enclosing his wrists. Heard the snap of them locking. Then he was yanked to his feet again. Enraged, he shouted, "This is police brutality. I'll have your damned badge for this! Dr. Seligmann is a witness!"

"What are you talking about?" Sam said, a small smile flitting over his lips. "I didn't see any police brutality. I saw a man resisting arrest."

"You kike bastard!" Jeff was practically screaming now, and his lips were flecked with foam.

"Let's go, Mr. Buckley," the police lieutenant said sternly. He was embarrassed by his prisoner's slurs on Sam Seligmann. Sam was the town doctor. Everyone liked him. He was a good man. What kind of thing was that for this jerk to say to him? He pushed Jeff forward a little harder than he might have under other circumstances.

Jeff whirled about, and his head butted the detective hard. "I want my lawyer!"

Two uniforms jumped forward and, each taking an arm, hustled Jeff Buckley from his house past a line of flashing cameras, and into a waiting police car. Left to regain his composure and his dignity, Lieutenant Barker stood up from the couch where he had landed.

"Are you alright?" the doctor asked him.

"I think he bruised my ego," the lieutenant said with a wry grin. "Nah, he just took the wind out of me. I didn't expect such violence from the guy."

"He's a man used to getting his own way, and used to having people do what he tells them to do. His wife really surprised him when she didn't cave easily to the divorce. He was tossing her out of her house. Cutting his kids off so they had no college tuition at the last moment, and he didn't want to pay alimony, or support for the younger kid," the doctor explained. "To his surprise, she got tough with him."

"Yeah, a woman will where her home and her kids are concerned. Nice guy, your neighbor. Wanted everything for himself, and the young girlfriend. Hey, wasn't his kid the high school's star soccer player the last two years? My kid really admired him. Went out for soccer just because of J. J. Buckley. Made junior varsity this year," the detective said proudly. "And he wouldn't help the kid go to college. What a shit!"

"J. J. got a scholarship," the doctor said.

"Well, I better take my prisoner down to the station and book him. You'll tell the wife? I hate stuff like this, and hell, you're a friend, right?"

Sam Seligmann nodded. "I'll tell Nora," he said.

The two men went their separate ways: Lieutenant Barker back to the Egret Pointe station house, Sam Seligmann across the street to his house, where he discovered his neighbors all gathered in the kitchen drinking coffee and eating Krispy Kremes. He laughed. He couldn't help it. "Rina! Rina!" he said to his wife.

"Well, we were all up," she replied, "and you were over there. This saves you telling the story four times, Sam." She handed him a cup of coffee, already creamed. "So?" she said, offering him a donut from the open box.

"I've got good news and bad news," Sam Seligmann said. "Which do you want first?" He took a sip of coffee, and a bite of his glazed donut.

"We know the good news," Rina said. "The cops arrested Jeff Buckley."

"No. The good news is Nora Buckley woke up this morning, and she is absolutely fine, my dears. It's as if she's been sleeping for eight weeks."

There was a collective shriek of delight from the assembled women, and their husbands smiled, nodding and looking pleased.

"So what's the bad news?" Rina asked.

"There is none," Dr. Sam chuckled. "Where is Heidi?"

"One of the young patrolmen got her into his car, and away to the station house before the news media started showing up. Rick and Joe went with her to make sure Jeff didn't bully her out of filing charges. She's hired them as her local counsel," Rina told her husband, who, nodding, was already turning to Carla. "Listen, Carla," Sam said. "I'd like you to go over to Shorecrest with me when I tell Nora. And bring your cell. There's no phone in her room, and she'll want to call the kids. I'll speak with them first with the news their mother is alright."

"When is she getting out?" Rina, practical as ever, queried her husband.

"I told her tomorrow. I don't understand it. She shows absolutely no effects of lying unconscious in a bed for all those weeks. It's a miracle."

"Let me bring her to my house today," Carla begged. "She must be frantic about the kids, Dr. Sam. Please!"

"Well," the doctor considered, "she is fine, and if she were anyone else, I'd say no, but why not? I'm just across the street if she should relapse. Alright, Carla, you can have her. Is an hour time enough for you? This is seriously big gossip, and I can guarantee it's all over town already. I don't want Nora to hear anything before I have a chance to speak to her. The shock could be very damaging."

"Ten minutes is enough time for me," Carla told him. "I'll just run home and throw on some sweats, okay? What about Nora?"

She can come home in her hospital gown and coat. It's quicker, and will get her out of the media eye. Jeff was a big shot in town. They'll be all over this one. Girlfriend beaten up. Wife comes out of coma on same day. Husband arrested. Oh, yeah. This has *Enquirer* written all over it," Dr. Sam said.

Carla was as good as her word. Dr. Sam came back from the Buckley house with a coat over his arm to find her sitting in his car, already belted.

"Let's ride, Clyde," she told him.

He laughed and, tossing the coat in the backseat, got in next to her. He turned the key in the ignition and backed out of his drive.

"She's really okay?" Carla probed him as they drove.

"She's amazing," he replied. "I don't know what the hell happened to her, and I don't know how she came out of it. But she did. And the entire time she appeared to be unconscious, her pulse and respiration were normal. It was more like sleeping."

"It was a heck of a nap," Carla said. She was just a little bit frightened by everything that had happened to Nora, yet it hadn't prevented her from visiting The Channel herself. And seeing

Nora on her beach, switching men with her, and drinking with her at the pirates' inn was a trip.

They were almost at Shorecrest Nursing Facility. The car turned down Shore Road. The morning sun was sparking on the water to her right.

Dr. Sam parked the car, and they entered the lobby of Shorecrest.

"Ohh, Dr. Sam," the receptionist at the desk said, "I hear there was a hostage standoff in your neighborhood!"

"Just came from Ansley Court, Judy, and all's quiet there," Sam Seligmann responded. "Turn right," he hissed at Carla. "She's on the main floor. Room 112 at the end of the hall. Ah, here we are." He knocked and then, opening the door, stepped inside. "Nora, I'm back, and look who I brought with me."

The two women hugged and sat down in the twin club chairs grinning at each other. They were sharing the most delicious secret.

"Listen, Nora, something has happened, sweetheart. I don't know how upset you're going to get over it, but . . ." He paused, trying to figure the most delicate way of saying it, but there just wasn't any. "Jeff's been arrested for beating up his girlfriend. She's at the station house now pressing charges."

"What?" Nora feigned shock. "When? Where did this happen? Omigod, the kids! I have to call the kids!"

"I've got my cell with me," Carla said, "but wait, and hear Dr. Sam out."

"The police think it happened during a bout of rough sex. He's mad as hell, of course, and threatening everyone," Sam said.

"My God!" Nora said slowly as if she were having difficulty understanding.

"That poor girl."

"I'm releasing you from the facility right now," Dr. Sam continued. "I'll drive you and Carla back to Ansley Court. This situation could generate some publicity given Jeff's position in Buckley, Coutts and Wickham."

Nora began to laugh. "They really are the most conservative of advertising firms. Blue-chip clients. Veddy proper. They weren't very happy with Jeff and Heidi and the divorce situation. That's how Rick was able to bargain for me. The one thing Messrs. Wickham and Coutts didn't want was a noisy, public divorce; this, however, will send them round the bend. A partner arrested for beating a female employee of the firm while his wife lay comatose! Poor old Jeff. How he looked to the world has always been so important to him."

"You're staying with me," Carla told her.

Nora stood up. "Can we go now, Dr. Sam?" she said.

He nodded, and wrapped her coat about her. "Shoes! Oy! I forgot shoes."

"Bring the car around to the entrance, and it won't matter. These little paper slippers are really warm," Nora said.

Dr. Sam tossed his car keys to Carla. "You get it while I check Nora out," he said.

Carla caught the keys and hurried out.

"You ready, Nora?" he said. "There shouldn't be anyone in the lobby right now. It's still early."

"I'm okay," she told him.

At the desk in the lobby Dr. Sam signed all the necessary papers, and Nora signed where she was told. They heard a car horn beep, and knew Carla was waiting for them. Dr. Sam escorted his patient to the car and helped her into the backseat. Then he climbed into the front seat, letting Carla do the driving this time. After they pulled into the Johnsons' driveway, the doctor helped Nora from the car and into the house.

"You're okay?" he asked anxiously.

"Yes," she said.

"Come on," Carla said softly. "We can talk inside."

They went inside, where everyone was now waiting in Carla's

living room. After the other women had hugged Nora and welcomed her home, Rina, Tiffany and Joanne left with their husbands, but not before Dr. Sam had checked Nora's pulse again. Satisfied, he suggested rest, and said he'd be back later in the afternoon. They went into the kitchen, where they found Rina had left a box of glazed Krispy Kremes and made coffee.

"Well, Rick," Nora said quietly, sitting down and reaching for one of the donuts, "what now? Do I sign the settlement agreement?"

"No," he said. "You're still legally his wife. Trust me when I tell you that Heidi Millar isn't going to back down. She hasn't just accused him of assault and battery. She's added rape to the charges. Says she came up to bed from watching the television, and he was hot to trot. She wasn't, told him so, said no, but he forced her anyway. Jeff is now in really serious trouble."

"Everything's still in his name," Nora said. "What if she sues him for damages?"

"No judge or jury will award compensation to a woman having an affair with a man who has a wife, especially when the wife and children are as presentable as you and the kids are. And especially if the circumstances are made public.

"I gotta go to the office," Rick Johnson said. "You two going to be alright?"

Nora nodded. "I'm going to call the kids. Carla will tell them I'm okay, and then I'll tell them what has happened. Thanks, Rick."

"I'm glad you're okay, Nora," he answered her, and then left the kitchen with Carla, the two of them talking softly.

"Thanks," she called after him.

Carla returned shortly. "Let go upstairs," she said. "You're staying in the guest room until Dr. Sam is certain you're okay. Rina brought some of your stuff over so you can get dressed."

"You know I'm absolutely alright," Nora said as they walked up the staircase.

"I know, but I can't believe this is happening. I just spoke to Heidi last night. I knew when she left, she was fascinated. I knew she'd try The Channel. Poor kid. She was bored to death out here. And Jeff was hitting the sack early, leaving her in front of the television. Do you know what happened to her? I mean you were there, in The Channel."

"I imagined someone like Caleb Snow to be her lover last night. I knew you would have enticed her with the fourteen-inch penis, and every little girl wants one of those at least once," Nora said as they entered the guest room. She sat down on the edge of the bed. "His name is Brad. He's a dominant, and I just somehow knew that while Heidi wants to be in charge in our reality, she secretly wants to be controlled when no one else can see it," Nora said with a small smile. "Of course if you ask for a favor you must repay it. Because Brad's bisexual he wanted my Rolfie. I can always get another masseur so I let Brad have him. I guess Heidi had a good time, considering what happened when she got back from The Channel."

"What are you going to do now that Jeff is going to jail? Rick will get the house for you, but I don't know about the rest of it," Carla said.

"Well, I am the poor wife," Nora replied with a twinkle.

"I'll share my Channel connection with you," Carla said.

"No, thanks," Nora told her. "I'm going home tomorrow, Carla. I want to be in my own house. Tomorrow I'll order The Channel just to be with Kyle for an evening, but I won't stay now. I'll be back by morning as always. I have to see what Rick is going to do to protect me now. What if Jeff insists the house be sold so he can pay his lawyers? I know he'll hire only the best."

"Too bad she didn't kill him when she beaned him with that vase," Carla said.

Nora laughed. "I can't say I disagree. Give me your cell. I'd better call the kids now, and let them know I'm okay. Were they too upset?"

"They wanted to come home," Carla replied. "I talked them out of it." She pulled out her cell. "Let me prepare them, okay?" Then she dialed.

J. J. cried learning his mother was awake and okay. He didn't want to let her go to talk with his sister, but he finally did. "Can I come home next weekend?" he asked her.

"I'm not certain, honey," Nora said. "There's something else I have to tell you," and she gently explained to her son that his father had been arrested for assaulting Heidi Millar. "I don't want the media jumping all over you, and they might if you come home."

"I'll make a deal with you, Ma. If they come to campus, I get to come home, okay?"

"Okay," Nora promised her son. "I'll call you later this week, honey, alright?"

Jill was more pragmatic about her mother's recovery. "I knew you'd pull out of it," she said. "Do you need me home?"

"No," Nora said, "but I've got something unpleasant to tell you, Jill," and she went on to explain what had happened.

"Daddy beat her up? Geez, I wouldn't have thought it of him," Jill said.

"I don't know," Nora said. "I'm not certain when he's being arraigned."

"They've got to charge him, or they can't hold him," Jill said.

"I'm sure they will charge him, Jill. I can't believe it of your father, but it does appear as if he is guilty," Nora told her daughter. "Watch out for the media. Daddy was prominent in his business."

"Roger!" Jill replied. "Sure you don't need me home?"

"I think under the circumstances it's better if we're scattered," Nora answered her daughter. "I've got to go, honey. I haven't called Grandma yet. Bye, now."

The last number Carla got for Nora was Margo's. "Hey, Margo, Carla. No! Everything is okay. In fact it's better than okay. Nora woke up. She's in terrific shape, and Dr. Sam let her come home. She's with me tonight. I'm going to put her on now. Bye, Margo."

"Mom?" Nora's voice was strong.

"My God, darling, you had us all terrified," Margo said. "What happened to you?"

"You got me, Ma," Nora told her mother. "Everyone is mystified, including me. How are you, and how is that sexy Southern gentleman of yours?"

"Taylor is just grand. Persistent, but grand," Margo answered her daughter. "Now, Nora, I want you to ask Dr. Sam when you can fly. You're coming down here to recuperate, darling, and I won't take no for an answer."

"Ma, I can't," Nora said. "A rather nasty problem has come up. It's Jeff. He's been arrested for assault with intent to do bodily harm, and rape. He beat up his girlfriend, and she says he raped her when she said no to sex."

"My God!" Margo exclaimed. "Thank heavens it wasn't you, darling. I never did like that man. I'm so glad your father isn't alive to see the truth. But why can't you come down? I mean surely you aren't going to defend him, are you?"

"No, no," Nora assured her parent, "but you see, Ma, everything is still up in the air. I never signed the settlement, and now Rick says I shouldn't until we see what's going to happen. So I'm kind of stuck here for the time being."

Margo Edwards sighed. "Well, I suppose you do have to stay until it's all straightened out. I'll tell you one thing, Nora. I am very glad that neither of Jeff's parents is alive to see this either. His father in particular would be mortified. I always thought the mother sweet, but a bit of a mouse. Oh, I have to go! Here's Taylor. I'll tell him the good news. And the bad while we drive to lunch. There is an absolutely darling new little restaurant on the beach about fifteen miles from here. Everyone says the food is heavenly. You're at Carla's? I'll call you later. Bye, now!"

Nora smiled to herself as her mother rang off. Margo was

Margo. She never changed, and it was certainly comforting. Everyone was fine, and her little adventure hadn't really harmed anyone. She looked around Carla's cozy guest bedroom. It was sweet, but she longed for her penthouse, or was it just Kyle for whom she was longing? Lord, she had only been gone a few hours, and she was already itchy. She needed him so badly. She wasn't going to sleep a wink tonight, she thought.

By evening the story was all over the news—print, television, and radio.

It was a slow news day and the arrest of the golden boy and partner of the most prestigious advertising agency in the country had great salacious value. A couple of Jeff's more clever campaigns were mentioned, and their commercials shown. Then came the tale of the wronged wife, just out of a life-threatening coma, and the ambitious blond mistress. The story had everything, and it took people's minds off the war and the economy.

The remote van from the city's two biggest stations appeared outside of Nora's house. She was glad she wasn't there. Eager young reporters began making the rounds of Ansley Court, knocking on doors and asking questions. The Pietro d'Angelo twins were surrounded as they got home from school, with one anchor badgering them until Tiff came flying out of her house, the protective and avenging mother to rescue her children.

"I'm calling the police," she shouted at the media.

"First-amendment rights, lady," one of the young reporters shouted at her.

"Fuck you!" Tiff yelled back as she hustled her kids safely inside.

Shortly afterwards the police arrived and set up barricades, behind which they moved the reporters and their trucks. The trucks were still there in the morning. One of the uniformed cops came to the Johnsons' kitchen door. He suggested that using the backyard might be a good way for Nora to get into her house without being annoyed. The barricades were removed to allow the residents out to go to their jobs, then put back. The police van departed shortly after eleven a.m. One cop remained on guard.

Carla was watching. "They're eating sandwiches and talking," she said. "I think we can get you home if you want to go."

"I want to go," Nora told her.

"I'll have to shop for you," Carla said. "I doubt there's anything in the house you can eat. Heidi didn't cook. They always had takeout."

"Jeff never wanted takeout," Nora noted.

"Heidi told me she didn't cook," Carla answered. "I guess she had other talents."

"She must have liked working alone," Nora remarked cattily, and Carla laughed.

Carla's cell rang. "It's Dr. Sam," she said. "Hi, Doc! What? Okay. Nora's going home now. We're sneaking through the backyard. I'll tell her. Bye." She turned to Nora. "Dr. Sam says the newspeople have Shorecrest staked out. They don't know you were released yesterday, and of course Shorecrest isn't going to give them any information. They're outside our street because they're waiting for you to come home."

"Let's sneak through the backyard, then," Nora said.

Getting their coats, the two women exited the back door of the Johnson house and ran quickly across the lawn. There was a large privet hedge between their homes. Their kids had worn a passage through the hedge over the years. They slipped through it, and removing her key from her pocket, Carla opened the kitchen door to the Buckley house. Entering quickly, they closed and locked the door behind them.

Nora looked about her, and smiled with pleasure. She was home. Removing her coat, she laid it aside and went to the fridge, opening it and looking in. There was a container of plain, fat-free yogurt, an open quart container of milk, and everything that had been in the fridge eight weeks ago. She laughed. "She was no housekeeper, poor Heidi," Nora remarked. "I'll spend all afternoon cleaning up this mess. If only J. J. needed a science fair project, we could do the wonderful world of mold. I'm just going to toss everything. The plastic containers will have absorbed the smell after this long. Who doesn't empty out a fridge of ancient food?"

"Will you be alright?" Carla asked.

"I'm fine," Nora assured her.

"Then I'll go do the shopping. Anything other than the basic supplies to get you through until the reporters go away?" Carla inquired.

"Get me one of those rotisserie chickens the market does. And a box of Mallomars," Nora told her with a grin. "I can survive on chicken and cookies."

"I'm glad you haven't changed entirely," Carla replied.

"Have I changed? Really?" Nora was surprised.

"Oh, yes. You're more assured, stronger now. I guess what I'm saying is that you're no longer a victim, Nora. You fought Jeff, and you've won." Carla buttoned her jacket as she spoke.

"I never meant for Heidi to be hurt," Nora said quickly.

"I know you didn't," Carla answered her, and then blowing a kiss to her friend, she went out the kitchen door.

Nora picked up her own coat and went to the hall closet to hang it up. Returning to the kitchen, she got out a large black lawn-leaf bag, and dumped the contents of the fridge into it, pouring the milk down the sink, washing the yogurt away. There was only one glass casserole in the fridge. She scraped the contents of it into the black bag and washed the dish by hand, noting that the dishwasher was full of clean dishes. She put everything away and cleaned the sink. She wiped down the walls and glass shelves of the empty fridge. Then she went upstairs.

The unmade bed showed signs of one occupant. They were the same sheets she had put on the bed clean on New Year's Day. Jeff's pajamas were on the floor. She picked them up and, going into the hall, threw them down the stairs. They would go in the black bag with the rest of the garbage. She opened her walk-in closet. Her clothing was gone, and in its place hung two pairs of trendy jeans, a pair of flannel slacks, two wool sweaters, and a silk shirt. Pulling the clothes from their hangers, Nora threw them down the stairs as well.

She pulled the sheets from the bed. She was going to get a new bed. In fact she was going to redo the whole bedroom. She had always hated the decor in this room, but Jeff had liked it. The headboard was even similar to the one his parents had. She considered what she would change it to, but she was too distracted right now by the fact her husband had been screwing another woman in the bed in which he had conceived children with his wife. "Bastard!" She wasn't going to sleep in this room until it was redone. She'd use the guest room.

"Where are you?" Carla's voice called.

"Upstairs," Nora said.

Carla's footsteps sounded, and then she came into the bedroom. "What are you doing, and what's all that stuff at the bottom of the stairs?"

"Garbage," Nora replied. "I'm moving into the guest room until I can redo this room. Where are my clothes?"

"Jeff had them packed up and put in the cellar," Carla answered. "I'll get the guys to bring them up this weekend. I got the groceries. They're in the kitchen. The reporters are still outside the street. When I went out they yelled questions at me. I just shrugged. Listen, Nora, if they don't go by evening, and you have the lights on in here, they're going to know you're back. I wouldn't put anything past them to get a picture or a story from you."

"I can live with just the television," Nora murmured.

"They could see the flickering from the outside," Carla responded.

"Tell Rick to issue a statement to the press that I will grant them a half hour tomorrow morning at eleven, and I'll answer questions. But this is on the condition that they leave with their trucks now. And Carla, my windows will be dark tonight. You know the den has those heavy short draperies with the lining. I'll draw them as soon as I go downstairs again."

"You're going to access The Channel? Nora, the cable operator might give that information out to make a few bucks if you call. Then they'll know you're home," Carla fretted. "What if someone tries to jump the gun and get an exclusive?"

"I think I can handle it," Nora replied quietly.

"I'll go call Rick," Carla said. "Do you want me to come back?"

Nora shook her head in the negative. "I think we're safer if you don't."

Carla shoved a cell phone at Nora. "Take it. I picked it up at the market. It's one of those ones with the prepaid minutes. You've got one hundred twenty. It's safer just in case someone is listening in on your line. And don't answer your house phone, Nora. I'll call the kids and your mom, and give them the cell's number, okay?"

"You're make this sound like a covert operation," Nora laughed.

"It is," Carla said, grinning. Then she hugged Nora. "God, it's good to have you back, and to know you're safe!"

"Rick still has to reason with Jeff, and Jeff isn't going to be reasonable in jail," Nora reminded her friend. "Now scoot, and leave me to finish cleaning up my house."

Carla departed, and then called Nora once on her cell to tell her she had gotten in touch with Margo, J. J., and Jill, and given them the cell's number. Then she had called Rick, and Rick had issued the statement. The media people and their trucks were now gone from the head of Ansley Court, but the cop and the barricade was still there just to ensure everyone's privacy for the interim. "Need anything else tonight?" Carla asked. "I mean that I could give you."

Nora could imagine her grinning. "Nope. I'm fine," she

replied. She had cleaned out the master bathroom, but she wasn't going to use it. She found a fresh tube of toothpaste, a new toothbrush, and her own hairbrush. She put them in the guest bath. Until the master bath was cleaned thoroughly and redecorated, she wasn't going in it. In fact she was going to gut this bathroom and put in all new fixtures.

It was getting dark now. Nora heard the clock in the foyer striking six p.m. She hurried downstairs, carved some chicken off the rotisserie bird Carla had brought, fixed a salad with some of the greens now in the clean fridge, made some iced tea, and sat down to eat. She wasn't interested in the local news. She didn't give a damn who did what to whom overseas. The world was crazy now. All she wanted to do was survive the madness, and she had her escape in The Channel. She picked up her cell and dialed the cable company, ordering The Channel for the evening. The operator seemed neutral, and uninterested in who she was. She had never considered it before, but she now suspected that the operators taking calls for Suburban Cable were located somewhere else. They didn't know her or the scandal now surrounding Ansley Court. She finished her meal, and put her dishes in the dishwasher. She hadn't had to turn on any lights, and in the den the curtains were drawn tightly. Nora went into her laundry room and, taking a few clothespins, returned to the den and clipped the draperies shut where they just might allow a crack of light through.

She plunked herself in Jeff's recliner. It was like new because he had hardly sat in it. The mantel clock struck eight. Nora turned on the television and waited. And then her penthouse living room appeared. Eagerly she put her hand on the screen, and was there. "Kyle!" she called.

He arose sleepily from the couch, the relief on his face evident. "God, Nora, I missed you," he told her, and wrapped his arms about her.

She held her face up to him for a kiss, and almost melted with the desire he instantly engendered in her body and soul. Their lips met, and when they parted once more, Nora said, "You owe me a massage, Mr. Gorgeous." She smiled.

"And afterwards, what would madam's wish be?" he said.

"To spend the entire evening with your talented cock in my pussy, my darling!" Nora told him. "I missed you!"

"What has happened on your side of reality?" he asked her, taking her hand and leading her into the bathroom, where the massage table was set up and waiting.

"So far everything has been just as Mr. Nicholas said. I woke up in a nursing facility. Heidi got beaten up and pressed charges. Jeff is in jail." She undid her robe and climbed naked on the massage table.

"Are you happy, Red?" he asked her softly, pushing her hair aside to kiss the back of her neck. "God, I missed your scent!" he groaned.

"Yes," Nora told him. "I've never been happier, although I wish Heidi hadn't been hurt. Use almond oil, darling."

He poured some of the heavily scented oil into his big hand and began to smooth it down her back. "I don't know how long I can do this," he whispered to her.

"I want the full treatment," she told him.

He laughed softly. "You're fully prepared to torture me, huh?"

"Maybe," she said.

Neither of them heard the elevator doors opening in the living room. The plush carpeting stilled the footsteps crossing over to the bathroom door, and then they heard Mr. Nicholas's low, cultured voice. "Good evening, Kyle, Nora."

She started, and blushed. Kyle's hands grew still on her body.

"No, no, my dear," he said. "Let Kyle finish what he is doing. I do so enjoy the sight of a beautiful female form. We can talk as he massages you. Carry on, Kyle." He came around the table and drew up a padded stool, upon which he sat. "Now, tell me, Nora—everything has gone as I promised you?"

"So far," Nora replied.

"And tonight as Kyle makes love to you, your husband will see it in his dreams. It will be the final straw for him. He has behaved quite badly during his short incarceration, I'm afraid. They have had to restrain him. He had been so unpleasant the judge refused bail. It really doesn't do to annoy these small-town judges. I actually have come to believe that no one has ever said no to Jeff, or refused him, in his entire life. He seems unable to cope. It will not seem odd therefore that they find him dead in the morning. It will seem the natural result of his choler. And then, my dear, you are a free woman."

"Thank you," Nora responded. His feet were very narrow, and he was wearing very well-polished black leather shoes. But then he tipped her face up to his. His fingers were very warm against her chin. Almost hot.

"So now, my dear, we must discuss your repayment of my kindness," Mr. Nicholas said. He averted his gaze from hers momentarily. "Turn her over, Kyle, so Nora and I may speak on this matter. You can finish the massage when I have gone."

Kyle turned her over, but as he did he wrapped her in the sheet that had been covering the table, thus preserving her modesty. Their eyes met in silent understanding. Nora sat up, swinging her legs over the edge of the massage table.

"Ah, excellent," Mr. Nicholas said. "Now, my dear, one must always pay the piper, and you have said yourself that you would meet your obligations to me. Is that not so, Nora?"

"Yes," she answered him. What was he going to ask her? Whatever it was, it was worth it if she could be free of Jeff, and her house and her children were safe.

"I am a man of many and varied interests," Mr. Nicholas began. "The Channel is just one of them. There are other things requiring my attention now, and I find I must choose someone to be the new administrator of this enterprise. I choose you, my dear Nora. You are exactly the person for whom I have been looking."

"You want me to be the administrator of The Channel? I can't!" Nora cried. "I wouldn't have the faintest idea of what to do. I don't even know how all of this is even possible. I've never held down a job in all of my life. I've just learned how to operate a computer. I know nothing of office procedure."

"You don't have to, Nora," he told her calmly. "You will have others to handle the mundane chores of The Channel. But you have what I want in my deputy. You are intelligent, and there is a well of anger deep down inside of you that exists. Your intuitiveness is most promising, my dear Nora."

She was astounded. She was frightened. "I can't," she said.

"Of course you can," he replied. "And you will. You owe me a great debt, my dear, and I have kept my word. Now you must keep yours. Why is it you humans take so greedily of what I offer and then demur about paying the price? Think, Nora! What would your life have been without The Channel? Without Kyle? Do you want to go back to the way it was? Your husband deserting you for another woman? Throwing you out of your house? Making you a penniless wretch. Your children's dreams destroyed. I can make it happen if that is your wish, and you will owe me nothing."

"The Devil and Daniel Webster." Nora was suddenly reminded. But she couldn't think of a way to talk herself out of this predicament. She looked directly at Mr. Nicholas. "Can I continue to traverse between these two worlds?" she asked him.

"Of course," he said. "At least until you are an old woman, and die."

"Then what happens to me?" Nora queried him, but she already knew the answer.

"You will remain here within The Channel," he answered her. "Think about it, my dear Nora. You will be forever young! Forever beautiful! Forever desirable!"

"And I will have Kyle?" Why was it you never knew when you were making a bargain with the devil? Nora wondered sadly to herself.

"Of course," Mr. Nicholas said. "He is yours for as long as you wish him to be. Consider, my dear, you will have the kind of power of which all rulers dream."

"But I don't really understand what it is you want of me, expect of me," Nora said.

"I will teach you everything you need to know, my dear girl," he promised. "Kyle will open an antique shop in Egret Pointe," Mr. Nicholas said.

"Kyle is human?" Nora was surprised.

"All too human, I fear, eh, Kyle?" And Mr. Nicholas laughed darkly. Then he continued. "He is quite the expert in seventeenth- and eighteenth-century English and American antique furniture, glass, and china. He will advertise for an assistant. You will answer the ad, and he will hire you. Although you will not need to work, your doing so will be but part of the metamorphosis you undergo in your friends' and family's eyes. People will admire you for your grit and determination despite all the tragedy that has befallen you. The shop will be quite successful in part to your presence. I do like an investment to pay off."

"I do know something about antiques," Nora said.

He laughed. "Whether you do or not isn't really important," Mr. Nicholas told her. "The office upstairs where you will work most days will be where you will manage The Channel for me. You may want to check into the office at The Channel in the evenings occasionally."

"Will I have Margaret?" Nora said.

"No, no, my dear. Margaret is far too valuable to me. She has been involved for years with my other interests. I shall give you Celia, who works at the desk across from Margaret's. Edna will remain, moving up to Celia's position, and I shall give you another girl as well. You and Celia will be in constant touch during the day."

"Wouldn't Celia be a good administrator for The Channel?" Nora ventured. "After all, she knows all about it, and how it operates. I don't."

"Celia would never aspire to such a position," Mr. Nicholas said. "Besides, she doesn't have your intellect, or depth of duplicity."

"You make it sound as if I am evil," Nora cried.

"All humanity has the ability to be evil, dear Nora," Mr. Nicholas told her. "How many of you can really turn the other cheek? A few, but not the majority. Could you really have stood by and said "So be it" if Jeff had taken your home, left you penniless, and destroyed your children's future? That is part of what being good is, but most people can't do it."

"Does everyone who is lured into The Channel end up damned?" Nora asked him sadly.

"No," he said. "Most people live their foolish fantasies for a time, and then grow bored with it and go away. Very few can be entrapped in this manner. And fewer yet with your potential. Don't look so distressed, my dear Nora. Being bad is far more fun than being good. Look what being good, being dutiful, got you."

"Then I have no choice," she said softly.

"You made your choice," Mr. Nicholas said quietly.

"What if I say no, I won't do it?" she asked him.

"It shall be as it was back just before J. J.'s graduation last June," he told her. "Of course you will remember all of this, and you will not be able to convince yourself it was your imagination, my dear. You shall know that you willfully threw this opportunity away. You shall lose your beloved house. Jill will not be able to finish law school for at least six years. She will have to work in order to pay her tuition, and of course she has no skills other than waitressing and temping as office help. As for J. J., he will give up his scholarship to help you survive. You see, Nora, you really do have a choice," Mr. Nicholas said. "If you take the path I have laid out for you, you will be a very wealthy woman in your reality. You will inherit everything that Jeff has amassed. Heidi will accept repayment with interest for the moneys she has expended on the bridge loan. Be generous with her. She cannot afford to retain possession of the co-op. Even if it is in her name, she will be glad to get her small investment back, and leave selling it to you. Surprisingly she feels guilt about the children's college funds. And of course she has other goals in mind now, which I will see she attains in return for her cooperation. Brad will make certain she understands, and does what she is told.

By the way, do get Rick to have Raoul Kramer negotiate the sale of your husband's partnership in Buckley, Coutts and Wickham. The senior partners will attempt to cheat you. And do invest the moneys conservatively."

Nora shuddered. It was like being on the other side of the looking glass. It was surreal. She was getting investment advice from the Devil. But how could she live with herself knowing what she had done to her children by refusing him? And she would remember, Mr. Nicholas said. Nora believed him. Everything he had promised her had come true. Why would any woman in her right mind give up all of this, all of what she could have, out of a sense of right and wrong? She looked at Kyle. His face was expressionless as if he didn't want to influence her. They would be together every day in his antique shop, and every night here within The Channel. "How long must I repay this debt I owe you?" she asked Mr. Nicholas.

"Does it really matter, my dear Nora?" he asked her with a small smile.

"No," she said with a deep sigh. "It doesn't."

"Then we are agreed, my dear? You will accept my offer?"

"Yes," Nora told Mr. Nicholas, "I will. How clever you are, sir, to seek out a weakness and use it to your own advantage."

"You will learn how to do that in time, my dear," he promised her.

"Will I learn all of your little tricks?" she queried him.

Mr. Nicholas laughed. "No," he said, "but you will learn enough over the coming years to be quite valuable to me, my dear

Nora. Oh, one small thing more, dear girl, employee. The Kyle who will exist in your reality, your world, will not know you other than as his employee. Only in The Channel will he be the man you have come to love, and who loves you. His memory of you in your reality will not exist. You must, after all, suffer some small punishment for your sins. Even I am not allowed to put the universe out of balance." He stood up. "I will leave you and Kyle to your private pleasures now." And with a neat little bow he departed the bathroom. They heard the elevator doors closing behind him as he went.

"Do you want to know?" Kyle asked her.

"I know what I need to know for now, I suppose," Nora answered him.

"I was never privy to what he intended to do with you," Kyle said.

"No, you wouldn't have been," she replied, lying back on the table, and unfolding the sheet that had covered her so that she was naked once again.

"I never lied to you when I said I loved you," Kyle told her.

"I know that too," Nora agreed.

"Are you angry?" he asked her.

Nora thought a moment. "No," she said. "Just sad."

He began to massage her again, and when he had finished they went into the bedroom, where they climbed into the king-sized bed and began to make passionate love to each other. And in his jail cell bunk Jeff Buckley dreamed that his wife, Nora, was screwing another man. He saw her plainly. Beautiful. Young. And far more passionate than he had ever seen her before. The horny little bitch, he thought, and he tossed restlessly. And then he heard her cries of pleasure as the dark-haired man used her mercilessly over and over again. He could feel his own heart beating violently in his chest as he watched them. How could she betray him like that? She was having a really hot fucking party with the guy, who behaved as if she belonged to him and it wasn't the first time he'd had his big cock up her wet pussy. He was going to kill the bitch when he got out of here. And all the while she had played the proper suburban matron. She sure as hell wasn't behaving properly now. How long had it been going on?

And then Nora's lover turned her over onto her stomach. She knelt with her deliciously round bottom toward him. Leaning forward, she balanced herself on her folded arms. The guy had the biggest dick Jeff had ever seen, and he slowly slid it into Nora's asshole. Jesus! She'd never done it for him that way. He'd never even suspected she was that hot. A respectable man's wife wasn't supposed to be like that. Jeff could see Nora's face. It was alight with her pleasure. A look he had never seen. The guy was reaching beneath her to get at her clit. Jeff's heart beat faster. He heard Nora's voice as plain as if she had been in the room with him.

"Do it!" she begged. "Do it to me, Kyle!" And then she looked directly at him. "Good-bye, Jeff," she said, laughing.

Jeff Buckley's heart felt as if it were being squeezed by a large hand, and then it stopped entirely. There was a white light ahead, and a well-dressed man came forward smiling at him.

"Hello, Jeff," the man said to him. "I'm Mr. Nicholas. I've been waiting quite a long time for you."

A Note From The Author

ℛ

The idea for this novel came about several years ago when I read about the long-time wife of a very wealthy businessman who was being divorced by her husband so he might take a younger wife. The gentleman in question wanted to give his wife a bare minimum of what he had. She sued for half of what he had, including an interest in his pension, and she won. And subsequent courts upheld her. Her attorneys had reasoned that the lady was responsible in part for her husband's success by being there to entertain his clients, raise their children, and give him the all around backup he needed to succeed.

The lady was very lucky. Most women being divorced don't have that option. Those who have been in long-term marriages, who have no work experience like Nora, or who have been out of the workplace for so long that their skills are no longer viable, usually end up barely subsisting. And the women with children generally find themselves in poverty, or just above what is called the poverty level in this country.

But what, I thought, would happen if the wife about to lose everything got to turn the tables on her unfaithful mate, and ended up with it all? And what if she also got everything she had ever secretly desired? But be careful, my friends, for what you wish. The road to Hell is more often than not paved with noble intentions, and in the end good must always win out over the dark side as Nora's tale has shown you. She was betrayed, and badly treated. But in the end she was responsible for the death of another human. And she is paying the price for it. But Kyle remains by her side.

He always will for if Nora did not find true love in her own reality, she has it now in the reality of The Channel.

ABOUT THE AUTHOR

ৡ৶

Bertrice Small is a *New York Times* best-selling author and the recipient of numerous awards. In keeping with her profession, she lives in the oldest English-speaking town in the state of New York, founded in 1640, and works in a light-filled studio surrounded by the paintings of her favorite cover artist, Elaine Duillo. Because she believes in happy endings, Bertrice Small has been married to the same man, her hero, George, for forty years. They have a son, a daughter-in-law, and three adorable grandchildren. Longtime readers will be happy to know that Nicki the Cockatiel flourishes along with his fellow housemates; Pookie, the long-haired greige and white; Honeybun, the petite orange lady cat with the cream-colored paws; and Finnegan, the black long-haired baby of the family.